"Who is he?" Lucia stood peeking through the shutter. "The one who gazes up like a sad puppy, waiting for your songs. He carries a sketchbook."

"Probably a French artist," I replied. "The king of France sent sixteen sculptors to study Rome's masterpieces, to duplicate them for his court, and their workshop is just across the street."

"Fiery eyes, black curls, strong arms." Lucia swooned, dancing her hips from side to side. "And his eyes light up whenever you sing."

Bianca looked up from her prayers. "Mother would never allow an artist to court my sister."

"Some things are worth risking your mother's scorn," Lucia said, motioning me toward the window. "At least take a peek through the shutters."

I stood behind Lucia, staring over her shoulder.

"See? Isn't he handsome?"

I confess he was most pleasing to look at, with dark eyes and a gentle smile. When he saw a movement at my window, he took off his wide-brimmed hat and, sweeping it through the air, bowed.

"Look, he bows to you." Lucia nudged me with her elbow. "Sing him a song."

But Bianca quickly closed the shutters. "Don't listen to her foolishness, Angelica."

THE QUEEN'S SOPRANO

THE QUEEN'S SOPRANO

CAROL DINES

HARCOURT, INC.

Orlando   Austin   New York   San Diego   Toronto   London

Requests for permission to make copies of any part of the work
should be submitted online at www.harcourt.com/contact or mailed
to the following address: Permissions Department, Harcourt, Inc.,
6277 Sea Harbor Drive, Orlando, Florida 32887-6777.

www.HarcourtBooks.com

First Harcourt paperback edition 2007

The Library of Congress has cataloged the hardcover edition as follows:
Dines, Carol.
The queen's soprano/by Carol Dines.
p. cm.
Summary: Seventeen-year-old Angelica Voglia lives in
seventeenth-century Rome and has the voice of an angel,
but because the pope forbids women to sing in public, she
must escape to Queen Christina's palace to become a court singer.
1. Voglia, Angelica, ca. 1670—Juvenile fiction.
2. Christina, Queen of Sweden, 1626–1689—Juvenile fiction.
[1. Voglia, Angelica, ca. 1670—Fiction.   2. Christina, Queen of
Sweden, 1626–1689—Fiction.   3. Kings, queens, rulers, etc.—Fiction.
4. Sopranos (Singers)—Fiction.   5. Singers—Fiction.
6. Sex role—Fiction.]   I. Title.
PZ7.D6119Que 2006
[Fic]—dc22   2005014760
ISBN 978-0-15-205477-9
ISBN 978-0-15-206102-9 pb

Text set in Minion
Designed by Lauren Rille

A C E G H F D B

Printed in the United States of America

The Queen's Soprano is a work of fiction based on historical figures
and events. Some details have been altered to enhance the story.

To Jack,
for opening so many worlds . . .

ACKNOWLEDGMENTS

I am so grateful to family and friends for their support, encouragement, and sustenance while writing this book. In particular, I'd like to thank Miriam Karmel for our many "writing" walks and talks and for her great insight into the writing process; Carol Bouska and Marcia O'Hagan for listening and believing in this book; the wisdom and encouragement of readers Barbara Graham, Donatella Izzo, and Margot Fortunato Galt. I owe much to Kate Harrison, my editor, for seeing what I had yet to see, and for her brilliant advice throughout the editing process. Many thanks, too, to Diana Finch, my agent, for her patience and wise counsel.

And a very special thank you to my mother, Bette Dines, who read every version and asked all the right questions; to my father, David Dines, who taught me to love music and to see it as a window to the world; and to my daughter, Hanna, a writer, artist, and thinker whose creative spirit inspired this story.

FOREWORD

Imagine, if you will, being born with a great talent for singing, only to be told you could never sing in public. If you dared to do so, you would risk your reputation and perhaps even your life. What follows is the story of one girl who was willing to risk everything to sing.

Angelica Voglia was born in Rome, Italy, about 1670, when Rome was the center of music in the western world, and musicians came from all over Europe to be trained there. However, Rome was also the capital of the Catholic world, and during Angelica's life, Pope Innocent XI and his cardinals created laws forbidding females to sing in public. Known for his strictness, the pope proclaimed, "Music is completely injurious to the modesty that is proper to the female sex, because they become distracted from the matters and occupations most suitable for them." Respectable women and girls were rarely seen outside the home, except to attend church, and even then, they had to be accompanied by relatives or escorts.

Any woman who dared to sing in public was automatically suspected of being a courtesan or prostitute because she was seen as "prostituting" herself onstage. If caught, she could be fined a large sum of money, arrested, expelled from the city, or placed in a convent for wayward women. A talented singer like Angelica had only two options if she wished to continue singing in safety: Join a nunnery or become a court singer. Entering a nunnery meant living behind walls, separated from the world, and following the strict rules of a religious order. Becoming a court singer meant serving a powerful patron in whatever way the patron desired, as well as giving that patron ownership over one's career.

During Angelica's life, Rome was divided into neighborhoods, called quarters, that were governed by foreign ambassadors and noble families. Since Pope Innocent XI had come into power, he had begun taking control of Rome's quarters and enforcing the church's laws. However, certain neighborhoods were still known for their freedoms, drawing people who wished to escape the pope's laws. Most famous for its "liberties" was the quarter governed by Queen Christina. Once the queen of Sweden (a protestant country at war with Catholic Europe), Christina shocked the world when she gave up her throne at the age of twenty-seven and moved to Rome, where she converted to Catholicism in a public celebration that lasted for days. A great patron of musicians in Rome, Queen Christina set up the first public opera house and even allowed women to perform, until the pope closed her opera house. She also began an academy of scholars that included weekly musical performances and launched the careers of musicians and singers, one of whom was Angelica Voglia.

One girl's story can reveal a whole world, and Angelica's story reveals much about Rome during the baroque period. Yet her story will not be found in history books. Indeed, had she not become one of Queen Christina's favorite sopranos, she would surely have been forgotten. What makes Angelica's story so remarkable, and what compelled me to write it, was not so much her amazing talent but, more importantly, the many obstacles she had to overcome to have her voice heard.

THE QUEEN'S SOPRANO

CHAPTER ONE

The first person to look inside my heart, to really see me, was a monk. He came to teach me how to play the harpsichord, and when he heard my voice rise above the chords, he put his hands over his face and wept.

I was eleven. Chubbier then. My hair was covered in a white scarf, and the gray smock I wore chafed my breasts. My mother and Father Zachary, the priest who acted as my patron, were drinking coffee in the garden. Father Zachary always waited while the tutors he had hired gave me music lessons.

When I saw the monk wipe the tears from his round face, I stopped singing. My heart pounded and my cheeks burned. Resting my hands in my lap, I spoke softly. "My song displeases you?"

The monk raised his watery eyes, then brushed his cheek with the sleeve of his brown robe. "Dangerous," he whispered, his eyelids closing.

"What is dangerous?" I asked.

"Your voice." He spoke with closed eyes. "You are a child…
but you sing with a woman's voice. It's unsettling…disturbing."

I shook my head; I didn't understand.

He was nervous. His lips trembled, and sweat glistened
above his thick brow. "Music awakens the passions…stirs feelings…" He stared at his hands, lying still on the harpsichord
keys. "Excuse me. But I have never heard a voice like yours. You
sing with such joy, it moves me deeply. I cannot stay here."

With that, he stood and stepped quickly across the room and
out the door. He did not ask Father Zachary to pay him, and he
did not say good-bye.

I have forgotten his name, but I remember his words, for
they settled inside me like a deep sigh. As a young child, I sang
before I could speak, humming the melodies I heard in church.
By the age of five, I dreamed of music while I slept, and when
waking in the morning, I would sing the songs that had filled my
dreams. I took to instruments naturally—the guitar and harpsichord—knowing how to play them by touch and sound. Father
Zachary brought tutors from the Jesuit College to teach me
the theories and practice of music. We always began with scales
and vocal exercises. Then I would sing whatever they put before
me—psalms, motets, arias—as if each melody had been born
inside my own heart. When I finished their lessons, they shook
their heads, refusing to return. They claimed their years of training had been wasted, that already I'd surpassed them in skill.

All my life, others had told me my talent was a gift from
God. But as I grew older, I felt my own power reveal itself in
song. I did not speak of this feeling. I didn't dare. Yet music was

as much a part of me as the air I breathed. It lived in my bones, my blood, my heart. No matter what I was doing—sweeping the floor, pulling water from the well, chopping onions—songs rose through me. I tried to rest my voice, as Mother commanded. I learned to hold a song inside my thoughts, swaying silently. But lately, with so many songs bursting inside me, I'd grown tired of living by Mother's strict rules.

No, I was not the daughter my mother thought me to be... wished me to be. I lacked obedience. And obedience, as Mother reminded me daily, was a girl's most valued quality.

Mother had many theories. About daughters, about marriage, about husbands. Only part of me still listened.

I was not like my sister, Bianca. She *was* obedient. She listened. She had the sturdiness of an iron plate, reflecting whatever stood above it.

Nor was I hardworking like my brother Franco, who spent his days beside Papa making windows for the most beautiful churches and palaces in Rome. I neglected my chores, preferring music to mending.

And I certainly wasn't sweet like my nine-year-old brother, Pietro. He'd been born with a deformed chin, a cliff of flesh and bone, made worse by the thrust of his bottom teeth. He hid his chin in public, trying to avoid the taunts of our neighbors who called his chin the devil's work, crossing the street to avoid him, calling out, "Hee-haw, hee-haw...it's the donkey boy." Often as we walked to and from church, Pietro took my hand and held it, as if by squeezing my fingers, he might soak up some of my good fortune.

And I was not patient like Papa. Good, kind Papa. He was shy with me, his eldest child. He called me his angel but watched me from a distance, as if he knew my talent would take me far away from him someday.

I loved my family, but I learned nothing of myself from them. If my family looked inward, they never spoke of their feelings. They spoke of the grape crop, the new priest who stuttered, the barber's wife whose body was barren. Mother and Papa spoke of my father's earnings, the nobles and bishops who failed to pay him. We spoke endlessly of food: Why is the soup watery? How tough, this mutton…how salty, these beans.

And we prayed. We prayed before the Virgin Mary on our wall. Sometimes I felt her eyes watching me, the left one chipped so that she always looked as if she were winking, telling me not to be afraid, to sing louder, to lift my voice to God.

For sixteen years, Mother had kept my sister and me enclosed in the house and courtyard, except for our frequent visits to church, and even then Mother made sure our faces were hidden, our cloaks pulled tight, always reminding us, "A gentleman prefers a modest wife."

On the morning of my seventeenth birthday, I woke to the sounds of chickens clucking, wooden wheels creaking on the cobbled street, the barber's wife weeping in the courtyard. I lay in bed listening to my sister's prayers as she knelt beneath the Virgin Mary, and my father's loud boots clomping below as he got ready to leave for church, which he and my brothers attended every morning on their way to the workshop.

Everything the same. Except for me. I wanted my life to be

changed on this day....I wanted to raise my voice beyond this house, this neighborhood, to sing in the grand palaces across the river!

I hurried downstairs, to find an orange, a chocolate, and a pair of leather shoes with shiny buckles waiting for me on the table. Papa lifted me off the floor with his hug. "Happy birthday, Angelica."

"*Grazie,* Papa." I tried on my new shoes with the square toes, the same gift I received every year. "Where do you go today, Papa...a church or a palace?" I always asked, I always wanted to hear about the palaces across the river.

"Palazzo Riario...Queen Christina's palace," my brother Franco told me. "The queen wants a glass house built over her garden shed, so her gardener can grow flowers in winter."

"Your brother's feet should move as fast his mouth." Papa pulled on his coat. "Come, Franco. You, too, Pietro. The church bells are already ringing!"

Pietro jumped from the loft above the fireplace, planted a kiss on my cheek, then rushed after them. But as Papa opened the door and stepped outside, mud poured across the doorway.

"*Gesummaria!*" Mother pushed my brothers into the rain and bolted the door behind them. "By your talents, Angelica, I hope one day we'll leave this neighborhood."

Our house stood in a small alley off the Piazza Santa Cecilia, in the quarter known as Trastevere. Here, the narrow winding streets were lined with workshops where glassmakers, wood-carvers, and stonecutters plied their trades. Even though this side of the river often flooded, Papa said we were lucky. Our house had a courtyard in the back, with a small well and a garden we shared with our neighbors.

As I sat drinking a cup of watery coffee and eating a slice of bread, I could hear the tradesmen on their way to work, calling out to me, "Sing a song for us, Signorina."

I stood quickly before the tall mirror that rested against the wall—a gift from Father Zachary so that I could watch my movements as I sang. Every day Mother advised me to hold my eyes open and avoid nervous habits. "Do not sway too much, and make sure your hands do not clutch your smock or dig into your pockets."

But music blinded me. As my voice rose, I saw nothing of myself in the mirror. I saw grief, joy, jealousy—whatever feeling existed in the words of the song. I learned more by ear than by formal training, and I never tired of practicing the music I heard in church, especially the solos sung by the castrati—those male singers who had been castrated as boys so that their voices would maintain the power and purity of the high notes. These days, whenever an oratorio was posted outside the church, Mother made sure we attended. I learned much from listening to the sacred music and poetry, performed free to the public.

As soon as I finished my song, I heard the crowd below my window calling, "Brava! Let us hear another song. Let us hear the girl with the miracle voice."

"They should know better than to call your voice a *miracle*." Mother frowned, shaking her head. "This pope doesn't allow for miracles, especially on our side of the river. Remember the lad whose father claimed God had given him the power to heal animals by his touch? Now he sits in the pope's prison."

But I was eager to sing for the crowd cheering outside. "Just one more song, Mother?"

Mother shook her head. "Luck is hard won in the city, Angelica. But I feel it in my bones. By your talent, luck will be ours."

"What if I'm not lucky, Mother? What then?"

Mother's sighs were weighted with purpose. "Never doubt yourself. Doubt is what corrupts talent." Then she called to Bianca to come downstairs, and when my sister pulled a chair beside me, Mother handed us a basket of clothes. "Your brothers' trousers need patches on the knees."

Holding up Franco's pants, I planted a patch of burlap over the crotch. "Franco's pants are worn thin, but not at the knee." Then I whispered, "And they smell of cheese!"

Bianca and I burst out laughing. I was speaking of the cheese-seller's daughter, who yesterday evening made eyes at Franco as we crossed the piazza on our way home from church. Mother, seeing the girl swoon, had raised her voice. "Some girls pretend to be modest but think nothing of lowering a blouse whenever a handsome boy passes."

Laughing, the cheese-seller's daughter had tugged her blouse lower. "Not a boy any longer, eh, Franco?"

Now, hearing our giggles, Mother scolded me. "Common girls think nothing of laughing with their mouths wide open. What an ugly sight, a girl's throat." She never lost an opportunity to teach us manners, and she raised her palm to cover her mouth. "If you must laugh, shield your mouth like this."

I shrugged off her words.

"You roll your eyes at my advice now, Angelica, but one day soon, when you have servants to do your chores and a coach to carry you across the city, you'll thank me."

Servants and coaches—that was Mother's dream, not mine. I'll admit it was common for a mother to rule her daughter's heart, making sure her daughter married a respectable husband. What was *uncommon* was Mother's determination to marry me off to a highborn gentleman and, by such a marriage, raise my family's station in life.

"You're no longer a child." Mother wrapped a scarf around my neck. "Seventeen years in the world, Angelica. Now is the time to show the world your talent for singing. Mark my words, by eighteen, you will be married to a nobleman who will guarantee a future for all of us."

As soon as she went upstairs, I leaned close to my sister. "I wish to sing in the courts of Rome, not marry my way into them." Unwinding my scarf, I told her, "Any husband I wed must share my passion for music, or I'll not bed him…I'll simply keep my legs locked tightly like this"—I pulled up my frock and twisted one knee around the other—"until he begs me to sing."

Bianca laughed. "Then I pity your husband."

"Pity me. I've never crossed a bridge…never strolled across the river…never left this neighborhood!"

Bianca blew strands of hair away from her face as she threaded a needle. "Nor have I, and you don't hear me complaining."

True enough, we were as different in character as in appearance. A year younger, Bianca was shorter and plumper. Like my brothers, she had Papa's round face, thick black hair, and olive skin, while I'd inherited Mother's pale complexion and honey-colored curls, along with her stormy green eyes and temper.

"Wait until Mother sets herself on finding *you* a husband," I whispered. "She'll stuff your ears with rules, and then you'll wish to escape, too."

Our whispers were interrupted by a loud knocking at the door, and Mother hurried down the stairs to peek through the shutters. "*Una pellegrina*...A pilgrim girl," she muttered, making sure the door was bolted. When the weather turned cold, pilgrims often knocked, begging a bit of warmth and a loaf of bread. They came to Rome seeking the pope's blessing, and many traveled from distant villages and countries. When the knock came again, Mother cried out, "This city has more churches than the pope has hair. Let the priests feed you...Their stomachs are full!"

"Caterina!" Father Zachary cried out. "Open the door, I have a surprise."

As Mother unbolted the door, the priest pushed a young woman into the room.

Mother planted her hands on her hips. "Who is this?"

"You've hounded me for months to bring a servant, Caterina. Well, now you have one. Her name is Lucia." Father Zachary took the girl's cloak and hung it behind the door.

The girl curtsied. "*Piacere*...It is my pleasure, Signora." Then, raising her eyes, she noticed the harpsichord and guitar sitting in the corner of the room. Her hands sprang to her mouth as she stared at me. "Oh my, I know who you are...the girl with the miracle voice! Everyone speaks of you...They say nobles and princes ride across the river in their coaches to hear you sing while you stay hidden behind shutters. Is it true that you were born from your mother's womb, singing like an angel?"

Bianca and I laughed, but Mother spoke sharply. "How dare you speak so boldly? It's true my daughter was born with a talent, but she wailed like any other baby. Her gift for music has been cultivated by hard work and the best tutors in Rome, thanks to her patron." Mother nodded at Father Zachary.

"Perhaps such a generous patron might ask for a glass of wine?" Father Zachary rested his gaze on the jug of wine. I often thought the priest resembled an owl, with his bald head, wide-set eyes, and long nose.

Mother stared at the girl. "We don't want a servant who spreads gossip, Father Zachary."

"Caterina," the priest replied. "She's an orphan. Give her time to learn. She's intelligent, and you'll teach her well. I'm sure of that. Now, show a bit of gratitude and pour me a glass of wine."

I stared at the shivering girl. She was my age, or nearly so, with long knotted hair the color of chestnuts, blue eyes, and chapped lips. Despite her runny nose, she was pretty. Her clothes were tattered and soaked through, but they were not the grays and whites of a tradesman's daughter. Under her black jacket, she wore a maroon skirt of coarse linen, a matching bodice laced tight over a faded white shirt, the wide sleeves rolled up, and a gray apron tied around her waist. Her skin was pale, not like the sunburned faces of girls who worked in fields. I glanced at her hands—smooth, uncalloused. Clearly she was not a girl who'd been raised in the country.

Sipping his wine, Father Zachary continued. "Her parents were pilgrims. They died of a fever outside the city gates. Their last wish was that their daughter find a family to serve in the pope's city." Father Zachary nodded. "The nuns told me she can cook and sew."

"The nuns will say anything to rid themselves of another mouth to feed." Mother stood up, circling the girl. "How do we know she doesn't carry the same disease that killed her parents?"

"You can see for yourself she is strong. Besides, she is well-spoken and presentable; good traits in a servant."

"Where was your family from?" Mother asked.

"Bologna, Signora."

"It's true, you do not garble your words as peasant girls are like to do." Mother nodded. "It's also true we need a servant. We cannot welcome Angelica's suitors without a maid to serve them. Even though we live on this side of the river, we can't be seen as common."

Father Zachary smiled. "Now Angelica will be freed from her chores and will be able to devote herself entirely to music, and this poor girl will have a roof over her head."

Mother crossed her arms. "And where do you suppose she will sleep? Certainly not in my daughters' room upstairs."

"A pallet on the floor will do." Father Zachary nodded to the space near the fireplace. "Here, next to the fireplace."

"I suppose a hot bath and clean clothes will help." Mother lifted Lucia's chin. "Lower your eyes when I speak to you."

She lowered her eyes, "Yes, Signora."

"Yes, *Mistress*," Mother corrected her. "That is how you shall address me. And my husband shall be Master."

"Yes, Mistress."

Smiling at me, Father Zachary leaned over and pulled a package from his satchel. "Did you think I had forgotten your birthday, Angelica? To be born on the Feast Day of Saint Cecilia, patron saint of music, that is a sign your gift is great."

My hands trembled as I took the package. I hoped for a new cloak. Perhaps now that I was seventeen and meant to marry within the year, the priest's gift would be a fine velvet cape with silk lining and embroidered trim, like the ones the noble daughters wore to church.

But opening the brown paper, my heart sank. I saw gray... the same gray wool worn by all the tradesmen's daughters, exactly like the cloak I wore now, only longer.

"*Grazie,*" I whispered, trying to hide my disappointment. I held a smile to my lips as Father Zachary draped the cloak over my shoulders and raised the hood around my face.

"The perfect length," he said. "It shall keep you warm this winter."

While Mother and Bianca admired the cloak, I turned slowly, keeping my back to the priest, not wanting him to see the tears brimming in my eyes, the wobble in my chin. Glancing up, I saw Lucia watching me, her eyes studying my face. She didn't look at the cloak but held my gaze...long enough for me to swallow my sadness. For the second time in my life, I felt a stranger look into my heart and know me. It wasn't the cloak that brought tears, but something else, something deeper. I had songs bursting inside me and dreams of singing in all the famous courts of Rome, but I was still a glazier's daughter dressed in a gray cloak.

Lucia stepped forward, and taking up the role of servant, lifted the cloak from my shoulders. "Best not to get it dirty, Miss. The floor being wet and all."

And with that simple gesture, I knew she understood.

CHAPTER TWO

Lucia was my first friend, the first person I came to trust outside my family.

She quickly took over my chores and proved herself such a worthy cook and able seamstress, she assumed some of Bianca's chores as well. In the morning, after she had stoked the coals and set the water boiling, she climbed the stairs with a pitcher of cold water and placed it next to a big bowl on the windowsill. After Bianca and I washed our faces, Lucia combed my hair and pinned it, while Bianca said her morning prayers.

I wasn't used to someone doing for me what I could easily do for myself. I was embarrassed to be waited upon, and those first days, when Lucia swept my floor, ironed my apron, and combed my hair, I tried to offer something back, my own bit of kindness. "Let me do your hair as well, Lucia."

Seeing my discomfort, she quickly set me straight. "There's no shame in hard work, Miss." And tugging my curls, added,

"And your head takes a fair bit of effort...I've never seen so many snarls, nor curls so tight they refuse a comb."

"Lucia." I frowned. "There's no need to call me Miss."

"It's best, Miss, with your mother listening through walls."

Each morning, while I rehearsed my songs, Lucia gathered the wash and took it to the fountain in the piazza, where she listened to the neighbors' gossip. Then, when she saw Mother leave to go to the market, she quickly returned so we could talk freely while she prepared the midday meal.

"Tell me what you saw today, Lucia?"

"A dog giving birth, Miss, under the lip of the fountain."

"What else, Lucia?"

"A family of pilgrims crawling on their bloody knees through puddles. That is how some see fit to show humility, Miss, though I believe God frowns on children doing such." Lucia shook her head. "The saddest sight, Miss, a husband, crazed by his wife's fever, who stole a wooden door off the side of the church to build a fire. He was arrested."

At first we stuck to subjects that had nothing to do with her life or my own. She spoke of the blind widow peddling teas and the castrato who had once sung for the papal choir, and now, having grown cobwebs in his voice, begged his livelihood on the church steps. I spoke of the barber's wife who often fled her husband's beatings and wept in our courtyard.

But by the third day, we had begun to build a trust between us, and when I asked if she'd noticed the crowd beneath my window, she drew close. "I shall tell you plain what I see, but first we must make a pact to hold what we say between us." She held out her hand in a formal way, and when I shook it, she told me, "Rich and poor lingered under your window today, Miss. There were many of the pope's soldiers, with their leather boots and swords." Chopping onions, she said, "A boy asked about you. He was dressed in silk breeches and a jacket that smelled strongly of church incense. A cardinal's page, I expect."

My heart pounded. Cardinals were the pope's princes. Along with the pope, they made the rules that governed our lives.

"What did he ask?"

"He wanted to know how you'd come to be trained in music. I told him you had a priest who acted as your patron." Glancing up, Lucia grinned. "He told me his master wishes to see your face."

"Lucia," I gasped. "What did you reply?"

"I told him that seeing as his master rode in such a fine coach, his wish wasn't to be taken lightly." And here she giggled. "I said plainly your mother guards you narrow as the space between teeth and you take no visitors as yet. So he asked me why you hide yourself, and I said out of prudence, for your beauty is unsurpassed, except by your own modesty."

"You said that?" I blushed.

"I said more, Miss," she continued. "I told him your hair was golden and your eyes green as a forest...skin like a pearl with the sun rising in it. I said there was no prettier girl in all of Rome."

"Oh, Lucia, you shouldn't make me into more than I am." I covered my face and groaned. "If he ever sees me, he'll surely be disappointed."

"No fear of that, Miss." Pouring olive oil into the kettle, Lucia tossed in the onions and stirred them. "I followed the cheeky lad to the unmarked coach. Black as a beetle's shell, with

16

red velvet curtains that stay drawn. The same coach comes every morning and sits in the piazza. Whoever sits inside must be very important…or very dangerous."

"Why do you say so?"

"Because the pope's soldiers circle nearby, and whoever sits inside never shows himself." Seeing my frown, she waved a knife. "Don't fret, Miss. I'll ask around and find out who he is."

I would've liked to find out more, but our chatter was interrupted by a loud knock and a familiar voice. "It is I, Prince Colombiere."

"The goat." I tugged my chin to imitate his fleshy neck. "He's old and shriveled and I despise him."

Lucia peeked through the shutter. "*Scusi*…Sorry, Signore, but my mistress is not at home."

It was not the first time he'd knocked at our door. The prince had taken notice of my voice months ago, but Mother had put him off until after my birthday. Now, seeing the prince pace outside our house, Mother hurried through the door, and closing it behind her, whispered, "Go and put on your church frocks… Bianca, too. He's a nobleman, so you'll give him one song, a fair enough trade for a box of chocolates. But don't show your faces. I've told him to go and stand in the courtyard, off the street."

Upstairs, Bianca and I stood with our backs to the window while Mother opened the shutters a crack. We sang a chamber duet, lifting our voices in harmony, and when we had finished, Mother leaned from the window. "My daughters must rest their voices. *Buon giorno*…Good day to you, Prince Colombiere."

As it happened, Father Zachary was just arriving, and seeing the prince exit our courtyard, he hurried inside and raised his voice to Mother. "How dare you let Prince Colombiere visit Angelica!"

Upstairs, Lucia and I knelt and pulled up the floorboard so we could see, while Bianca stood over us, listening.

"He drinks and gambles, Caterina. I know this man's debts!" Father Zachary was an accountant for the Bank of Mount Piety, so he was in a position to know a man's worth in coins. "Why do you waste your daughter's reputation on such scoundrels?"

"Why?" Mother laughed. "He's a prince; that's why. Besides, I only let him into the courtyard so he might listen to Angelica through an open shutter. She didn't show her face but kept her back to the window." Mother's voice softened. "He brought us a fine box of chocolates...here, try one."

"Chocolates! You risk your daughter's reputation for chocolates?" Father Zachary's fists hit the table. "Crowds already gather each day to hear Angelica sing."

"How else will her talent be discovered?" Mother stared at the priest.

"Perhaps you don't understand, Caterina. This pope governs strictly." Father Zachary paced the floor. "They call him *Papa No* because he has ordered all the naked statues painted over, closed the opera houses, banned street festivals...even Carnevale!"

I remembered Carnevale from my childhood, a whole month when the streets were filled with singers and musicians.

"There are still those who perform," Mother replied.

"And risk their lives to do so." Father Zachary took a kerchief and wiped the sweat from his forehead. "This pope has issued a decree, forbidding women from performing in public. Female singers caught disobeying his laws are heavily fined, and if they cannot pay their fines, they are jailed. Or worse, they are sent to convents for wayward women, where they are put to work tending to the sick. Believe me, their lives are quickly shortened." Father Zachary rested his eyes on Mother. "Is this what you wish for Angelica?"

"Don't preach to me, Father. My daughter sings only sacred music, and she sings behind closed shutters."

"She would be better off in a convent."

"She would be better off married to a nobleman." Mother's voice grew shrill. "A girl is nothing without a husband. We both know that!"

"I fear greed commands your duty as a mother—"

"How dare *you* speak to me of duty, Father...I'll tell *you* about duty. I have four children, and none but the eldest benefits from your generosity, so I must seek to guarantee my other children's futures as well."

"Heed my warning, Caterina. If you don't protect Angelica from swine like the prince, I'll place her in a convent myself, away from your schemes." Then, turning, Father Zachary stomped across the floor and out the door.

I shivered and planted the floorboard back in place.

"He's right," Lucia whispered. "Your voice is worth far more than a box of chocolates."

"Lucia," Bianca interrupted, "are there no chores to be done?" My sister disliked the way Lucia spoke so openly about our family, asking questions and voicing her opinions.

But Lucia ignored her and pressed me with another question. "Does the priest always speak so freely with your mother?"

I nodded. "He is my patron."

Bianca rose and, with a stern glance, brushed past us. "Surely Mother needs help in the garden, Lucia, and since you seem content to idle away the morning, I shall go myself."

As soon as my sister's shoes could be heard on the stairs, Lucia leaned close. "But how did your mother come to know the priest?"

"Mother was five when the fever took her parents," I whispered. "She was sent to the convent for orphans, Poor Saint Clares...famous for its choir. Father Zachary was the convent priest. Lucky for me, he is still friends with the abbess and borrows music for me to copy."

"The convents for orphans are the worst for scandals." Lucia held my gaze. "I saw with my own eyes, before I was brought here. The girls have no families to visit them...to protect them. Not like the fancy convents for noble daughters."

"At least Mother learned to read and write."

Lucia paused, her mouth drawn tight, as if she were troubled. "If she was raised in a convent, Miss, how did your mother come to know your papa?"

"Father Zachary arranged their marriage."

Lucia's eyebrows lifted. "The priest found her a husband?"

I nodded. "Before their marriage, Papa was an apprentice to a master glazier, and after, with the dowry paid him by Father Zachary, Papa bought his own shop."

Lucia gave a sharp laugh. "An orphan with a dowry?"

I felt my face turn hot. "Don't laugh at me, Lucia. It's true, I haven't seen much of the world. But you needn't treat me as a child, plying me with questions in order to be amused by my answers."

Lucia's smile quickly faded. "I only meant to understand—"

"Understand what?" I replied curtly. "What is it you wish to know, Lucia?"

She took my hands and stared at me squarely. "Don't you wonder why this priest provides for you and not for your sister or brothers?"

"I did ask...once." I hesitated, remembering. "I asked Mother why Father Zachary didn't bring gifts for Bianca. She told me Bianca did not have such a great talent as my own."

"Did you ask anything else?"

"Why Father Zachary only visited us when Papa was at work."

Lucia's eyes widened. "What did she reply?"

"Mother said I asked too many questions. She said curiosity is a man's right, a girl's fast ruin. She said I'd never find a husband if I didn't learn to hold my tongue, that no gentleman would marry a girl who makes herself his equal by asking questions."

"Have you never wondered why the convent priest made it his task to find your mother a husband?" Lucia stared at me. "Do you know how long it was after your mother married before you came along?"

I lowered my eyes, feeling my blood rush.

Lucia squeezed my hands. "You yourself have spoken of Father Zachary's generosity...the pouches of money he brings to your mother...the tutors, the music, the instruments he provides—even a harpsichord!"

I could not cease shivering. Perhaps I'd always suspected the truth and hadn't wanted to admit it, but now, my voice trembled. "You mean to say...you think the priest is my blood father?"

Lucia didn't speak. Not then. She let the truth sink in.

As I breathed in Lucia's words, I felt a deep sadness. *I don't want any other father...Papa is my father...the kindest man I know.* As tears slid down my cheeks, I closed my eyes.

"Makes sense, if you don't mind my saying so. And that's why your mother guards you so close. She doesn't want you to suffer the same ruin." Lucia reached into the pile of clean laundry and, taking a fresh handkerchief, wiped my tears. "At least the priest did his duty by you. He found you a decent papa and did right by your mother."

I took the handkerchief and turned away. I couldn't listen to Lucia anymore. There was too much truth to her words. And I could only handle so much of the truth at one time.

CHAPTER THREE

Right off, Franco couldn't take his eyes off Lucia. True enough, Lucia had an ample bosom and sturdy hips, with no need of a corset to make her curves. And though she did well to hide her feeling in Mother's house, she yet found ways to return my brother's affections, playing proper all the while. Tucking a curl behind her ear, swaying her hips as she swept, licking the sweat from her lip, she offered up glimpses of herself.

Franco thought himself a man now that he worked beside Papa. Indeed, he had a man's body, broad shoulders, black eyes, and a wide, open smile, which gave many a girl a fluttering heart. Even the noble daughters giggled behind their veils as he passed them in the church courtyard.

And yet he had a boy's playful spirit. He made it a game to bring a blush to Lucia's cheek. As soon as Mother's back was turned, he winked, pleading for a lock of her red hair, counting the freckles on her nose, pretending to read her thoughts, saying they were always of him. And though she couldn't hide the flush he brought to her face, Lucia feared Mother would discover his game and send her packing, so she busied herself. "My thoughts are on the beans that need shelling, the potatoes that need skinning, and not on the lad who makes himself a nuisance."

One such moment, Pietro fell laughing so hard at Franco, he spilled a cup of milk down his front. When Lucia leaned over to mop Pietro's shirt, Franco snuck up behind and, grabbing her at the waist, turned her toward him. "And my shirt, will you wipe it?"

Meaning to set him straight, Lucia raised a pitcher of cold water to pour over his shirt, but Franco was quick and steadied her hand with his own firm grip.

"Clean enough, is it?" She smiled boldly.

"For now." Franco used his strength to draw her closer. "But with you to distract me, I fear I'll spill often."

If it hadn't been for Mother's heels clicking on the cobbled stones outside, I think Franco would've swept Lucia up, right then and there, and kissed her on the lips. Hot shivers! Mother might be able to stop their words, but she couldn't stop their feelings.

I could see well enough that Franco's affections hadn't yet cooled that evening as Lucia prepared the dinner. Until then, I hadn't fancied myself a jealous person. But as my affection for Lucia grew, so did my fear of losing her friendship because of my brother. Already I wished her all to myself.

As Lucia stood by the fire, stirring the soup, Franco made eyes at her. Meaning to warn him that Mother had entered the room, I gave him a sharp kick under the table. But he ignored me and patted his stomach. "*Che fame*...I've never felt such hunger."

Just then, Lucia was taken in a fit of sneezing and covered her nose with her sleeve, giving Mother good reason to scold her. "Your nose is the dirtiest fountain in Rome, and your sleeves wetter than our piss pot. If you can't stop your sniveling, take your meal in the courtyard."

Mother often spoke the same to Bianca and me, so I knew she meant no harm by her words. As Papa often whispered, her bark was worse than her bite. But as a child, she'd watched the fever kill her parents and empty her world of all but grief, and I knew she had no sympathy for those who might spread sickness.

But Franco's feeling for Lucia turned him bold. "Perhaps if you didn't work her so hard, Mother, she wouldn't suffer the cold."

Mother's eyes widened. "Since when do you concern yourself with a servant girl?"

Papa, meaning to shift the conversation, cleared his throat and bent his head to recite the evening prayer. "And may we *all* be thankful for our many blessings."

"*Amen!*" Franco said it louder than anyone. "I am most grateful for the soup in our bowls." And wishing to show his praise of Lucia's cooking, he drank his soup so quickly, a piece of mutton lodged in his throat and he was taken over by a fit of coughing.

I poured him a glass of water, but as soon as he took a sip, his eyes strained. Reaching two fingers into his mouth, he made a gagging sound, but he couldn't reach the chunk of meat.

"Help him!" Mother screamed. "Do something, Giorgino!"

I stared in horror as my brother's face paled and he pounded his chest. As he gasped for air, Bianca closed her eyes and began murmuring a prayer, while Papa hammered Franco's back with loud claps, and Pietro yelled, "Breathe, Franco, breathe!"

Franco's eyes bulged, and his face turned a shade toward gray, as he stomped his feet. Then he leaned over, forcing himself to gag, but all that came out was a bit of drool, and still the piece of mutton stuck.

Lucia had been watching from the doorway, and now she took a large cooked noodle left over from the midday meal, poured oil on it, and hurried over to Franco, placing it close to his lips. "Swallow this quickly."

He did as she told him.

"Now another noodle," she spoke gently, pouring a cup of wine. "Then drink a whole glass of wine behind it." When the second noodle had gone down his throat, he straightened and chugged the wine. Already, his eyes relaxed and his breath returned. He stood erect and breathed deeply.

"Lucia, you saved him." I hugged her.

But Mother pulled me aside and raised her voice to Lucia. "How dare you leave large chunks of meat in our soup!"

"*Mi dispiace...*Sorry, Mistress." She lowered her eyes.

"As a punishment for your carelessness"—Mother took the pot and poured the last of it into Franco's bowl—"you're to go without dinner."

"Caterina," Papa whispered. "It was an honest mistake. Give her time to learn."

"And reward her for her mistakes? Never."

Papa's fists shook the table. "Caterina, no child will go hungry in my house—daughter, son, or servant!"

Franco took his bowl and handed it to Lucia. But she set it down on the table and made herself busy at the fireplace. Mother sat rigidly at the table as the rest of us ate our meal in silence. In the corner, Lucia filled the *scaldini* with coals, then carried the heavy porcelain pots up the stairs to warm our rooms.

Before retiring upstairs to bed, Mother stuck her hand in Lucia's apron pockets to make sure they were empty. Then she handed Lucia the bowl of cold soup. "You're lucky your master is so generous."

Small mercies, Mother didn't see her bulging socks, stuffed with bread crusts.

I hid my smile. *Brava, Lucia!*

∽∾∾

During Advent, the days were short, the nights long. Mother didn't like to waste our candles or coal, so most evenings, we went to bed directly after dinner. But I was prone to lying awake and thinking in the darkness, while Bianca was quick to fall asleep. Tossing and turning, I thought about my future and listened to the sounds outside my window—groups of men leaving the corner tavern, courtesans laughing as they hurried toward the bridge, the church bells sounding the hour.

But that night, as the city fell into silence and the wind died, I heard something else in the distance…music! Not religious music. No, this was far more passionate, solo voices singing to

27

each other, with a chorus echoing their words. After a few moments, I realized it was an opera, seldom heard in Rome these days, at least not in public.

Meaning to hear more, I wrapped myself in a shawl and tiptoed down the stairs. Then, feeling my way along the wall, I opened the back door and stepped into the courtyard. I could hear the music better in the open air, but I also heard another sound...closer. Perhaps a dog panting...or a pilgrim sleeping?

The moon was full. As I stepped toward the sound, my eyes adjusted, and I saw a shape moving beneath the pear tree. Drawing closer, I recognized my brother...and then, by her sighs, knew it was Lucia in his arms. She was pinned against the tree, with my brother's arms around her. He buried his face in her hair, kissing her neck. My heart pounded as I stood still, watching. They didn't hear me. They didn't hear anything beyond their own loud breathing, their own deep kisses. Which meant they might not hear Mother, either. It was the fear of them being caught that made my breathing stop until I gasped.

Seeing me, my brother dropped his hands from Lucia's waist and whispered angrily, "*Vattene*...Leave!"

But Lucia pushed him away and came to my side. I was trembling, and tears stung my eyes. Lucia hugged me close, as if she knew my feeling. "Don't worry, Miss. Your brother and I have an understanding."

Embarrassed, I turned to leave, but she pulled me back. "Did you hear the music?"

"Yes," I whispered. "An orchestra and chorus!"

Then Lucia pulled me into the center of the courtyard,

where the moonlight was shining brightest. The music was still faint, but with bursts of joyous sound. Never before had I heard such a concert outside a church, the higher voices reaching our ears more readily. And when the music fell silent between songs, I asked, "Where do you think it comes from?"

"Queen Christina's palace," Franco whispered. And wishing to boast his knowledge in front of Lucia, he told us, "When I was measuring for the queen's glass roof, the gardener told me that ever since the pope closed the queen's opera house, she plants her singers and musicians on the balconies to mock his new laws."

Here I must say that although my brother didn't know how to read or write, he had an uncommon talent for learning. Franco had been everywhere in Rome, and unlike Papa, who didn't bother himself with other people's business or enter into idle chatter, my brother had an ear for listening and a mind for remembering what he'd heard.

Wherever he went, whether it be a church or a palace, people talked to him. Bishops, monks, maids, gardeners, footmen—they whispered their bits to him. Like most men, his learning was more inclined toward politics, battles, and loose women, but I couldn't be choosy about the subjects he wished to share with me. He helped me to know the life around us, sometimes drawing maps of Rome in the dirt of our courtyard, showing me how the city had been divided into franchises, quarters controlled by kings and queens from Catholic countries, like Spain and Portugal, who sent their ambassadors and soldiers to oversee their quarters. Though the kings and queens swore their allegiance to the pope and promised to obey the laws of the church, they had governed freely until now…until this pope, Innocent XI, had come to power.

I learned from my brother that the present pope had made it his mission to take control of the city during his reign, and each time an ambassador died or was recalled, the pope sent his soldiers to take over the quarter. I knew there were still neighborhoods free of his rule, but I didn't know there was a queen so forceful she might challenge the pope's laws.

"Who is this queen?" I asked him.

"Her father was the king of Sweden. He led the Protestants in the Thirty Years War against Catholics. When he died, his daughter was crowned queen and ruled until she was twenty-seven. Then, she gave up her throne to her cousin, and disguising herself, snuck out of her country and came to Italy to convert to Catholicism." Franco had a way of telling what he'd heard so that it sounded like he had been there watching the stories unfold. "The queen was welcomed by a grand procession through the city. Alexander VII was the pope then, and he made a great show of the queen's conversion, honoring her as a heroine to all Catholics. The celebration lasted for five days!"

"And now?"

"The queen has fallen out of favor with this pope. But as long as she governs her own quarter, she can do as she likes. There are only two quarters left outside the pope's control—the French quarter and the queen's."

"If the pope wishes to take control," Lucia asked, "why doesn't he send his army?"

"Queen Christina has too much power," Franco replied.

"She aligns herself with the French king, Louis XIV, who would gladly send his troops to protect their rights to govern their own quarters. The pope doesn't wish to divide the city by a bloody battle." Then, pulling Lucia close, he whispered softly, "But if there ever is such a battle, I'll protect you."

Embarrassed, I turned to leave them alone and hurried upstairs to bed.

∾

The following morning, Lucia came into my room to hang laundry. She took her time, waiting for Bianca to leave, and when we were finally alone, she whispered, "Are you disappointed with me, Miss, that I let your brother kiss me?"

"I wish you'd told me."

"I wanted to, Miss," Lucia blurted. "Only I wasn't sure, and now I am. When your brother's near, my heart beats fast and my skin burns and my head grows light and every moment I can think of nothing else but his smell and his curls and his soft dimpled cheek and the sound of his voice when his lips press to my ear." She took my hands squeezing them. "It's the sweetest ache, Miss. And it makes me wish for nothing else in all the world! Just wait, when you meet your own true love, you'll feel the same."

But her words planted a great sadness inside me, and I grew silent.

Lucia read my thoughts. "What will you do, Miss, if your mother finds you a noble husband who is not to your liking?"

I shrugged. "What can I do?"

"If you don't mind my saying so, Miss, a girl who marries up is like to suffer more."

I did mind her saying so. Mostly I welcomed Lucia's advice, but sometimes her opinions crowded my heart and kept me from knowing my own feelings. "*Per favore*…Please, Lucia, do not speak on subjects you cannot understand."

Her face turned a deep shade of red. "Just because I have no mother to arrange a husband for me does not mean I know *nothing* of marriage."

"That is not what I meant."

"I listen to the women at the fountain," Lucia replied hotly. "Some are domestics in the palaces along the river, well positioned to see how noble husbands treat their wives. They say that even if a wife comes from a noble family, but is not so highborn as her husband, he will use her past against her, rid himself of her faster than a fly on a horse's tail. And then, Miss, she must fear his fists or worse!"

"Worse?"

"Rich or poor, a husband rules in his own house, and if he beats his wife to death, not even the priest will interfere."

"Mother will see that I marry a decent gentleman," I told her.

"It's odds against us, Miss." Lucia shook her head. "Do you know what the blind widow told me? She says that if a wife doesn't die in childbirth, she's lucky. If she doesn't get beaten to death for giving her husband daughters instead of sons, she's even luckier. And if by some miracle, her husband doesn't spread his whores' diseases to her, she's the luckiest wife of all."

Her words sent a shiver through me.

"I have seventeen years in this world, same as you," Lucia told me. "And if what the widow says is true, then half my life is over. I tell you plain, I'd rather have one day of happiness with a lad I truly love than years of loneliness in a nobleman's palace."

Hearing her speak so forcefully on the topic, I asked, "What do you know of a nobleman's palace, Lucia?"

She hesitated. Until that moment, she hadn't spoken of her life before coming to our house. But now she sat beside me, keeping her voice low. "I knew a duke well-learned in sins of every sort, and after he grew tired of his wife, he discovered that thrush can be cooked to look like woodcock, his wife's favorite dish. He also learned that thrush, raised in captivity, can grow fat on poisonous berries, without themselves being harmed by it. But whoever should eat the thrush served in a gravy would be dead within the hour. Well, Miss, this duke raised a flock of poisonous birds in secret, and when they were good and fat, he told the cook they were fresh from his hunt and to cook them up as woodcock, his wife's favorite dish, because she wouldn't know the difference under gravy."

My eyes grew wide. "Did she die?"

Lucia shook her head. "The duchess suspected his intentions and never ate except what her own chambermaid prepared in secret. But I tell you plainly, Miss, what the duchess told me...A man who marries beneath him is like to blame his wife for all that goes wrong in his life."

"How did you know this duchess?"

"You must promise not to say a word of it to anyone." She glanced up, and seeing me nod, continued. "My mother was the chambermaid to the duchess. My papa ran the stable." Then, swallowing: "When his own wife failed to give him a son, the duke turned his attentions to me—"

"*Gesummaria!*" I clasped Lucia's hands.

"I was fourteen," Lucia said softly. "The duchess, being a kind woman, wished to spare me her husband's cruelties, and she gave my parents money to leave. That is why we came south."

CHAPTER FOUR

"Who is he?" Lucia stood peeking through the shutter. "The one who gazes up like a sad puppy, waiting for your songs. He carries a sketchbook."

"Probably a French artist," I replied. "The king of France sent sixteen young sculptors to study Rome's masterpieces, to duplicate them for his court, and their workshop is just across the street."

"Fiery eyes, black curls, strong arms." She swooned, dancing her hips side to side. "And his eyes light up whenever you sing."

Bianca looked up from her prayers. "Mother would never allow an artist to court my sister."

"Some things are worth risking your mother's scorn." Lucia motioned me toward the window. "At least take a peek through the shutters."

I stood behind Lucia, staring over her shoulder.

"See? Isn't he handsome?"

I confess he was most pleasing to look at, with dark eyes and a gentle smile. He had a chiseled face, as the French are like to have, and he dressed the way common to artists—high leather boots, loose breeches, and a billowing white shirt under his jacket. When he saw a movement at my window, he took off his wide-brimmed hat and, sweeping it through the air, bowed.

"Look, he bows to you." Lucia nudged me with her elbow. "Sing him a song."

But Bianca quickly bolted the shutters closed. "Don't listen to her foolishness, Angelica."

Seeing the movement at my window, the Frenchman ran through the narrow passage between houses, hoping he might glimpse me through a window overlooking the courtyard. Unfortunately, he didn't notice Mother standing on the stairs behind the reed curtain, and she, thinking he'd come to relieve himself, as many pilgrims tried to do in the privacy of our garden, quickly dumped a bucket of water over his head, crying, "Out of our courtyard, dirty foreigner."

Dripping and shivering, he ran to the street and stood under my window, laughing and calling out, "Do you have a song for the dirty foreigner, Signorina? Oh, take pity on me. Your mother has punished me for admiring your song."

"You're soaking, Theodon." His friends laughed at him. "Caught pissing again?"

Theodon wrung the tails of his shirt. "The singer's mother must believe me very stupid to think I'd piss in the courtyard of the girl I mean to court."

Lucia opened the shutter a crack. "They call him Theodon, did you hear? And he means to court you."

"Perhaps she has only one eye or is missing all her teeth," his friends teased. "And that's why she stays hidden."

"Show me your face, Signorina," Theodon called out.

Oh, how I longed to open the shutters and apologize for Mother's harsh ways. I would've liked to tell him that I didn't share my mother's view of happiness—fancy clothes, fine jewels, and a title of lady or duchess before my name. Her view of happiness had nothing to do with music, which was my life. Would he think me stupid if I said such a thing? *Music is my life.* Ah, well, I felt stupid. How could I not? I'd seen nothing of the world beyond this house, this neighborhood.

"You should make him a sign," Lucia whispered.

"A song?"

She nodded. "Even through the closed shutters, he'll hear you."

Closing my eyes, I sang to him, feeling my own blood rush. Despite Mother's rule to sing only sacred music, I sang a song I'd heard years ago during Carnevale when the young men used to serenade their sweethearts in the street. *"Il cielo non tiene tante stelle... The sky does not hold as many stars, nor drops the sea and rivers; April holds fewer lilies and violets, the sun fewer rays than the sufferings and pain felt at every hour by a gentle heart that falls in love."*

"Stop this, Angelica." Bianca tried to put her hand over my mouth. "Do you want Mother to hear?"

But I pushed her away and kept singing.

My sister threw a blanket over the shutters to muffle my sound. She pleaded with me to stop. "The pope forbids women from performing!"

Still I lifted my voice. I sang so freely, I brought my sister to tears. Seeing I wouldn't listen to her reason, she knelt to pray. When I finished my song, I touched my heart. "I cannot help myself, Bianca. I have so many songs inside me, it hurts."

❧

The next morning, as soon as the rain quit, Lucia went to the piazza with a basket of clothes. When she returned, her smile had changed. I could read her face now: *I have something to tell you.*

"I'm off to the market, then." Mother gathered her basket and glanced at Lucia. "You washed the tablecloth? We might not have another warm day."

"Yes, Mistress."

"And the two gowns? They must be ready for Nativity. You'll add the lace and iron them today?"

"Yes, Mistress."

As soon as the door closed, Lucia tiptoed to the shutters and peeked, just to make sure Mother was at a safe distance. Turning, she dug her hand into her pocket. "Oh, Miss, I have something for you, something from *him*."

She handed me a small scrolled paper, tied with a silk ribbon. Holding it, I felt my heart beat so fast, I couldn't catch my breath.

"Well, go on!" Lucia urged. "You don't have all day. He said he drew the prettiest view in all the city."

My fingers shook as I untied the ribbon and unrolled the paper. "He draws *me* through the shutters," I gasped.

Lucia leaned over. "A good likeness, Miss. How well he captures your features. Look how he's shown your hair, with light inside each curl. And your chin lifted. It's the way you truly look, Miss, your eyes searching through the window. The sun lighting up only half your face, the rest of you in shadows. That's it, Miss. That's you...lips open, ready to sing."

"I don't understand how he can draw me. He's only seen me behind shutters."

"He has an artist's eye." She grinned. "Trained to see what others cannot."

I took the pot of steaming water and pinched some dried mint leaves.

Lucia gave me a sly grin. "I did think to tell him that I do the laundry at the fountain in the piazza every morning there's sun, Miss, if you wish to send him a message."

I turned, astonished. "But he'll think me too bold!"

"Oh, Miss." She shook her head. "If he pleases you, then make him a sign of it."

"What would I say?"

She paused for a moment. "You might tell him your songs are meant only for his ears."

"Oh, Lucia." I threw my arms around her. "You do have a way with words."

∽∾

The future arrives, I think, on a day like any other, except the heart finds something new to care about, something new to believe in. Each day, Theodon went to the fountain to sketch, while he and Lucia whispered back and forth. I filled Lucia's head with questions to ask him, and then waited impatiently for her to return with his answers. Through Lucia, I learned he had twenty-three years in this life. I learned, too, that his father was a horse merchant and sold horses to the king of France. He had two older brothers, who followed in his father's trade, but he, having an artist's character, had been sent to a monastery to study. I learned his preference for soft cheeses, the smelly kind, and red Burgundy wine. I learned, too, that he loved crossing the mountains on horseback, waking up to the scent of pine trees. He loved the autumn season best, when the air turned brisk. I learned he missed his mother's cooking, trout in mustard sauce and scalloped potatoes, and the scent of his father's pipe smoke after dinner.

"Does he have a sorrow…a grief?" I asked Lucia.

She rolled her eyes. "Surely his sorrow is to be kept apart from you."

"And his hope?"

She laughed at me. "His hope is to earn your love, Miss. That's plain enough."

"What did he ask about me, then?" It seemed to me there wasn't much Lucia could say about my life.

Lucia's eyes twinkled. "I told him you are not so grand when you first wake up, with your hair snarled and your muslin frock hanging loose with the coffee stain on it."

I fell on my bed, laughing. "You didn't—"

"I did." She grinned. "But I also told him you are surely the most talented singer ever born."

"Oh, Lucia." I pulled her next to me. "How you lift my spirits."

❧

I didn't know Theodon, except through Lucia's words. But her words made my longings grow, and these longings were made more real by the gifts Theodon sent—small sketches of the places he'd visited, a libretto from a French opera, chocolate wrapped in gold paper. Even though Lucia warned me to hide the gifts in my trunk, away from Mother, I carried the smallest sketch in my pocket and slept with it beneath my pillow at night.

As the Sundays in Advent passed and the days grew colder, I thought of nothing else but Theodon. Waiting for Lucia to return each morning from the piazza, I paced the floor, peeking through the shutters. Once she arrived home, there was still the task of finding a moment alone, when she could whisper their conversations to me. I grew impatient and took risks, pulling Lucia aside in the courtyard, tugging her up the stairs the moment she returned. As soon as Lucia whispered her secrets, my mood soared and my songs grew more intense. Whenever Theodon listened from the street below my window, I heightened my voice in new ways. Even though I performed only sacred music, I sang every word to Theodon. *"La mia anima perduta piange…My lost soul cries, waits for the love you alone can give. Hear my prayers…"*

Bianca saw my life was splitting. I had two lives now, the one I lived by Mother's rules and the one inside my heart, fed by Lucia's secrets and Theodon's gifts.

41

"If I notice," Bianca warned me, "then surely Mother will, too."

Although Bianca was pious and tried to speak kindly of others, my sister did not trust Lucia. "She fills your head with false hopes, uses you to win our brother's heart. She hardly prays, except at church."

My sister had always been cautious toward the world. But now that Lucia lived with us, her fears grew. One morning shortly after Lucia arrived, my sister woke to find the shutters blown open, shadows moving across our wall. "See that?" She shook me awake and pointed at the shadow. "It is the shape of the Virgin. She comes to warn us against Lucia."

A few days later, Bianca screamed when she saw a spider weaving its web in the wood beams above our bed. Trembling, she said, "God is warning you, Angelica. The web is right above you. Don't you see? This is a sign. There is danger in this house. Lucia has brought bad luck."

At first I laughed. But three Sundays after Lucia came to our house, my sister and I were carrying water in from the well, when a black cat with yellow eyes arched its back in front of our doorway, refusing to move. I took a broom and shooed it, but the cat stared at me without blinking. Neither one of us dared step past the cat, and so we stood frozen in our steps. Only when Lucia took the bucket of water from our hands and splashed it toward the cat did it leap across the wall.

"This is your doing," Bianca told Lucia.

Lucia laughed. "So now I am to blame for every hungry cat on your doorstep?"

Bianca took my hand and tugged me toward the door. "The cat stared at you, Angelica. Come inside and pray with me."

But I shook my hand free and hung back. "Bianca has always been fearful," I whispered to Lucia. "She prefers a life that doesn't change, and you brought change into our home."

But I knew I wasn't speaking the whole truth. Bianca had good reason to resent Lucia. Before Lucia came, my sister and I had been closer, a closeness brought by singing and sleeping side by side, year after year. Now that Lucia had arrived, I felt my sister's presence as an intrusion. When Bianca was near, Lucia didn't speak openly, and I blamed my sister, feeling she deprived me of the moments when Lucia and I might talk.

One such morning, when my sister's prayers droned on and I wished a moment alone with Lucia, my impatience turned to cruelty. I mocked Bianca behind her back, rubbing the space above my upper lip as if tweaking a mustache, for indeed she'd grown a line of fine dark hairs, which she'd tried to lighten with lemon juice. Looking up, Bianca caught me making fun of her. She rose to her feet, and her eyes filled with tears. "It's you!" she faced Lucia. "You've turned my own sister against me. Do you think you can live inside a family for the space of three Sundays and know the truths of our lives?"

Lucia shook her head. "I didn't mean to, Miss—"

"Mother has sacrificed everything for my sister." Bianca's lips trembled. "God willing, her hopes will be well served."

After that, when Lucia and I were in the same room, Bianca hurried away from us. More often now, when she and I weren't rehearsing our hymns together, she prayed downstairs or spent time in the courtyard. And that gave me more opportunity to sing to Theodon.

⌒∞⌒

Perhaps that's how love takes its shape...bit by bit, secret by secret, until the feelings grow, leaving room for nothing else. Theodon was my secret. And I liked that, having some part of myself hidden from Mother. But I also had to be careful not to let Mother discover my favorite time of the day—when Theodon stood beneath my window and I sang to him.

That, too, had changed. Now, when I sang an aria, I added my own ornaments, trilling longer, suspending the dissonant notes into silence, then leaping into passionate sound. I sang of love, filling the air with our secret life. And yet, as the days passed, I worried that my songs would not be enough, that he would tire of so much secrecy, that Mother's rules might drive him away.

When today's song ended, I peeked through the shutters. Theodon stood below, his face raised to my window. When he saw my shutter open a crack, he smiled slightly. How I wanted to throw open the shutters and sing openly. But he was late for work, and nodding once toward my window, he turned quickly and hurried into his workshop.

I threw myself on the bed. "How slowly time passes inside this house."

Bianca caught me staring at myself in the iron plate I'd borrowed from the pantry. "You look the same, Angelica. No better, no worse than yesterday. You think overly much about what *he*

44

sees." Mocking me, she sang the scale in thirds, up and down. "Me, me, me, me, me, me, meeeeeeee."

Irritated, I couldn't hold my tongue and sang higher. "Plump, plump, plump, plump, plump, plump, plummmmmp." (For it was true, her hips had widened.)

My sister's face reddened. "It's the Frenchman who lingers beneath our window. You sing louder the moment *he* arrives, and the moment he leaves, you get very cross and are impatient the whole day."

"You imagine such things. You're jealous."

"You should be careful, Angelica." Bianca's round eyes stared into my own. "He changes your song. You sing for *him* now. And Lucia encourages these feelings." Bianca knelt down at the foot of our bed and closed her eyes to pray.

"Why must you pray so often?" I said teasingly, "God doesn't forget your prayers, does he?"

She opened her eyes. "I pray that you, Angelica, will not stray from God's path."

"Perhaps God has willed me to fall in love with the Frenchman."

"Don't be foolish."

Closing my eyes, I thought, *But I am foolish. Foolish enough to believe in myself, my song, my future.* I imagined Theodon taking me to France, where I'd heard that all forms of music were permitted. I imagined him as a famous sculptor, and I, as his wife, singing operas to the French king and his courtiers. I thought of all the songs I'd be permitted to sing far away from this pope and his laws.

CHAPTER FIVE

Two days before Nativity, Lucia came home from an errand looking worried. As soon as Mother stepped out into the courtyard, she quickly drew me near. "I know his name. The one who comes every day in the unmarked coach and doesn't part the curtains as he listens to your songs. A Spanish cardinal, Tomas de Cabrera."

"A cardinal?" My eyes grew wide.

She gave a quick nod. "Much in favor with the last pope but at odds with this one. Rumor, mind you, I'm told he's squandered his reputation. But"—she glanced up—"here's where you fit, Miss. I'm told his passion is for music, not women."

"Who told you?"

Making her mouth as if to offer up a kiss, she batted her eyes. "His cheeky valet."

"Lucia, you let him kiss you?" I thought of Franco, how angry he'd be.

"No, Miss. But I let him think I might." She fixed her eyes

on me. "The valet told me the cardinal's niece lodges nearby, in the convent Saint Ruffinus, and he uses her as his excuse to come and hear you sing. Five mornings last week, he listened while you practiced."

"Mother says it's good to have someone high up in the church take notice of my talent."

"Not if he neglects his duties!" Lucia leaned closer. "His valet says you've cast a spell...stolen his master's reason. He says your songs drive the cardinal to weeping. And even though the pope's spies circle his coach, he still can't stay away."

I felt the blood drain from my face, my throat grow tight.

"Perhaps your sister is right, Miss. Perhaps you shouldn't sing so freely to Theodon."

Lucia's words troubled me, but I had no time to dwell on her meaning. That morning, when Mother came inside from the courtyard, she sat down and couldn't stand up. She asked for a cup of water. Drawing close, Lucia saw the flush to her face and called to my sister to bring blankets from upstairs. We knew right off Mother was ill. Soon enough her breathing turned shallow, and one dry cough followed another. I put my hand to her forehead. "She has a fever."

Even after Lucia stoked the fire and wrapped blankets around her, Mother shivered so that her teeth chattered. She didn't seem to be awake, though her eyes were open. Lucia fanned the coals, trying to coax more heat. I tried to get her to drink warm tea, but Mother pushed me away. "Angelica,"—her voice was a hoarse scratch—"keep away from me. Stay in your room."

"All of you, keep away," Lucia said. "I'll put her to bed."

When Lucia had tucked Mother inside her sheets and filled

her *scaldino* with coals, she came downstairs and whispered to me, "We need Saint-John's-wort and peony root to ward off the fever."

It was decided that since Bianca feared such outings and Lucia needed to stay by Mother's side, I would go to the apothecary's as soon as Pietro returned and could accompany me. I draped a scarf round my chin, then lifted the hood of my cloak so that my face would remain hidden. I confess I had my own reasons for wishing to go, as I hoped to glimpse Theodon. But I was not so lucky, as the weather was brisk and the workshop doors were closed.

The apothecary's shop stood under the sign of the leeches, and as we entered, Pietro covered his chin. The apothecary had a gold tooth, which he could take from his mouth to amuse and frighten children. With his bulging eyes and thick lips, he had the dry croak of a man who lectured more than he listened. He stared at his customers—their feet, knees, stomachs, necks, and eyes—reading their bodies out loud. "I see by the yellow around your eyes, too much wine." He was apt to tell exactly what ailed his clients, even before they felt their symptoms. "Are your toenails curling?" he asked a young priest ahead of us. "I thought so. You need more green vegetables."

When it was Pietro's turn, the apothecary's gold tooth shimmered. "Giorgino's boy, no? I see by the squint of your eyes, you don't see well. Drink your own urine mixed with honey. It will improve your sight by the grape harvest."

Then he turned his gaze to me. "Perhaps, Signorina, you need something for your *miracle voice*?"

Pietro, acting the part of my escort, spoke up. "Our mother suffers a fever. We need Saint-John's-wort and peony root."

"How much can you pay?" The apothecary rubbed his mustache.

Pietro emptied three small coins from a pouch.

The apothecary shrugged. "I have no peony root, but the Jew down the street will give you some free. He has bundles. Tell him I sent you." Then he scooped the coins off the counter and pocketed them. "Here's the Saint-John's-wort. Boil the leaves, add wine, and have your mother drink it." He held the door open. "Go ask the Jew for his peony root."

Pietro and I stood outside the Jew's shop. Mother claimed that Jews carried diseases, but I also knew that peony root worked best for warding off a fever, so I took Pietro's hand and hurried inside. A man with a long black beard and a round black hat looked up from a book.

"The apothecary sent us for peony root," Pietro stammered, holding his scarf over his chin.

"He doesn't have his own supply?" The Jew narrowed his eyes at us. "Did he ask to see your coins first?"

When Pietro nodded, the Jew shook his head. "Yes, it is always so. He has plenty but prefers to keep his peony root for the bishops who have coins to spare. Here"—the Jew reached inside a jar and took out two roots—"two *paoli*."

Pietro blushed, lowering his eyes.

"Signore,"—I stepped forward—"we have no more coins."

"Ach!" The man threw up his hands. "That gold-toothed thief took your coins, then sent you to me? Am I supposed to give my medicines away for free?"

An old woman came through a curtain and muttered a few words in their language, and the Jew handed Pietro the peony root. "Take it, but do me a favor. Tell the apothecary I sold my last peony root to the cardinals." He grinned. "Tell him that."

As we turned toward home, the apothecary stood waiting in his doorway. "Did you get your peony root?"

Pietro shook his head. "There was none left. The Jew sold it all to the cardinals."

Turning red in the face, the apothecary slammed his door in our faces.

That gave us a good laugh, and as we turned down our street, I slowed my step, hoping that I might see Theodon. But again, my luck was off and the doors were still closed. I might have lingered, but Lucia was waiting in the doorway, motioning for us to hurry. As I stepped inside and heard Mother's coughing upstairs, my thoughts of Theodon were quickly replaced by worries for her.

Right away, Lucia carved the peony root into pieces and strung them on thread. We all wore a piece around our necks to keep the fever away. Bianca and I kept the pot of water boiling, and Papa carried her bowls of soup and sat beside her. "Drink it, Little Goose," Papa whispered. That was his nickname for Mother. He stayed by her side, spooning broth into her mouth until the bowl was empty.

❧

The following morning, as church bells rang throughout the city to celebrate Nativity, Mother was still burning with fever. Her face was flushed, her mouth dry. Lucia kept by her side, encouraging her to drink tea with Saint-John's-wort, but Mother was so weak, she could only take small sips. She slept with her back propped against the wall, to keep herself from coughing.

We went to church without Mother, leaving Lucia sitting outside her door. Crossing the piazza, we saw a crowd gathered near the fountain. From behind, we could see that a man with dark curls had been arrested. He stood inside a *berlina,* a cage on wheels, with a sign around his neck. His back was to us, but I could hear the crowd jeering as someone read the sign out loud. *"Hereby punished for tampering with the weights and swindling the cheese-seller on the Eve of Nativity."*

"Leave it to a Frenchman to steal cheese," someone called out.

A Frenchman! My heart froze, and I tried to stand on my toes to see his face. Lifting the hood of my cloak, I stared through the black veil to get a better view, but it was impossible to see over the tops of heads to glimpse the man's face. Nearby were two *sbirri,* the pope's police, walking slowly around the piazza, waiting the designated time before they could free the man.

As the church bells tolled, Papa called for us to hurry.

Bianca gripped my hand. "Come quickly. The church doors are open, and the nobles have already begun arriving. If we don't get there soon, we'll not get a pew near the front."

"I must see who he is," I whispered.

"Oh, Angelica," Bianca said crossly. "Look inside the church gate and stop lingering."

There he was... *Theodon.* Even with my face veiled and my cloak pulled tight, he knew me, smiled at me. It was true what Lucia said: His eyes were trained to see what others could not. He wore a loose scarf around his neck, and his wide-brimmed hat matched his dark wool coat. His smile was soft, framed by the beginnings of a goatee. I dared not lift my veil but let my gaze hold his for a few seconds as we passed through the gate, long enough to feel my heart quicken. As I entered the church, I heard the rustle of his coat and felt his presence behind me.

Just as Mother would have wished, we arrived early, claiming the first pew behind those reserved for noble families. The church smelled of incense and candle wax. The choirs were already singing. In the front pews, the noble families displayed their velvet coats lined with fur. The men came with powdered wigs, their coats opened, their boots polished. The women carried fur muffs suspended around their necks on ribbons. They wore their hair parted, coiled ringlets pinned either side, pearls dangling from their ears.

Behind the nobles sat the families of tradesmen, all of us cloaked in black and gray. Farther back sat domestics, who worked in palaces and returned to our quarter to attend church with their families. Outside the doors, beggars and orphans stood shivering.

The Church of Saint Cecilia was known for its music. On religious holidays, there were always two choirs, one made up of nuns, singing in the balcony, hidden behind the wooden grille, the other, a male choir. For the concerts on Nativity and Easter, both choirs blended their voices, with several musicians accompanying them, playing lute, keyboard, violin, and organ.

After the priest had said the offertory, I followed Papa toward the front of the church to take communion. But as we approached the sacristy, the line stalled, and next to me, two young noble brothers were whispering. "There she is, behind her father…the girl with the miracle voice. Every morning a crowd gathers outside her house."

"Go on," one of the brothers dared, "lift her veil so I can see her face."

Even if the priest heard their whispers, he would do nothing against them because the nobles paid his wages and repaired the roof. I blushed and kept my head lowered. I tried to edge my way forward, but there was no room to kneel at the sacristy. I heard laughter, and out of the corner of my eye, I saw a hand dart out and reach toward my veil, trying to lift it.

I lurched forward, almost tripping, but a hand caught me, steadied me. "Mademoiselle."

Lifting my gaze, my heart stopped—Theodon smiled at me. Even through my black veil, our eyes met. A moment only, but how warm his hand felt where it touched me, a warmth that stayed, even as he released my arm and I moved forward to take communion. Trembling, I glanced at the priest, wondering if he could hear my heart pounding beneath my cloak. When I walked back to my pew, I knelt. Moments later, I heard the soft squeak of the wooden pew behind me. I didn't need to look. I knew it came from Theodon.

As the choirs sang the processional, we stood, bowing our heads as the priest and his acolytes carried the cross down the aisle. I knew that women were forbidden to sing in church, unless they were nuns singing from behind the grille. But with Theodon standing behind me, I hummed softly, singing along with the nun's voices. I kept my voice faint, believing only those closest would hear. But with my heart so full, the feeling spilled over, and for a moment, my harmony separated from the choir's.

Papa turned, his eyes furious. Bianca gripped my hand,

squeezing it. Even Franco gave me a harsh stare. Their meaning was plain enough. *Stop this freedom of sound!*

I fell fast into silence. Even so, I saw the noblewomen staring at me as they left their pews, making their whispers heard. "Even in church, she sings to arouse."

For once I was glad my head was covered, my face hidden. As we started home, Papa gripped my arm. "It is one thing to mock your mother's rules, Angelica, another to disobey the church's rules. If you wish to sing in church, then we'll have the priest place you in a convent." It was rare for Papa to speak so forcefully, and his words wrenched my heart. Now that I knew I was not his own blood daughter, I felt the need to prove myself worthy of his love.

When Lucia returned from the fountain later that afternoon, she pulled me into the courtyard. "I'm told, Miss, that even in church you sing to perfection!" At first I thought she meant to scold me, but then her face softened into a smile. "Must've been the Frenchman, made you forget yourself."

⌒∞⌒

The morning after, Mother's voice rang out. "Angelica, do you know how they celebrate Nativity in the palaces?"

"Your mother has recovered." Lucia grinned as she swept the floor.

I hurried upstairs with a cup of tea and a plate with bread and jam.

"Grand balls," she told me. "Gowns, orchestras…You must sit near the front of the church on Nativity, Angelica, where the nobles will see you."

I set the tray on her lap. "Nativity has come and gone, Mother."

Bianca stood at my side. "You slept through it. You slept four days."

Confusion filled Mother's face. "New Year's Eve." Her eyes grew doubtful. "Has that, too, passed?"

I shook my head and, surprising myself, threw my arms around her narrow shoulders and hugged her. "Oh, Mother, you had us all so worried."

She laughed, embarrassed by my affection. On occasion, Mother could be tender. Not that she would kiss or hug us, but she would show her affection in other ways—offering up a bigger portion of soup, sewing a pair of socks double to keep our feet warm, wrapping her only silk shawl around my throat. That was my mother's way.

"By this time, next year, Angelica, you'll be married. Married to a noble husband. Think of Nativity then…in your own palace!"

Bianca caught my eye and gave me a meaningful stare. *Stop this foolishness with the Frenchman.* I thought of Theodon, and then I made my thought disappear. I should be grateful. Mother had recovered, and no one else had caught her fever.

That night, when Mother joined us at the table, Papa had a gift for her. Unwrapping the brown paper, Mother gasped, holding up the most beautiful cloak I had ever seen, blue velvet with red silk lining and trim. It was the sort of cloak I had wished for on my birthday.

"Try it on." Papa draped it around her. "As pretty as any noblewoman's."

"Prettier." Mother stared at herself in the looking glass. Bianca and I reached over to feel its softness, but Mother's eyes narrowed on Papa. "It must have cost a month's wages."

"He traded for it," Franco blurted. "Installed the tailor's glass windows in exchange for the cloak."

I saw Mother's face twitch, as if some tenderness for Papa was trying to show itself. But instead she turned her gaze to me. "It will be wasted on me. Angelica must wear it on New Year's Eve. If the nobles see her in this, surely they'll invite her to perform in their palaces."

The room grew quiet. My heart squeezed as I thought how her words would make Papa feel.

Only Franco dared speak. "Five days' work, Mother. Papa and I spent five days so he could give you this cloak."

"I do not care about cloaks," Mother whispered. "I care about Angelica marrying—"

Papa's eyes flashed. "Do you think of nothing else, Caterina? Nothing but Angelica's future?" Then he took the cloak from Mother's shoulders and held it near the fire. "This cloak is for you. My gift to you. If you do not want it, no one in this family will wear it. I will burn it."

Grazie a Dio, there are those who know how to handle such situations, and Lucia was one of them. She moved swiftly from the corner and lifted the cloak from Papa's hands. "*Per favore*, Master, it's the fever that makes the mistress say such things. The fever turns a heart weary...so weary that even a gift so grand as this cloak cannot be accepted properly."

Then, turning, she draped it around Mother's shoulders. "How well it suits you, Mistress. Now you'll be taken for a noblewoman when you enter the church, and Angelica and Bianca will be seen as noble-daughters by your side."

We all needed to pretend her words were true, and so we nodded.

Mother's face softened. "Yes, perhaps it is the fever." Then she stepped to Papa's side and planted a kiss on his cheek. "*Grazie*, Giorgino." It was an uncommon thing for Mother to speak his name so softly, to show him tenderness in front of us, her children.

Now, lifting his eyes, Papa whispered shyly, "It will keep you warm so your fever doesn't return." Then Papa sat at the table, folding his hands, and we joined him.

A chilly stillness had settled into the city. There was only one sound that echoed loudly when the bells stopped tolling—the wailing of babies left on church steps. It happened every year between Christmas and New Year's, when the weather turned cold and parents too poor to heat their houses left their babies on the church steps, hoping for charity this time of the year.

We could hear them crying now, across the piazza.

We bowed our heads as Papa said grace. "We thank God for blessing Caterina with good health again. Bless them, too, who cry this night. It be love that drives mothers and fathers to wrap their babies in their last blanket, leaving them swaddled on the church steps. Them who have nothing left but hope...May the church keep us all warm and in good health."

Even Mother, glad to be feeling better, nodded. "Amen."

CHAPTER SIX

New Year's Day brought with it a great surprise.

We attended church in the morning, then returned home to Mother's feast—roasted chicken and potatoes, her special torte of ricotta and almonds. Afterward, we were all in need of fresh air and bundled ourselves warm for a stroll. As Papa draped Mother's new cloak around her shoulders, Mother raised herself on her toes and planted a kiss on Papa's cheek. My parents rarely showed their affection for each other in front of us, and now Papa blushed and said, "Surely you are the finest wife in all of Rome." Then, looking very proud, he took Mother's arm and led us out the door.

Dusk was already casting shadows in the piazza. On top of the hill stood a row of cypress, standing tall against the setting sun. Smoke rose in angles from the chimneys, and the brisk wind made my eyes water. Other families were out strolling, too, and we stopped often to wish them *"Buon anno."* As Mother gossiped with the other wives about the length of the new priest's sermon, and Papa spoke with the husbands about the heavy rains, I found myself peering from inside my hood, searching for all things French—French boots, French coats, French hats.

Just when we turned back toward home, we heard the faint rumble of wheels and horses' hooves crossing the nearby bridge. Two runners, dressed in billowy cotton shirts, came running through the crowd. "Let the coach through," they cried. "Move aside!"

"I want to be a runner," Pietro said, and darted ahead.

But Papa yanked him back. "It's no job for a son of mine, Pietro. They hire orphans, then run the lads into an early grave."

"If you marry a nobleman, Angelica,"—Pietro hid his chin behind his hand—"can I be your coachman?"

I gently pulled his hand away from his face and, thinking of Theodon, spoke loudly so Mother might hear. "I don't want a husband so highborn he treats me as a servant. Besides, idle hours turn men ugly. Haven't you noticed the nobles in the front pews? Withered eyelids, loose chins, and foamy mouths."

"Haven't *you* noticed the furs that keep their wives warm?" Mother remarked, before she rounded the corner, then stopped in her tracks. *"Mio Dio!"* There, standing in front of our house, was the coachman, rapping his gloved hand against our door. Mother gathered her skirts and stepped quickly toward the house. "I am Signora Voglia, mistress of this house."

It pained me to hear Mother imitating the upper classes— rolled *rrr*s, clipped words, her chin held higher than necessary. The coachman handed her an envelope without so much as a smile. Then, bowing curtly and without a word, he hurried past us toward the coach. As soon as he mounted the back, the curtains stirred inside the coach windows and a hand reached out to signal, as a deep voice cried from within, "Move on!"

We held our breath as the air filled with dust.

"Did you see it?" Franco whispered. "Did you see the cardinal's ring?"

Gesummaria, my heart raced.

Bianca, always thinking the worst, made the sign of the cross. "I pray it isn't a warning from the pope, Angelica. Perhaps you have sung too freely, and now a cardinal comes to deliver a fine for your foolishness."

I hung back, but Papa tugged me toward the door. "They don't deliver fines on New Year's Day, Angelica, and never in fancy envelopes."

Inside, Mother held the card in front of the candle. She gasped. "Oh my. Angelica is invited to sing at Palazzo Pamphili for the Music Academy, Sunday next. Maestro Arcangelo Corelli will conduct the orchestra." She hugged me fiercely. "Soon all of Rome will know your name."

My stomach fluttered with excitement. I'd spent my whole life preparing for this opportunity, and now it had finally arrived. I felt happy...but also nervous. It was one thing to sing to a crowd on the street, quite another to perform before an audience of cardinals and nobles.

"This is your opportunity," Mother said as she lifted my chin. "Someone high up has taken notice of you. Once you perform at Cardinal Pamphili's Sunday concert, every noble in the city will know your name. And then the suitors will be lining up."

I drew my head away. I didn't want to go alone to the palace, and now I stepped closer to my sister. "Bianca reads music far better than I do and has such a gift for harmony. Perhaps she might come, too?"

"You can't lead your sister around like a stray dog, begging bones," Mother replied. "Besides, I'll accompany you."

Bianca smiled. "I'm happy for you, Angelica. Truly I am."

And relieved, I thought. I knew my sister did not like to leave the house, except to go to church.

"Your sister knows that if you marry well, Angelica, her prospects for the future will also be improved."

I had never seen Mother so excited, her eyes all lit up as she stood in the door calling the news to our neighbors. "Have you heard? Angelica is invited to sing at Palazzo Pamphili!"

Lucia took my cloak. "Congratulations, Miss." Then she gave me a meaningful glance, and by that, I knew she had something to tell me.

∞

Later, after Lucia had scoured the pans, she carried the *scaldini* full of coals to warm our rooms. When we were finally alone, she handed me a square of green marble. Etched into its smooth surface, I read: *Buon Anno, 1688.*

"Look at it, Miss. Isn't it the loveliest green? He gave it to me this morning on our way out of the church, but with your family being home all day, I had no chance to give it to you."

"Oh, Lucia." I rubbed the smooth stone. "Engraved by his own hand... It's the sweetest gift I have ever received!"

"I must say, Miss, he was so reluctant to take his eyes off you, he nearly tripped over the priest's cane."

I wanted to hear more, but Bianca came into the room and, seeing the marble in my hand, cast us both a sharp glance.

After Lucia left us alone, I dressed for bed and climbed under the covers. Before Bianca blew out the candle, I held the piece of marble near the flame. "It's a gift from Theodon. Isn't it lovely?"

Bianca ignored my question and blew out the candle. "I'm tired, Angelica."

"Tired or angry?" I tugged her braid, meaning to tease her into a better humor.

"Does it matter? I am sure there's no muzzle that can stop your chatter...Theodon, Theodon, Theodon."

I put my feet against the backs of her knees, to warm them, for her body was always warm, while mine shivered at night. "Seeing him, my blood rushes with its own song."

"And if you continue to sing to him? Have you given a thought to the future?" Bianca turned over. "Today you were lucky. It was a coach delivering an invitation. Next time, it might be the pope's police coming to cart you away to a convent for wayward women."

I touched the marble to her arm. "His feelings are true, Bianca. And so are mine."

"Lucia feeds such dreams; I've seen her. But I'll not lie to you as she does. I'll not raise false hopes. This affection between you and the Frenchman has no future."

"What if Mother wishes you to marry the candlemaker's son?" I spoke of the young man with greasy hair and coarse skin who often gave Mother free candles, asking after her younger daughter with the sturdy hips. "Would you do your duty then, accepting Mother's choice of a husband, with no thought to your own feeling?"

Bianca kept her back to me. "God gave you a great talent, but I fear you mean to use it to your own purpose."

"Saint Bianca of Piss Pots." I mocked her preachy voice and flopped over, rolling to the other side of the bed. "What great wings you have to crush my happiness."

We lay clutching opposite sides of the bed, her silence pulling tight around my heart. As I listened to her breathing slow to the heavy sighs of sleep, I tossed and turned. I could never sleep with bad feelings between us, but Bianca snored to the heavens.

The next morning, we heard a loud knock, followed by Father Zachary's booming voice. "I warned you, Caterina. Your daughter's reputation for singing grows too quickly!"

I reached for my smock and hurried to the top of the stairs, where I knelt behind the reed curtain to listen. Each time Father Zachary came to visit now, I could no longer think of him as priest or patron but saw instead my own blood father. I felt uneasy, not knowing how to act in his presence, as if knowing the truth had turned everything else between us into a lie.

"All of Rome knows about the invitation, but that's not what they're talking about!" Father Zachary stood by the fire, warming his hands. "It's rumored a cardinal comes each day and sits in an unmarked coach, listening to Angelica rehearse. This very morning, on this cardinal's gates were placed *cartelli infamanti,* posters showing the cardinal praying on his knees to an angel wearing the cloak of a tradesman's daughter. Need I say that his manhood was displayed rising beneath his robes!"

I couldn't see Mother's face to know her feeling, but she spilled the coffee as she poured it, so I expect she wasn't pleased by his words.

"The pope is outraged." Father Zachary lowered his voice. "He has sent his spies to listen to Angelica, and they've reported back to him. They say she lures men. They say her voice is so full of passion, not even a cardinal can resist her song. They say that she makes honest men forget their senses, that she's dangerous—"

"Then we must hurry and find her a suitable husband, Father. As soon as she's married, the rumors will die down."

"Are you deaf, Caterina? This is most serious. If it's true that a cardinal sits each day, neglecting his duties, then your daughter will be blamed for his faults." Father Zachary paced the floor. "I tell you, she'd be better off in a convent, where she could sing every day without risking her reputation."

"A convent does not always protect a girl, Father. You and I both know that." Mother's voice rose. "Angelica will sing at Palazzo Pamphili. Once the nobles hear her voice, I am confident the suitors will be lining up."

"Then she must be beyond reproach, Caterina." Father Zachary took a book from his satchel and handed it to Mother. "All the guests will be watching to see if the rumors are true, if she corrupts this cardinal. You must prepare her well."

"A book of manners? This is the same text the nuns used when I was a girl in the convent—"

Father Zachary nodded. "Used to train noblemen's daughters in courtly behavior. Angelica must memorize the rules. These Sunday academies are a stage for new composers and singers, and they are well attended by those nobles and cardinals who take music seriously. There will be a small chamber orchestra. After her performance, she will be expected to take refreshments—"

An orchestra...refreshments! I flew down the stairs. "I cannot...I am not prepared."

Father Zachary held my shoulders. "Rest assured, Angelica, you will be. I'm on my way now to visit Maestro Corelli, and I'll hire one of his musicians to rehearse with you."

I stared at the floor and held my fears still. I tried to act the same—grateful to my patron. But now that I knew the truth of our relationship, I could not look the priest in the eye. I'd never once spoken my heart to him, and even now, I hid my truest feelings. *Yes, Father. Thank you, Father. I'll do my best, Father.* I showed him half of who I was, only half. Gratitude, not affection. Respect, not doubt. Obedience, not love. We'd never spoken as father and daughter. And I could only guess he preferred it so.

❧

Mother set to work immediately, insisting that Bianca learn the manners, too. Running her finger under the print, she read slowly, *"Avoid yawning at all times."*

Mocking Mother's seriousness, I yawned excessively, planting a smile on Bianca's lips.

"Even if the soup is hot," she read, *"it is impolite to blow on it."*

"What if I burn my mouth?"

Mother ran her finger across the page. *"If you have the misfortune to burn your mouth, you should endure it as patiently as possible."*

I rolled my eyes. "I'd rather eat with the servants who lick their fingers and wipe their sauces with bread crusts, thinking nothing of their reputations and only of their hunger."

Mother opened to another page. *"Among refined company, it is decent for a prince to drink first and then to offer the same glass to his guests, for it is considered a mark of candor and friendship."*

"Mother, if I must relieve myself, how will I know where to go in the palace?"

Mother thumbed through the book and found the right heading. *"Regarding Natural Functions of the Body...In palaces, chamber pots are provided in rooms with curtains. If you pass a gentleman who is relieving himself, it is impolite to greet him."*

Bianca and I smothered our giggles as Mother continued, *"It is very impolite to blow wind from your body when in refined company, either from above or below, even if done without noise. Do not move back and forth on your chair, for whoever does so gives the impression of trying to break wind."*

Bianca and I could not hold back any longer, and we burst out laughing.

Mother slammed the book closed. "Go ahead and laugh. But you, Angelica, must understand that every gentleman will be watching you, and judged more harshly is the conduct of a girl like yourself who has talent and beauty but lacks position."

Perhaps it was our frayed nerves, but Mother's chiding only made our laughter swell. Each time I glanced at my sister, we were taken in another fit of giggles until tears ran down our cheeks and we had to hug our stomachs.

Mother's face turned red, and all at once, she leaped up. "If you don't behave properly, you won't get another chance. How dare you throw away this opportunity after all we've done for you!" Then, turning on my sister, she paddled Bianca's arms with the book. "You stupid girl! Can't you see that without your sister, we're doomed to this life? I, too, was pious as you are, praying morning, noon, and night. Prayers got me nothing but thankless daughters!" With each word, Mother slapped the book against Bianca's arms until my sister folded, covering her face.

Hearing Mother's shrieks, Lucia came running, and together, we held Mother's arms while she vented her fury. "It's not blind ambition that makes me command your future, Angelica. It's fear. That alone marks my purpose. I know what can happen…do you understand? I *know* what this world does to girls with talent and beauty. The only safety is to rise in this world, to secure a marriage that protects you."

Then, breathing heavily, she sank onto the bed and buried her face in her hands. Only when she began shaking did I realize she was crying. I'd never seen Mother cry before.

Lucia glanced at me sadly, then quietly left the room.

Mother cried silently, her shoulders lifting and falling like the handle of a milk churn. Then, sitting up and wiping away her tears, she took my hand and squeezed it. "This life can destroy you. You have beauty and talent, Angelica. So did I...*So did I! Now* look at me." She smiled bitterly, glancing at her stained apron. "I'm mother to four children, and I must count every coin to keep them fed and clothed through winter." Rising from the bed, she stroked Bianca's hair. "I fear I know grief better than love. If I seem overly harsh, it's because I don't wish the same for you." Then, she planted the book on my pillow. "Do as you like."

Bianca and I didn't speak, didn't move. We listened to the *swish, swish* of Mother's skirt as it brushed the doorway, the stairs. Bianca wept quietly, and I hugged her close, brushing her hair with my fingers.

I didn't want to memorize rules or manners. But for the first time, I understood how much hope was pinned upon my talent. Hands trembling, I reached for the book. I opened it to the first page and started at the beginning.

CHAPTER SEVEN

The following afternoon Father Zachary introduced us to Stefano Gasparini. "He will prepare Angelica for the Sunday concert."

He looked a boy still, with his pale skin, blond curls, and serious gray eyes. Mother took one look at him and laughed. "How much have you paid *him*, Father?"

"He has twenty-two years, Caterina, and is reputed to be the finest musician in Corelli's ensemble." Father Zachary gave Mother a stern look. "We are lucky he's willing to help Angelica for the sum we can offer."

Hearing himself talked about, Gasparini's ears turned the color of beet water. After Father Zachary and Mother stepped into the courtyard, he lifted several sheets of handwritten music from his satchel and handed them to me. "I'm told you read music?"

I nodded and took my place next to the harpsichord.

Then he sat on the bench and rolled up his sleeves. After clearing his throat, he began playing the opening notes and nodded for me to begin. But as soon as I raised my voice, he stopped playing. "You must listen to the notes."

He played the same measures a second time while I sang along, but again the harpsichord fell silent. "You cling to the notes like sap to a tree. Sing softly, one note at a time. Hold the high notes steady, without fluttering."

"You hardly let me begin," I muttered.

As soon as his hands struck the keys, I leaped, but this time with too much effort. Then, meaning to slow my phrasing, my voice missed the notes he played.

"No, no, no!" His hands flew up in the air. "Have you no ear for music? Can't you hear the heaviness of your sound?"

"I must have time to learn the music."

"You don't *learn* the music...you *become* it! Look over the notes and read through the words before we try again." He breathed in deeply, then stood and paced in front of the keyboard, hands clasped behind his back, while I looked over the pages of music. When I had finished, he remarked, "Perhaps with the church music you have performed, freedom of sound is undesirable. But Maestro Corelli expects his sopranos to interpret the librettos with their own feeling."

Then, eyes closed, Gasparini hummed—first the way I had sung, then in his own way. "Do you hear the difference?"

My cheeks grew hot as I tried to imitate his sound.

"Not this pecking of girlish sound! You are too controlled. The song must live inside you. That is how you awaken affections...passions!"

I could not help myself. As tears rolled down my cheeks, I turned to hide my face.

"Sopranos!" He threw his arms in the air. "Always a surplus of tears. Why do you cry? You are fortunate. You will sing for the greatest composer in Italy." Handing me his kerchief, he said, "Never, *ever* cry in front of Maestro Corelli. Do you understand? Now try again." When I had gathered myself and stood ready, Gasparini took his seat and held his hands above the keyboard. Then, nodding, his fingers flew across the keys. Humiliated, I could not imagine myself singing any worse, so I stopped caring, stopped trying to sing as he wished me to sing. Instead, I closed my eyes and sang the words as if they sprang from my own feeling.

And then?

Gasparini looked up, a smile stretching wide across his face, and when the song ended, he nodded. "You see? You must *be* the song. Practice this afternoon, and I'll return tomorrow morning."

For five days we practiced the same way—trills, mordents, staccato ornaments, slides, cadences. He cursed me with sighs and impatient glances, forced me to begin each song again until I had perfected the notes. I wept often, both from nerves and from fatigue. And the final day, when he didn't criticize me once but played through the music until the end, I feared I'd wasted his time. He didn't speak as he packed up his music. Then, standing, he bowed. "I never doubted your gift for music, Angelica. But it is not easy to sing for those born to a higher station in life, and I wanted to make sure you would not break under the pressure. I see now that you are ready. I shall be honored to play for you on Sunday."

It was the first time a professional musician had regarded me as his equal, and his esteem did much to raise my confidence. I curtsied. "The honor is mine, Signor Gasparini. And if my voice pleases the audience on Sunday, it is your doing. You have taught me well."

As soon as he left, Mother's voice rang out. "Angelica, come quickly while the water's hot!" She meant to bathe me in advance and try out my hair in ribbons, so we wouldn't be rushed the following morning when the coach came to collect us.

Lucia was busy carrying pails of boiling water from the fireplace to the tub that stood hidden behind sheets in the courtyard. Seeing me, she grinned, excited as I was. I lowered myself into the large wooden tub. *So hot!* Mother scattered rose petals so my body would soak in the sweet-smelling perfume.

"*Porco...* Swine!" Mother's shrieks suddenly pierced the air as she yelled at the barber who shared our courtyard. "You, Vittorio, I'm talking to you...I see the reeds part upstairs. Keep your bloodshot eyes away from my daughter, you ignorant toad! Curse you and your pickle...or I'll chop it off and put it in a jar for the whole city to laugh at!"

Lucia burst out laughing, and Bianca gasped, while I quickly lowered myself beneath the rose petals. "A loose tongue tells the truth, that's all." Mother poured hot water over my hair, then washed my back, all the while humming and smiling. Nothing could dampen her spirits, not with her daughter singing in a palace the very next day.

While I was soaking, Mother hurried inside, and when she returned, she drew back the sheets and held up the loveliest gown I'd ever seen.

"For me?" I gasped, blinking my wet eyes.

She nodded. "It belonged to a duchess. Father Zachary brought it early this morning. Those noblewomen who live in the country need a place to store their gowns inside the city so that they need not carry them back and forth. They pay the nuns to store them at the convent, and then, with much secrecy, the nuns rent the gowns to women like us."

Women like us. Mother calls me a woman now.

"What if the duchess is there and sees her dress?" I asked.

"Dead, three months ago." Mother fingered the fine lace. "She died in childbirth. This gown has never been worn, which is why it cost so much. The nuns are very careful. This is how they put bread on their table."

After I'd dried myself off inside the house, Lucia helped me into the lace corset before I slipped on the dress—a sky blue mantua, its boneless bodice gathered at the waist with a girdle opening over the hips, revealing a petticoat with bright red lining. Trimmed with a silver brocade against the blue, it shimmered. Each sleeve had three-tiered ruffles, and the bottom was tiered as well. She stood back. "*Bellissima*...My, Miss, you look like a real princess."

"Truly," Bianca whispered.

Mother also tried on her gown, yellow with inlaid blue silk, borrowed from Father Zachary's cousin who had married a wine merchant. Then she pinned my hair in different ways. Lucia and Bianca agreed with her that curls suited me best, but when she'd finished pinning my curls, Mother stood frowning.

Lucia ventured, "Perhaps, Mistress, if we took the sashes

from their church dresses and cut them short, then sewed bows out of them, they would heighten the colors of the gown."

Mother didn't like such brilliant ideas coming from a servant and watched with narrowed eyes as Lucia turned the sashes into small bows. But when Lucia pinned the blue and yellow bows to my curls, Mother admitted, "They do heighten your color."

Then she pulled out a long hairpin, worn for protection.

"Surely I won't need that tomorrow," I protested. "I'll be among nobles and cardinals."

"A girl's honor is everything." Mother stuck the pin carefully in my hair. "Don't forget the girl who stuck her pin in a prince's eye to save her honor, and then, two Sundays after, married him."

I nudged Bianca, giggling. "Though his eye was sewn closed the rest of his life."

My sister kept a smile to her lips, offering up encouragement. Only later, when we were readying ourselves for bed, would I glimpse her true feelings. It was when Lucia brought me Theodon's gift, after making sure that Mother was nowhere near. She closed the door tight and, glancing quickly at Bianca, whispered, "He sends you this for luck."

She handed me a garden pansy with a note wrapped around it:

> *Dear Angelica,*
> *I give you this flower as a sign of my admiration. Known as the flower of thought, I hope you shall carry it close to your heart and know that my thoughts are with you.*
>
> *Respectfully,*
> *Jean Theodon*

Bianca stared at the flower. "You pretend to do your duty by Mother, and yet you let this man court you in secret. It's a cruel game."

"These feelings are real," I told her. "He makes me feel I can do anything, sing to anyone—"

"You don't even know this man, except for Lucia's whispers."

Only then did Lucia raise her voice. "Perhaps God plants these feelings inside your sister's heart."

"It is you who plants these feelings, not God." My sister lifted her chin.

"Such a pious spirit as yours is dangerous." Lucia did not blink. "If we all lived as you do, hidden from our own true feelings, there would be no hope for a better world."

"I may be hidden from my own feelings, but I do not hide from God, as you do. Perhaps if you prayed more often, you would know God's will—"

"Who are you to preach God's will?" Lucia's voice took on a hardness I had not heard before. "Was it God's will that my parents should shiver and purge from fever outside the pope's gates for five days? Was it God's will that not one priest found it in his heart to offer them water as they lay there dying?" She shook her head. "I don't believe it is God who fills this world with suffering, but ourselves, by failing to know and speak our hearts."

Bianca didn't speak but walked to the door and held it open. Lucia had no choice but to leave, and she hurried through the door. As we climbed into bed, Bianca blew out the candle. I wished to calm the rift between us, but I dared not speak, for fear of making matters worse. I was not gifted in words unless they were sung. For a long time I lay awake in the darkness, feeling caught between Lucia and my sister. I was more inclined to think as Lucia did, and yet I knew my sister to be uncommonly good in her intentions. Try as I might, I could not find a way to ease my position between them, and I fell asleep with a heavy heart.

CHAPTER EIGHT

With her prim smile, Mother carried on as if riding in a coach were natural for us. But I leaned toward the window and parted the curtain—how different the world looked from inside a coach. Riding so high off the street, I felt like a real lady. That is, until Mother pulled me back from the window. "Don't act a child, Angelica. Close your mouth."

Inside, our crinolines formed a wide arc. Mother had talked to a neighbor who worked as a stable boy in one of the palaces across the river. Now Mother repeated his words. "The coach comes to a halt inside the carriage *portone*, a circular drive inside the palace gates, and the doors are opened by gentlemen escorts, waiting at the bottom of the marble steps." Here Mother used her own words to warn me. "The escorts are parasites in fine dress, Angelica. They exist for show, like fine horses in a stable, but they can't provide for a girl with your talent."

As we came to a stop, we saw the escorts standing stiffly, wigs plumped, faces powdered, their jackets displaying rows of shiny gold buttons. Following Mother's lead, I took my escort's arm and stepped out of the coach. But just as he introduced himself, Mother interrupted. "Do not think to take liberties with my daughter, or your patron shall hear of it."

My face burned...Mother's voice rose so loudly, heads turned. I couldn't help but see my mother as others must see her—*a tradesman's wife, trying to seem a lady.*

Skirts lifted, heels clicking, up, up, up the staircase, we walked as daintily as we could, trying not to stare at the statues of Roman gods. My escort saw me glancing sideways. "These statues were recently excavated by Cardinal Pamphili's own archeologists." His perfume was so strong it made my eyes water. No doubt he meant to hide his breath, reeking of yesterday's garlic and today's brandy.

As we walked through several large anterooms, Mother's escort led the way and announced the artists by name. "Titian... Lanfranco...Cortona...The most famous artists in the world are in this room." How I wished Theodon might stand beside me now. I tried to memorize the names of the artists, so that one day I could tell him I had seen their paintings. Surely he would be impressed by my knowledge. Between the paintings, gilded mirrors were tilted to reflect the mosaic stone floors. One wall was lined with ornate glass windows, tall as the ceiling, framed by red silk curtains. They were the kind of windows Papa and Franco made, and I stared at them now, searching for Papa's mark on them.

"Close your jaw." Mother nudged me. "You look like a peasant reading the future in the stars."

My escort smiled. "Everyone stares at these curtains. Seven

hundred scudi paid for each curtain of Venetian silk, and all of them hang thirty feet tall."

Seven hundred scudi…My heart stopped as I calculated: In the best of years, Papa earned no more than eighty scudi, and only after he and Franco worked six days a week from sunrise to sunset.

"Perhaps you now understand what might be ours by your talent," Mother whispered. "My escort tells me the pope's own nephew shall be attending today's performance, a great admirer of music…and of marriageable age."

As we entered the *Grande Salone*, a large hall with an elevated stage and rows of chairs, my escort handed me over to a maid, and I was separated from Mother. The maid led me through a door and up a staircase. "This is where the soloists prepare themselves, Signorina." Then, without another word, she closed the door behind me.

Alone, I breathed deeply. Next to the marble dressing table was a curtained space with a beautiful chamber pot made of blue and white inlaid stone, standing on tall silver legs. I saw a cord hanging on the wall, and thinking it drew the curtain, tugged it. A bell rang, and a small door opened.

A young girl crouched inside the narrow space. "*Prego*, Signorina, are you finished?"

"*Scusa*…I'm sorry…I didn't use the chamber pot."

The girl's eyelids beat furiously. "Are you the commoner what sings like an angel, then, Signorina? Are you the girl with the miracle voice?" A thin, frail thing, she was, but with ears well positioned to hear what others said.

Laughing, I plucked a perfumed kerchief from my sleeve.

"Here, take it. You've given me a better feeling for myself, and I thank you."

The girl smiled so many crooked teeth, I nearly caught my own breath. What a life, scurrying up and down a windowless staircase, carrying pots filled with the stench of those born to a higher rank.

"Has the singer arrived?" The doors flew open and four ladies entered. I immediately curtsied, holding my gaze to the floor. I feared such ladies might mock a glazier's daughter for daring to sing beside them.

"So here you are, Angelica Voglia," said the prettiest. Her dark eyes met my own as she smiled warmly. "I'm Mariuccia Landini. I'll sing mezzo soprano beside you today." She nodded at the two eldest women. "Octavia and Portia are sisters. We three are ladies-in-waiting to Queen Christina." They curtsied while Mariuccia introduced the fourth lady as her half sister. "This is Clarissa del Monte. She visits from Frascati."

Mariuccia gestured for me to sit in front of the mirror lit by candles. "Portia is an artist when it comes to our faces."

Portia sat beside me, then removed brushes and jars of powder from a small box she carried with her. She wiped my face clean and applied a cream before brushing my cheeks and nose with a silky powder. "Ground seed pearls give a luster to the face."

"Real pearls?" I gaped at the fine powder in her bowl.

She nodded. "Also good for a rotted stomach. Pope Clement VII took forty thousand ducats worth of ground pearls within fourteen days of his death."

Mariuccia handed me a glass of wine. "We call this *Corpo e*

Spirito…Body and Soul—orrisroot, three grains of musk, and wine. It relaxes the throat." Then, raising her glass to mine, she toasted, "May we ravish noblemen's hearts!"

I sipped the thick liquid, then dared to ask, "How do you find Maestro Corelli?"

"The best composer in Rome…perhaps in all of Italy." Mariuccia sat next to me while Portia brushed her face with the same powder. "And gentle in his genius."

"As if she truly cared." Clarissa rolled her eyes. "She's only here to find a husband."

"You might find a husband by your title, sister"—Mariuccia raised her glass, then puffed out her chest so that her bosom nearly burst from her gown—"but I must rely on my virtues."

Laughter filled the room as Portia whispered in my ear, "Same father, born of different mothers, each seeks to outdo the other."

When Portia had finished making up our faces, Mariuccia took my arm and, bidding the others good-bye, led me through a hidden door and down a circular stairwell. At the bottom, we waited behind the curtain.

"Look through the crack," Mariuccia whispered. "There is Queen Christina, seated between Cardinal Pamphili and Cardinal Azzolino. See the queen's cup engraved with stones? She carries it everywhere. Blessed by Pope Clement IX, it protects her from poison."

"Why would anyone poison the queen?"

"Have you no ear for gossip? Her Highness has many enemies, especially this pope, Innocent XI, for she refuses to give up control of her quarter." Mariuccia leaned closer. "We, too, are pawns in their games. By inviting you here this day, Cardinal Pamphili is siding with the queen, sending a message to the pope—"

"What message?"

Mariuccia raised her eyebrows. "You're a tradesman's daughter trained in music outside the convent, Angelica. By inviting you to perform, Cardinal Pamphili is telling the pope that he believes women should be permitted to perform, at least in the privacy of palaces."

My heart tightened. *How little I understand of this life of cardinals, queens, and nobles!*

"I'm sure you know that this pope bans opera, which the queen dearly loves. Queen Christina opened the first public opera house in Rome, Teatro Tordinona, and she even permitted women singers to perform. This pope closed her opera house, claiming that Queen Christina offers refuge to enemies of the church."

"Are the rumors true?"

Mariuccia batted her eyelids. "If you mean sopranos like us, then yes, the rumors are true. Our queen serves God more readily than she serves this pope. *Grazie a Dio,* I count myself lucky to be in service to the queen. Her Highness is a great patron of music, and even now she encourages women like us to perform in her palace."

I stared through a crack in the curtain. The queen was dressed in a black velvet waistcoat with a long velvet skirt, lace shirt, and large flat black shoes. Her ample waist was loosely belted. Her long gray curls, pinned with jewels away from her forehead, exposed her long nose. What a face on this queen! Such an intensity of expression, one could hardly look away from her. Even surrounded by beautiful young ladies, it was Her Majesty, with her large eyes, smooth complexion, and warm smile, who seemed the force of life within the *Grande Salone.* I took deep breaths....I was about to sing for this famous queen!

And then he arrived...black tails flying. Maestro Corelli was small, shorter than me, with a face full of pinch and pull, as if great forces were caged beneath his expressions. "Ah, you!" He stopped abruptly and fixed his stare on me. "I don't want my music overshadowed by gossip, Signorina Angelica. Music, *not admiration,* is the door to God."

Then, turning, he took his position in front of the orchestra. My heart pounded as Mariuccia took my hand and led me to the front of the small stage. Gasparini had told me to watch for the signal: Maestro Corelli would clear his throat before he raised his baton to begin. Eyes glazed in concentration, he drew his stick in a sweeping, upward slice, like a bird leaping into flight, and the trumpets sounded.

My voice rose above the instruments, as we opened with "Occhi Immortali" by Caccini. "*Occhi immortali d'amor gloria e splendore*...Immortal eyes of love..." Mariuccia and I sang as two feet on the same body, one leaping while the other caught up... echoes springing, one from the other. Corelli, red-faced, breathless, conducted masterfully, his baton striking the air, his waist bending side to side, coaxing the sounds from his musicians.

When we finished, thunderous applause filled the ballroom.

Feet stomped, hands clapped, ladies drew out their kerchiefs and dabbed at their eyes. I let my eye wander to my friend, Gasparini, whose smile burst across his red face while he nodded at me. As the audience continued clapping, Maestro Corelli turned and bowed, face glistening, then lifted his hands to Mariuccia and me. We curtsied, then waited until the audience grew quiet.

Our voices rose again, this time singing in rivalry with the violin, played by Gasparini. I'd never sung in response to an instrument, but Gasparini had coached me well. As Mariuccia stood beside me, echoing my trills, I felt my voice swell, matching the power of the violin.

As soon as we'd finished singing, the audience jumped to their feet. "Brava... *Bravissima!*"

I took a step back so that Mariuccia, who was my elder, might stand in front. But she took my hand and pulled me forward beside her.

"Angelica... the angel sings!" the voices cried.

"Such clarity!"

"Purity!"

"It is true, her voice is a *miracle!*"

When I looked up, the queen's gaze met my own, and she smiled, nodding once.

"Do you see? The queen honors you." Mariuccia led me behind the curtain. "It's *your* greatness, Angelica, that makes my own talent shine. How I wish I might always sing beside you." Mariuccia hugged me then. "Should you ever desire a place in the queen's court, I'd be honored to act on your behalf."

I was touched by her affection and smiled gratefully but made no reply. It was one thing to sing in a palace, another to leave my family, my home, and Theodon.

"Your silence is plain enough." Mariuccia smiled. "Just remember what I've said. These are difficult times, and the only safety for a woman singer outside the convent walls is in the court of Queen Christina, who protects us."

She led me up the circular stairs to the room where we'd been before, and sitting at the dressing table, Mariuccia faced the mirror, pinning curls that had fallen free. "Now we must go and make witty conversation. I tell you plainly, my motive is to find a husband."

"Is there a gentleman you prefer?"

"Flavio Odescalchi, the pope's nephew…Surely you know his story?" Seeing my blank expression, she explained. "Ten years ago, when this pope was elected, he called all his cardinals to his side, along with Flavio, and proclaimed publicly that neither his nephew nor anyone else in his family would gain by the pope's name or seek a position in the church. He was the first pope to ban nepotism, and Flavio, poor boy, was the first nephew in history not to benefit from his uncle's power." She smiled coyly. "And that leaves him free to marry."

The trumpets sounded, and Mariuccia jumped. "Quick, before the queen enters."

Down the stairs, through the doors, we flew…and entered another world. I clasped my hands over my mouth to hide my amazement. The centerpieces stood seven feet tall and were spun from sugar and marzipan in the shapes of female figures. "Signor

Donato Romagnoli, the confectioner, cannot read or write but imagines these figures from ancient myths," Mariuccia told me. "He's a genius, no?"

There was more food than I'd ever imagined, an abundance of everything. How I wished Theodon were here beside me to see such a feast. My eyes couldn't settle but tried to take it all in: meat pies of roasted swan covered with clouds of dough, burnt sugar on top. Basins of prosciutto, melon, and cheeses. Platters steamed, with roasted swallows, partridge, and duck, surrounded by sculpted rice, whipped potatoes, and stuffed peppers. Around the centerpieces sat lemons, oranges, Spanish limes, pomegranates, and bitter mandarins. At the last table, the finest sweets lay waiting: cannoli, chocolate tortes, and candied fruits.

Hurrying to my side, Mother held her fan high. "You've done well, Angelica. Several nobles already seek your company. Don't forget yourself now!"

Portia and Octavia came to congratulate me, their fans fluttering. "The queen was greatly pleased by your performance, Angelica."

All at once, the horns trumpeted, doors opened. Mariuccia tugged me into a deep curtsy. Queen Christina entered, flanked by the cardinals, with the nobles following behind. We kept our heads lowered until they had taken their seats, and then, with a flurry of excitement, Mariuccia introduced me to the gentlemen who quickly crowded around us. "May I present Angelica Voglia."

Surrounded by nobles, I fanned myself, feeling a lack of air.

"I shall be paying you a visit," one gentleman said, then pressed my gloved hand.

"In my dreams, I have never witnessed such beauty," said another.

"Your voice, a miracle," whispered another in my ear.

Turning one direction, then the other, I repeated the words I'd heard Mariuccia reply. "Sir, the pleasure is mine." Fan upright, oh, my wrist ached. I felt myself caught in an endless performance, like a marionette dangling on strings, tugged in all directions. Finally, unable to stomach the wine-scented breath of another nobleman, I turned—and found myself face-to-face with Flavio Odescalchi, the pope's nephew.

I tried not to stare at the three beauty patches attached to his right cheek, cut in the shapes of a rabbit and two birds. Mariuccia had already pointed him out and explained that these shapes, cut from velvet, were the latest trend from the French court, often used to cover a blemish or scar.

Taking my hand, he kissed my glove. "Such a great pleasure to meet you, Signora Angelica. I am Flavio Odescalchi, nephew to the pope."

Fanning my face nervously, I created such a movement of air, the black velvet rabbit was blown off his cheek. I saw it was meant to cover a large pimple and, raising my fan to hide my smile, anointed him Prince of Pimples.

He made himself bold and took my wrist, lowering my fan and exposing my face wholly. "Where have you been schooled in music, Signorina Angelica?"

Rule number forty-seven in the *Book of Manners: Never turn away from a noble who asks a question, but answer him as he wishes to be answered.* His privileged position allowed him to break all the rules, and without waiting for my answer, he lifted a canapé and placed it in my mouth. *How dare he!* Shocked, I couldn't move or speak. In one swift gesture, he had made his claim.

I heard the gasps, giggles, and twitters around us. "Did you see?"

"She favors him, no doubt. Such familiarity."

"A common girl, looking for a way up."

"Perhaps she's not such an *angel*, after all."

By this remark, I knew they spoke of the posters placed on the cardinal's gate, and my face burned.

Flavio heard, too, and grew bolder by their words. He sipped from his cup, then handed it to me. "Tell me where you have been hiding?"

I lifted my skirts and turned away. I would run, *yes, run!* But Mariuccia caught my arm and whispered, "Turn back and sip from his cup. Then curtsy to Flavio, excuse yourself, and look around as if there is someone else waiting. Remember, a lady doesn't hurry."

I did as she told me, waving to no one in particular. Then Mariuccia took my arm, and we exited the room together, sauntering, swishing, as if we were on our way to meet secret suitors. But as soon as we were beyond the doors, I cried out, "Mariuccia, I did nothing to encourage his attentions—"

"I don't blame you, Angelica." Mariuccia handed me a handkerchief. "He was playing games, dangerous games, for they mock and admire at once. The performance doesn't end when we leave the stage—it continues until we're wed. Never forget that. We're easily ruined, girls like us. These nobles will marry the Countess-of-Many-Acres, or the Duchess-of-Gold-Castle, or the Princess blah-di-blah-di-blah, whose title stretches from here to Naples."

"Then why do you search for a husband here?"

She shrugged. "Perhaps there will be a gentleman so bored by his life, he wishes to cause a bit of scandal by marrying the illegitimate daughter of the Marquis del Monte."

My mouth fell open.

"My frankness shocks you? Why should I pretend? Everyone knows. The Marquis del Monte, my father, is first gentleman to Queen Christina. When he met my mother, he was already married to Clarissa's mother. My mother died giving birth to me, and I'm told he wept for days after."

I could not help thinking that we were the same, she and I. But, *grazie a Dio*, I'd been lucky enough to have Papa marry my mother and raise me as his own.

"I'll go and find your mother while you wait here"—Mariuccia nudged me playfully—"unless you want your mouth stuffed with more canapés."

I was glad for a moment to myself. I took a deep breath, trying to sort my feelings. Yes, I was pleased by my own performance and happy to have made a friend of Mariuccia. But afterward, the pressure to behave like a lady—that part filled my heart with doubt. I knew nothing of the world, but already the world knew of me. I felt the danger of my own ignorance...that I might be used by others in ways I couldn't understand.

"Signora Angelica?"

I was startled by the husky whisper.

"Signora Angelica, might I have a word with you?"

I turned and saw a cardinal's red berretta. Falling on my

knees, I kept my face lowered as he offered me his ring. I kissed it, saying, "Your Holiness."

"Raise yourself," he commanded gently, helping me to my feet. Then he led me behind a pillar so we were hidden. I'd never stood so close to a cardinal before and was surprised he smelled of tobacco and brandy. Glancing up, I saw his dark bushy eyebrows rise as he smiled. "I am Cardinal de Cabrera." He had a Spanish accent. "It's my coach that comes each day and sits in the piazza. I mean only to admire your talent." Straightening himself, his eyes grew serious. "If it is in my power, I shall not let your voice be silenced or corrupted by the evil that exists around us."

Evil...I glanced up.

He looked nervously toward the doors. "Your voice...your songs...There are those who would gladly see you silenced. They do not wish to see a girl from your station in life rise by her talent unless it is inside the walls of a convent. They claim any woman who sings in public is corrupted and should be locked away. They do not understand the new forms of music. If they did, they would know that your talent is a gift from God. A voice like yours lifts us toward heaven...Believe me, I shall do everything I can to help you."

I didn't understand, and yet I managed to reply, "I'm grateful, Your Holiness."

For once I was glad to see Mother burst through the door. "Angelica...where are you?"

Raising my fan, I stepped out from behind the pillar. "Mother, I am here."

I heard the swish of robes behind me, glanced back, and

then breathed a sigh of relief. Cardinal de Cabrera had slipped through a side door and was gone.

Mother opened her purse, displaying cards and introductions from gentlemen. "Well done, Angelica. We'll be welcoming numerous suitors in the days ahead."

CHAPTER NINE

The next morning, I was awakened by a faint knock, and Lucia pushed open the door, carrying a pitcher of fresh water. "Sang to perfection, Miss. That's what they're saying in the piazza."

"Oh, Lucia, I'm so relieved to see you." I climbed out of bed and washed my face.

"Is it true, Miss? The pope's own nephew stuck a canapé in your mouth?"

"I did nothing to encourage him." I turned and faced her. "He wears little velvet patches to cover up his pimples. Prince of Pimples, I call him."

She grinned. "The gossip flies this morning. They say he courts you openly."

"None of the nobles stirred my heart as Theodon does." I sat on the side of my bed. "Oh, Lucia, nothing pleases me more than singing. I fly inside the music—"

"Then why do you look so sad?"

"Because...I despise what follows the performance—the refreshments, the endless chatter. It all feels like a game, and I will never understand the rules. All those gentlemen pressing their lips to my ear, whispering their praises...I will never belong to their world." My throat tightened. "But what if I *must* play their games, Lucia? What if that is the price I must pay to sing in the courts of Rome?"

Lucia didn't laugh as I expected, but breathed deeply. "Oh, Miss, it was the same for the duchess. My mother always told her to hold herself to what she wished and not become what others expected of her, which was to play cards and laugh at others less fortunate."

I rose and opened the shutter a crack. "Was Theodon at the fountain? Have you seen him?"

"Not as yet, Miss."

"What if he hears these rumors and believes them?"

"Don't fret. I'll set him straight."

Just then we heard a loud knock below, and Father Zachary called for me to hurry downstairs. "Angelica! The whole city sings your praises. Come hear what they write about your performance."

After Mother poured him a cup of coffee, he opened today's *Gazzetta*, a gossip paper read by the nobles and clergy. "*Yesterday, at Palazzo Pamphili, the surprise performance was none other than a new talent, Angelica Voglia, whose voice and beauty ravished the hearts of gentlemen. No concert has so inspired love as this one, and it is said that the rivalries have already begun for Angelica's song...as well as for her heart.*"

Bianca hugged me. "Angelica, you are famous!"

I laughed...and flushed with excitement. I could hardly believe it myself. And yet my thoughts also turned to Theodon—once he heard these rumors, would he ever stand beneath my window again?

"You should have seen the nobles crowd around her, Father." Mother embraced me. "Angelica will have her pick of husbands now!"

We'd barely finished our coffee when a page knocked on our door and delivered an invitation requesting me to sing at Queen Christina's palace. By the way Mother and Father Zachary carried on, you would've thought it was Saint Cecilia herself, flown down from heaven.

"*Grazie a Dio,*" Mother exclaimed. "Invited to sing for the English ambassador...one of three soloists...in one month's time."

"This calls for a toast!" Father Zachary picked up the jug of wine as Mother took glasses from the cupboard. "To Angelica's future!"

Mother took a sip, then set down her glass. "We have much to do before the pope's nephew visits tomorrow, Father."

"You must manage these gentlemen carefully, Caterina. The pope bans public performance, so Angelica must sing with the shutters closed and only for those suitors who come by invitation."

"You must provide the refreshments for their visits, Father...pastries, wine. And Angelica will need another gown."

Listening to them talk, I felt my heart tighten. How quickly they forgot about last night's performance. It was not my voice they prized, but the future that could be bought with my talent. Just like the chickens at the market, I, too, could be sold for the right price. And Mother's price was plain enough—a highborn husband and the promise of a palace life.

❦

The next morning, before the pope's nephew arrived, Mother gave me a lesson on smiling. "Don't let your teeth show too much…keep your chin tilted down. Yes, that's it…never lingering too long in a gentleman's gaze."

When she'd finished with me, she turned to Lucia. "Make sure you use the cups without cracks for our guests. And pronounce his name distinctly."

"Yes, Mistress." Lucia winked at me, mouthing, *Prince of Pimples.*

All of it planned, all of it rehearsed, down to my curtsy and tone of voice, which should not be so loud as to seem bold, nor so soft as to seem timid. "How kind of you to honor us with a visit, Signor Odescalchi."

Of course, the pope's nephew saw how simply we lived—a pantry, a table, two chairs, two benches, and a harpsichord. And yet, Lucia's presence made us seem less common. Dressed in a gray smock and white apron, her hair pulled back in a white cloth, she put everyone at ease, passing a tray with sweets and liqueurs. As I played the harpsichord, and Bianca and I sang together, Signor Odescalchi's eyes did not stray from my face. I wasn't used to performing for a gentleman inside my own house, and I stiffened under his gaze. When we finished singing, Bianca and I sat on a bench across the room, while Lucia refilled his glass and passed the pastries.

95

"I am told your daughter has been asked to sing at Queen Christina's gala for Lord Castlemaine." Signor Odescalchi took a bite of pastry, the crumbs flaking across his goatee.

Hinting, Mother wiped her chin excessively. "My daughter is greatly honored to be one of three soloists for the English ambassador."

"Signora Voglia, are you sure you wish your daughter to sing for this notorious queen? If I can be candid"—and here Signor Odescalchi's smile faded—"it's no secret that Queen Christina loves nothing more than to torment my uncle, the pope, with the scandals in her quarter. The pope seeks to bring order to this city, which, as you know, is filled with thieves and wayward women who take refuge in the queen's quarter. My uncle has tried to convince Queen Christina to renounce her rights to control her quarter so that the whole city can be united...But this queen provokes my uncle at every turn and will surely use your daughter in her schemes."

Listening, I recalled Mariuccia's words: *We, too, are pawns in their games.* I wondered if the pope had sent his nephew to dissuade me from performing at the queen's gala.

"My daughter has an upright character, sir," Mother replied. "In strict observance of the church's rules."

"I am most aware of your daughter's virtues," he assured her. Then, setting his teacup on the saucer, he pulled a small package from his satchel. "Indeed, I have brought a small token of my esteem."

"Surely your presence is gift enough," Mother said to be tactful, though I knew well enough she expected a gift.

Signor Odescalchi stood and presented Mother with a small velvet box. Opening it, she lifted a pearl bracelet into the candle-light. "Pearls...How lovely—"

"May I?" He took the bracelet from Mother's hand, then crossed the room to my side. Leaning close—*too close*—he glanced down my dress and breathed in the scent of my hair, as he clasped the bracelet round my wrist.

"*Grazie,* Signor Odescalchi." Opening my fan, I waved it briskly...so briskly, it might scratch his nose if he didn't allow for a distance between us.

Thinking me modest, he chuckled and lifted himself away.

"My daughter is most grateful, Signor Odescalchi, but with the chill in the air, we must protect her voice. Angelica must rest now."

"Just one more song?" He sat back down in his chair and smiled at the bracelet: *Surely pearls are worth another song?*

But Mother rose and stood by the door. At first her firmness surprised him, but then he seemed to admire her for it and re-luctantly lifted himself out of his chair. "Perhaps I might return tomorrow afternoon?"

I glanced at Mother, wondering how she would handle his request. This was the pope's nephew, after all. "Tomorrow my daughter is fully occupied, sir," Mother replied. "But the follow-ing morning, we should be very pleased to welcome you again."

Signor Odescalchi buttoned his coat and wrapped a scarf around his neck. Bowing first to me and then to Mother, he stepped outside, letting a gust of cold air sweep through the door. Already the sun was lowering, casting the streets in shadows.

Mother quickly bolted the door and leaned back, sighing with relief. "A good thing days are short this time of year."

⌘

From that day on, the suitors arrived—dukes, princes, even a merchant who had bought his title of "marquis." Mother scheduled their visits carefully, so that they would not meet each other on the street near our house. Morning and afternoon, they came dressed in the latest fashions—breeches to the knee, tied with lace garters; brown waistcoats, worn open with white ruffled shirts; swords, hung low on the hip, attached to fringed sashes bordered by silk. Only the nobles were allowed to wear swords, as a sign of their power. They tried to dazzle me with their smiles, but I saw only their stained teeth, soft bellies, and fleshy faces.

"Which suitor comes this morning, Mother?"

"Bishop Vanini."

Bishop Wet Lips, I called him. He was the worst—potbellied, with beady eyes. As a bishop, he couldn't marry me, but he brought the most lavish gifts...enough silk and lace to make several new gowns. And at the end of each visit, he always promised Mother that, next time, he would bring a gentleman friend, perhaps a suitable future husband.

As soon as they left, Mother would display the gifts—swaths of silk, silver candleholders, satin ribbons. "See what your music earns?"

But I turned away. "It is more than a song they want."

"Let us hope so." Mother ignored my grumbling. "Let us hope they want you for a wife."

Mother kept the gifts of those she preferred. But as soon as she had dismissed one suitor as too old, or another as too cheap, she would give their gifts to Father Zachary to sell across the river, giving him lists of necessaries to buy with the money.

Nothing slowed Mother down—not the wintery rains, not my voice cracking, not my sister's headaches. Indeed, as the days passed, Mother displayed a new vigor, as if *she* were the one being courted. The suitors' visits put a blush to her cheeks, a smile to her lips. One morning, as Lucia polished the table with lemon oil and Bianca and I washed our hair in a large bowl, we heard Mother humming. Our mouths fell open as we stared at one another—*Since when did Mother hum?*

Most daughters would probably feel grateful to a mother so bent on finding a decent husband for her, but I was burdened by Mother's hopes. I spilled my heart to Lucia. "I despise these men. Their eyes rove up and down my dress while I sing."

"They like nothing better than an intrigue, Miss. The more you try to ignore their eyes, the more they take you for modest. You cannot play their games. It's the pursuit, Miss, and you are the prize."

I peeked out the shutter. "Where is *he*? For two days, he hasn't shown himself beneath my window."

"And why should Theodon stand in the street…with all your suitors coming and going?"

"Did you see him this morning?" I asked.

She nodded. "I told him that none of these nobles commands your heart as he does." And here Lucia offered up the whole of their conversation, telling me that Theodon was under pressure at the workshop. The new director was gravely ill and had to decide soon who should take his place. Theodon and another sculptor were being considered for the job. "He says if he is to earn your love, Miss, he must first raise himself in his career."

"Oh, Lucia, I don't want him to think he must earn my affections."

"I didn't take that to be his meaning, Miss. Only that he takes his prospects seriously, which, if I may say so, is a good thing. He is not a man of trivial feelings."

"Not like Mother's suitors." My eyes filled with tears as I thought of Mother's prospective husbands—Flavio Odescalchi and the Duke of Mantua, the wealthiest of all. "Duke of Dobble-chins." I laughed bitterly. "How could I bed a man whose neck dobbles like a turkey? His wife lies dying in a convent in the north, while he is here, laying a plan to replace her! Oh, Lucia...you must make Theodon know that I care nothing for these suitors."

Lucia laughed. "Don't fret, Miss. I told him your days are filled with pimples, wet lips, and turkey chins."

&

In the days following my performance at Palazzo Pamphili, a sparrow lay dead in the garden, an armless woman jeered outside my window, a cracked cup that had held together for years finally shattered. Signs, yes. Change was all around us.

Yet no one spoke of it. Not until the morning Papa reached for his jar behind the pantry and discovered half the coins had gone missing. "Half the weight it was last Sunday." His eyes settled on Mother. "Where has the money gone?"

She lowered her eyes. And by that small gesture, Papa

knew…knew that his own wife had deceived him. Never before had I seen Papa so angry…so angry he could not find words, but threw the jar, shattering it, scattering the remaining coins across the floor.

Pietro hurried to pick them up, his eyes filling with tears. Franco shook his head at Mother, for he, too, had added his earnings to the jar. Lucia stood still in the corner, her gaze lowered, while Bianca closed her eyes and took out her rosary, her lips moving silently. I trembled and didn't move from the bench. I wanted to cover my ears, or better yet, run out of the house. I feared that Papa would blame me for Mother's deceit, since she had spent the money to entertain my suitors.

But he didn't speak. Not one word. His eyes, his nose, his mouth grew hard as he stared at Mother. It seemed as if he couldn't move, as if a great weight covered his heart, and it took all his effort to keep breathing.

Later, at our midday meal, Papa didn't speak of the coins. But glancing at me, he shook his head. "She's too young for your schemes, Caterina. You can't use her to buy yourself another life. I won't stand for it."

I kept my eyes lowered, my face burning. I didn't want to be used in their battles.

Mother rose from the table and went into the courtyard. They didn't speak the rest of the day, but the following morning, their angry words filled the house.

"Is this all the coal we have?" Mother counted what was left in the coal bin. "I need Franco and Pietro this morning. They must come with me to carry coal. The pope's nephew visits us tomorrow."

Papa's eyes darkened. "I, too, need my sons."

"Once Angelica marries a nobleman, our sons shall become gentlemen's valets. Then they'll not have to rush out in the rain to fill orders."

Papa's fists hit the wooden table. "How can a man find pride if his meaning comes from serving others, Caterina? My sons are better off as glaziers."

Mother crossed her arms over her chest. "Each serves the rich."

"But a tradesman has a skill."

"And works himself into an early grave."

As I listened to them argue, my heart grew tight. Papa worked so hard, he didn't deserve Mother's scorn. I looked at Bianca, who read my thought and tightened her lips, warning me to keep quiet.

Papa's voice rose. "You scorn our neighbors who dip bread in chicken fat. You mock the women who serve the local priests on cracked dishes. You look down on families that eat off the same platter."

"They're peasants," Mother said.

"Yes, and their manners match their hunger. They have no illusions about moving across the river. But I'm one of them, Caterina, and you are my wife."

No one spoke. No one moved. Like my brothers and sister, I sat still, feeling the weight of their words. I'd heard Mother and Papa argue before, but never like this. Always before, Mother gave in and tried to coax Papa into a better mood. But not today.

Today Mother lifted her chin. "You sound like the dog who

finds happiness in a bit of shade. Or the fish who finds happiness swimming downstream. Are we no better than the beasts? Have you no dreams, Giorgino?"

"Not like yours! I dream of what I might make with my own hands, God willing."

"Then I pity you, and our sons if they hope for nothing more."

Papa rose from his chair. "There is honor in a hard day's work, Caterina. If you can't see that, then I pity *you*!" Shaking his head, he glanced at me, then back at Mother. "But most of all, I pity Angelica... You use *her* future to make up for your own disappointments."

I froze. It pained me deeply to hear my name flung back and forth.

"How dare you!" Mother screamed.

Then Papa stormed into the street without looking back.

"Go on, Franchino." Mother handed Franco his coat. "Help your father fill his orders so he won't return in such a bad humor."

That day, and the next, whenever Papa and my brothers were home, silence filled the house. Mother was no longer Papa's Little Goose. And Mother no longer gave Papa gentle pinches every time he snuck a taste of her cooking. These days, they regarded each other with hard eyes and bitter silences.

Father Zachary came often to visit, always bringing something new from Mother's list of necessaries—a pair of blue stockings, a new rented gown, white gloves that stretched past my wrist to my elbows, a shawl of silk.

But whenever the conversation turned to my suitors, his smile faded, as if he knew such men would not guarantee my happiness. "Do you see the gray circles beneath your daughters' eyes? Angelica is growing thinner, paler. Bianca suffers headaches. You're keeping your daughters inside too much. They'd benefit from a convent in the country, where they could rest and breathe fresh air."

"Let them sit in the courtyard and breathe fresh air," Mother always replied.

One morning, when we had not yet boiled our coffee, the priest arrived breathless, bolting the door behind him. "This time, it's serious, Caterina...very serious." He paced back and forth as Lucia set the pot boiling over the fire. "Yesterday, a shipment of silver was stolen from the docks...liturgical vessels, chalices, candlesticks, and crosses from the silversmiths on Via Pellegrino."

"What does that have to do with us?" Mother asked.

"Cardinal de Cabrera was supposed to go with the shipment, to sign the papers...but he was here in the piazza, listening to your daughter sing."

Mother glanced at me. "Surely Angelica cannot be blamed."

"The pope is furious. He believes your daughter corrupts even the most pious of men." Father Zachary's voice grew firm. "I tell you, Caterina, we should send Angelica to a convent until the scandal dies down."

"Even enclosed in a convent, a girl can be compromised." Mother's chin lifted. "We both know that, Father!"

Father Zachary grew silent. Now I understood why he caved to Mother's demands. But knowing what I did, my heart pinched more in the priest's presence. I wished my life were built on truths, not lies.

That morning, when Lucia returned from the bakery, Mother opened the pastries and found them crawling with ants. "*Gesummaria*…how did the ants get inside?"

I knew they must have crawled inside while Lucia traded secrets with Theodon.

Lucia kept her eyes lowered. "*Scusi*…Sorry, Mistress. I stopped for a drink at the fountain. I can fix them." Lucia kept her back to me as she scooped off the whipped cream and opened the pastries, one by one, picking out the ants. Then she peeled a lemon, chopped the rind, and added sugar, butter, and a spoonful of lemon liqueur. When the syrup had thickened over the fire, she drizzled the sauce over the pastries, then added the whipped cream and a twist of lemon peel on top. They looked even better than before, and despite faint praise, I could see Mother was pleased. "You were lucky this time, Lucia. But from now on, I expect you to come directly home."

Later, when we were alone, Lucia whispered, "We'll have to figure another way, Miss. If your mother knew the secrets I carried back and forth, she'd send me packing faster than a bell's toll. I can't take the risk."

I understood. But as the days passed with no word from Theodon, my heart began to feel small. Each morning, I searched through a crack in the shutters, but there was no sign of him. As the suitors came and went, I sang what Mother wished me to sing. But without Theodon to spark the feeling inside my songs, my heart could not breathe life into the music. Performing became a dull habit—every song felt the same, an exercise of words and notes. I didn't want to wake up or dress in gowns or comb my hair. And for the first time in my life, I didn't want to sing.

∽∾∽

On certain days, the egg woman who lived behind us made her special ointment, and the courtyard air grew thick with her potion—gander's fat, watercress, wormwood, primrose, and strawberry vine. She put the mixture into a gander's bowels and roasted it all afternoon. Then she scooped out the grease, put it in pots, and sold it at the market. Often the pope sent his own apothecary to buy the egg woman's potion, for it was rumored to be the best cure in Rome for stiff joints and aching bones.

When the heavy stench filled our courtyard, it irritated my voice and kept us all coughing, so we had no choice but to keep the shutters closed. One afternoon, lying on my bed upstairs, I heard the egg woman call out, "I'll be there in a moment."

"*Merci*, Madame."

A Frenchman's voice. Immediately I understood that Lucia had told Theodon to come when the stench was strong, because she knew Mother would have the shutters closed and wouldn't see him in the courtyard. I rushed to my window and opened it. Theodon stood smiling below, and he quickly lifted a scrolled paper from his bag and tossed it through my window.

I unrolled the paper and read:

> *Dear Angelica,*
> *I'm told your mother would stop at nothing to see*
> *you marry a noble, and I cannot avoid seeing the*

*train of suitors entering your house. I am forced to
show signs of my feeling in secret, praying you will
not take offense by my words. Monsieur Errard, the
director of our academy, who suffers from an excess
of stone dust and drink, has promised that I shall
become the director when his time is done. I tell you
this now, for I want you to understand that, though
I cannot offer you gifts of jewelry and silver, my future holds promise. Inspired by your song, I shall
earn your love through my own merits. If you lower
a twine after dark from your window, I will send
you signs of my admiration.*

> *With deep respect,*
> *Jean Theodon*

Shaking, I quickly took a scrap of paper, and after dipping
my quill in ink, I wrote:

*Please do not think me too bold if I say that when
my eyes fall upon you, I feel the most perfect happiness. By our talents—yours for sculpture and
mine for music—I believe our hearts speak the
same language. May my songs find wings to your
ears.*

> *A.*

A toss of the paper, and my words fluttered to his feet as I
sang, "*Paratum cor meum...my heart, my heart is ready.*"

CHAPTER TEN

From that day on, I woke before sunrise and, after making sure that Bianca was still asleep, hurried to check the twine. Each morning, Theodon had left sketches of the places he'd visited—the church of Santa Maria della Pace, Fontana dei Fiumi, Ponte Sant' Angelo. Better than jewels and silk, these sketches brought his life to me and allowed me to see the world beyond my house, my neighborhood. Not even Theodon could know how I treasured these gifts. Nor could he know what pain they would cause me.

The knock came one morning, right after Papa and my brothers had left. "Open up...I know you are home!"

"It is the pope's nephew...Get dressed." Lucia quickly handed us our gowns, then hurried downstairs. She waited until Mother gave her the signal, then slid the bolt.

Drunk and swaying, Signor Odescalchi flung himself through the door. "*She* prefers a *Frenchman*."

Mio Dio.... My heart froze as I stood at the top of the stairs, peeking through the reed curtain.

"What Frenchman?" Mother held a smile to her lips. "What are you talking about? Perhaps the wine has made you imagine things?"

Signor Odescalchi tried to focus, but his eyes could not stay still. Waving a finger at Mother, he collapsed onto the chair. "I took my coffee at the corner *osteria*...I heard *them*."

"Who?" Mother stood tall, arms folded across her chest.

"The artists." He leaned against the wall for balance. "The *French* artists who work across the street. Your daughter, *An-gel-ica,* drops twine at night...leaves him notes."

"Angelica!" Mother called me down the stairs.

As I descended, Mother's face grew hard. She didn't look at me, didn't question whether his words were true. She *knew.* But his words didn't matter; saving my reputation mattered. Mother held a firm smile. "These men speak of someone else, not my daughter."

"She sings for him, a sculptor called Theodon." His voice crumbled. "Do you know what they said of me? That I arrive with a gift in my hand and leave with a gift in my pants." He laughed bitterly. "And you...they say a mother like you would be the curse of a lifetime."

I stared at the pope's nephew. I didn't like to think of the Frenchmen across the street speaking of me in public, as if I were no better than a whore. I blamed myself for singing so freely.

"Have a cup of coffee, Signor Odescalchi." Mother handed him a steaming cup. "We must sort out this mess of rumor.

You've clearly been misled. I guard Angelica with my life. My daughter has no opportunity for intrigues." Nodding at me to sit beside him, she gripped my arm. "Tell him the truth."

I didn't want to lie, not about Theodon. And so I stayed silent, even as Mother's hand squeezed the blood from my arm.

"You see?" Signor Odescalchi stammered. "She does not speak because it's true. She's no better than the courtesans, accepting gifts from nobles while promising her heart to a foreigner...a bloody *Frenchman,* whose loyalty is to the French king, not to our pope, my uncle." Smirking at me, he rose from his chair. "I'm the pope's nephew, and I shall not forget this. Nor shall your Frenchman. He'll pay for his treachery."

It was one thing to suffer Mother's fists, another to ruin Theodon's future. "*Aspetti... Wait!*" I breathed deeply. "You misunderstand. The Frenchman courts my sister. I didn't speak because I wished to protect her reputation."

Signor Odescalchi leaned toward me. "Is it true?"

I nodded. "Though it pains me to betray my sister's confidence."

"Give me proof." He sat back, arms folded.

Mother hurried up the stairs, and when she came back, Bianca in tow, I could tell by the way my sister rubbed her arms that Mother had found her proof—*Theodon's sketches.* Handing the pile to me, she commanded. "Throw them on the coals. Show Signor Odescalchi you care nothing for this man."

I had no choice and tossed the sketches onto the coals. Watching the embers curl the paper, then break into flames, I swallowed my tears and forced a smile to my lips. Lucia saw me grapple with my feeling and quickly refilled Signor Odescalchi's cup of coffee, standing between him and me, in case I should need to wipe my eyes.

"Perhaps your song is for me, after all." He waved Lucia away.

Mother rose and stood by the door. "There now, I am glad we have this matter sorted through. When can we expect your next visit?"

"You hurry me away?" The pope's nephew sat back in the chair. "Perhaps I will take another cup of coffee after all."

"Signore, it would be better to return this afternoon."

But he had no intention of leaving. And Mother didn't think it wise to press him to leave in his drunken state, and so we were forced to drink our morning coffee and make polite conversation until the bells tolled the end of morning mass and the wheels of a coach could be heard at the end of our street.

"Do I hear a coach?" Signor Odescalchi chuckled and stepped outside. "Yes, it is the coach of my old friend, the Duke of Mantua. We often play cards together."

Mother watched from the doorway, while Lucia, Bianca, and I stood behind, looking over her shoulder. The duke stepped down from the coach and bowed, surprised to see the pope's nephew step from our doorway. "Usually they keep our appointments far apart."

"She does not permit me to leave...She sings songs of such a romantic nature that I can hardly keep away...whispers words so close to my ear, my eyes water!"

"So close, her breath warms my neck." The duke joined the game, boasting, "And when she leans down to serve me a sweet, she means me to see her secrets."

"How dare they!" Mother moaned, wringing her hands. "Their games shame us...and now a crowd gathers to listen." Indeed, our neighbors liked nothing better than to see men of quality reduced to bickering, especially over a woman.

"I should think you too old for such a young woman"— Signor Odescalchi tapped the duke's cane—"though her song might serve you well in your later years as you lay upon your bed."

The duke laughed. "It isn't her song I intend to make use of as I lay upon my bed, Signore."

"I hope you prove yourself more honorable in courtship than in cards...You fell asleep during our last game and failed to pay your debt—"

"Now you insult me," the duke cried out. "You're drunk!"

The neighbors cheered them on, for among nobles who insulted one another publicly, the only way to restore honor was a duel. And now the pope's nephew put his hand on his sword. "Blade to blade...this evening at the Ponte Sisto."

"When the sun falls below the clock tower." The duke stood tall, straightening his coat, before he turned toward our door. With the duke approaching, Mother could not vent her fury, but I saw the effort she spent to hide her rage.

Only after I'd sung for the duke and she'd heard the coach wheels drive away did Mother turn on me. "Do you realize what you've done? If one kills the other over you, no man will come near this house, out of respect for the noble families!" Then her hands flew at me. "This is all your fault. Now I know who inspires that stupid smile on your face—that artist who paces like a hungry dog outside our door. You think I haven't noticed him? His greasy curls, stone shavings covering his clothes. Believe me, I'd sooner be dead than marry you off to the likes of him."

Bianca pleaded for Mother to stop, and Lucia reached for her fists, but Mother kept her palms flying. "If they duel, your future is ruined…ruined…do you hear me? All the sacrifices… your papa's earnings, Father Zachary's gifts…and this is the thanks we get…Ruined!"

All at once, the door flew open and a hand caught Mother's arm. "How dare you!" Father Zachary squeezed her wrists until she sank into a chair.

"She has ruined us!" Mother cried out.

"*Taci*…You be quiet!" Father Zachary commanded Mother in a tone I'd never heard before. Then he turned to Bianca and me. "Your mother has done enough harm to your future. I'm taking you to a convent, away from your mother's suitors and the scandals that surround this house. Lucia, go and help them pack their necessaries."

Upstairs, I lifted the floorboard to peek. Mother didn't move from the bench while the priest paced in front of the fire. Once, twice, Mother lifted her head. "*Per favore*…you cannot take them."

"I can, and I will." Father Zachary spoke the truth, for a priest in Rome could do as he pleased, unless a bishop or cardinal, someone placed higher in the church, stopped him.

Again, the room fell quiet except for the creak of the wooden planks under the priest's feet. Only when Papa and my brothers entered for the midday meal did Father Zachary speak, extending his hand to Papa. "Giorgino, we must talk."

Lucia, Bianca, and I hurried down the stairs. Papa took one look at my swollen eyes. "What has happened now?"

"There's no justice in this world." Mother threw herself against him, telling Papa everything. "You must stop him, Giorgino. Her talent will be wasted in a convent."

"Sit—all of you." Papa gestured for us to sit at the table, then raised the flask of wine and poured a glassful. "A drink, Father Zachary?"

Father Zachary took the glass and drank it all. "I'm afraid there's no choice, Giorgino. Surely you know about the cardinal, the stolen shipment, the posters displaying your daughter's likeness—"

"Angelica is innocent," Papa told him.

"Do you know what the pope calls her voice? The *devil's breath*!"

"'The devil's breath!'" Bianca gasped, pulling her rosary from her pocket.

"We should send for Flavio Odescalchi," Mother suggested. "He might intervene with his uncle—"

"That would only make matters worse." Father Zachary shook his head. "Do you think the pope wishes his nephew to take the side of a girl who has caused such scandal? It's too late; they must go to a convent. For their own good, they must be kept away from these suitors. It's the only way to save their reputations." Then, breathing deeply, he stared at Papa. "With your permission, Giorgino, I'll make arrangements—"

"The convents are full," Mother whispered. "And we have no money for the dowry."

"I saw this day coming, Giorgino." Father Zachary ignored Mother and addressed his words to Papa. "I've placed some money in the bank. I know the abbess at the convent Saint Ruffinus. I've done her the favor of balancing her books and helping her pay off certain debts. She'll make room for both of your daughters, and that way they will have each other."

In truth, I did not reject the idea of entering a convent close by, at least for a short while. It would remove me from Mother's suitors, and perhaps Theodon would attend mass, and I could sing to him from behind the grille.

"But Angelica must sing at Queen Christina's gala," Mother protested.

"And sing her way into the pope's jail!" Father Zachary's voice exploded. "Is that what you want? Unless Angelica lives under the queen's protection, she risks her whole future singing for this queen. Don't you see, Caterina? If we wait for the pope to arrest her, he will send her to a convent for wayward women, outside the city's walls."

"Let them go." Papa put his arm around Mother's shoulders. "A rest will do them good, Caterina. This convent is nearby. Let them go until the rumors die down."

∞

"No silk stockings, no ribbons, no petticoat, Miss. They'll take them away." Lucia shook her head. "Leave your heeled slippers, your colored shawl."

"What do I take, then?"

"Flat shoes, your Bible, a comb."

"That is all?"

She nodded. "They'll give you clothes to wear…a habit, a headpiece."

"Maybe it's for the best, Angelica." Bianca spoke excitedly. "At least in the convent you'll be safe from Mother's schemes to marry you off quickly."

"You pray all the time, anyway," I snapped. "What difference will it make to you if you are here or there?"

Bianca had always dreamed of entering a convent, and now she quickly wrapped her things in a white apron and hurried downstairs.

All my life I'd heard stories about convents—how some women chose the life behind walls, while others suffered it. "You've been inside a convent, Lucia. What will it be like?"

"Depends on the convent, Miss. From the talk at the fountain, it seems like half the women in Rome live in convents at one time or another. Some are run by charity for orphans. Others take in beaten women and beggar women. I'm told the convents for wayward women are worse than prisons." Lucia shrugged. "But some women prefer the enclosed life. The duchess once told me she was never happier than in the convent. Her family had a whole wing, handed down for generations. Her cousins were there, and the duchess took her favorite maid and her pet dog—"

"I won't have servants or pets," I responded sharply. "I'll have my comb, my flat shoes, my Bible." I tied them in my apron and knotted it. "What if Theodon gets tired of waiting?"

"He'll be glad that you are far away from your mother's suitors. If you write him a note, I'll see he gets it."

I sat down and, taking a piece of parchment and dipping my quill in ink, wrote:

> *Dear Theodon,*
> *It grieves me to say that we have been discovered. There is much I would add, if time permitted, but I must be quick as this evening my sister and I shall enter a convent. I do not look forward to the cloistered life, except that it may spare me the suitors my mother welcomes. I wish you to know that your eyes, your words, and your talent for drawing have sparked a flame in my heart that cannot be extinguished by time or distance. I hope that one day soon, we might see each other again.*
>
> > *Fondly,*
> > *Angelica*

I folded it quickly and handed it to Lucia.

She smiled. "With you gone, your mother won't watch me so closely. I'll tell him all about you, Miss, and I'll ask him to sketch his life for you. When you come back, all the sketches will be here waiting for you."

I should've been comforted by her words, but knowing that I would soon be leaving Lucia made me even sadder. I hugged her close.

Father Zachary came after sunset and brought good news, assuring us that the duel hadn't taken place. "The pope learned of it and sent his guards to stop it. But His Holiness was so angered by his nephew's behavior that he sent his pages throughout the city, reading aloud his newest decree." Father Zachary glanced at me. "From this day forward, girls are banned from musical training outside the convent and are not permitted to learn instruments of any sort...punishable by imprisonment."

Hearing his words, Mother embraced me, then Bianca. "Watch over Angelica," she told my sister. "She doesn't have your pious spirit or your common sense."

"Stop fretting, Mother," Bianca said. "We'll look after each other."

Papa and my brothers kissed us good-bye, then Father Zachary opened the door and led us into the dark streets.

CHAPTER ELEVEN

The convent, surrounded by a high stone wall, was nestled into a hill. When we arrived at the entrance, Father Zachary rang the bell, then quickly embraced us both. The portress opened the gate, and we stepped from one world into another, my heart pounding. The portress, a tall nun with a manly jaw, locked the gate behind us, then held a candle to our faces. "Hear how the winds ring the church bells? An omen. A dark omen. We don't need women of scandal to use our convent as a refuge. We'll be watching you."

Women of scandal! I reached for Bianca's hand and squeezed it. *How could rumors have already made their way inside these walls?*

Without another word, the portress turned and led us through several doors, locking each one behind us, then up two flights of stairs, where the abbess waited.

Inside her apartment, the abbess told us to sit, then poured us each a cup of chamomile tea. A woman with small eyes and pasty skin, she hardly seemed pleased by our arrival. "As you know, our space is extremely limited. You, Angelica, will be housed upstairs. There's a spare room in one of the apartments. Your sister will sleep in the dormitory—"

"My sister and I have never slept apart," I told her. "Isn't there another bed in the dormitory?"

"There is not." The abbess's lips tightened. "Many of the novices had hoped their own family members might join them. This is a delicate matter. Even here in the convent, there are extreme loyalties within families…and a long waiting list." The abbess smiled coldly. "I am making space for you both, only as a favor to Father Zachary."

Bianca's eyes widened. "Will the other sisters be angry with us?"

"No doubt some will resent your presence here. You must understand that inside these walls, we have over one hundred girls. Some are religious, some not; some are here by choice, others not; some are enclosed for the remainder of their lives, others will leave to marry." She spoke in a solemn voice. "Even though we live cloistered lives, rumors find their way inside."

My voice trembled as I asked, "Are you warning us?"

The abbess directed her gaze at me. "There are jealousies… often petty, sometimes cruel. In this convent, music is taught as a profession. We have two choirs, and each choir seeks to better the other. I have given your situation much consideration, Angelica. Normally we would welcome a girl with your talent, but Father Zachary wishes your presence here to remain a secret. I have decided you will not sing with either choir but will teach music instead—"

"I *must* sing," I told her flatly.

"You *must* do as you are told." Her eyes flashed. "And for the time being, until the scandals die down, you and your sister will teach music to our youngest novices." She stared at me. "I can see by your boldness, Angelica, you'll be tested by the principles here: humility, duty, obedience."

⌘

The next morning, two hands shook me awake. Opening my eyes, I saw a nun leaning over me. "I am Sister Serafina. Get up...hurry." Speaking in a wheezy voice, she told me to wash myself with the cold water she'd brought in a bowl. Then she handed me a robe and a head covering. As soon as I pulled on the habit, it began to itch, and the headpiece slipped forward.

Serafina tightened the band until it pinched. "You'll get used to it."

Now, with the sun rising, I was pleased to see a window set high in the wall. I did not yet know that all the windows in the convent were placed high so that our eyes would always be turned toward God and heaven. Besides the small bed, there was a wooden desk, a chair, and a rug woven with green and yellow threads. On the wall hung a small statue of the Virgin Mary.

"Where are we going?" I followed her down a hallway.

"To your sister's dormitory."

"What is that smell?"

"Boiled cabbage and eggs." Serafina put a finger to her lips to silence me. The heavy odor hung in the air. Other nuns passed us, but they did not lift their eyes or speak as we passed

121

them. They walked silently, with their heads lowered, their hands folded.

"Don't they speak to each other?"

Serafina gave me a stern glance. "It is a purposeful silence, meant to empty us of thoughts...meant to fill our ears with God's words."

I listened. Shoes clicked, doors opened, but there was no laughter, no whispers, no arguments. No human voices.

Bianca was waiting for us. "My bed is there in the corner." She pointed. Next to her bed stood a small chest with a candle on top.

Staring at the high ceilings and tiled floors, I felt cold drafts around my ankles. "There's plenty of room for your bed in my apartment. You can sleep with me upstairs."

Serafina shook her head. "The abbess will never allow it. She claims blood sisters do not enter their life here if they're knit together."

Serafina adjusted the rope around my waist. "Loose enough?"

"Certainly more comfortable than my corsets and gowns."

"You shouldn't talk openly about such things."

"What things?"

"Gowns. We don't speak of the world beyond these walls." Glancing around us, she whispered, "Never speak your heart, except in the garden."

Later, when Serafina was showing us the orange grove, she raised her eyebrows and smiled knowingly. "We're not stupid. We know the reason you sleep upstairs in the nobles' wing. You're here because of the Spanish cardinal. We heard all about the posters placed on his gate. You're not the first to hide from a scandal inside these walls."

My face burned. "You're mistaken. I'm here to rest my voice."

Serafina rolled her eyes. "I tell you what I've heard. The same cardinal visits his niece here, and one of the nuns saw him scraping lichen off our church bell and drinking it in wine—"

Bianca's eyes widened. "Why would a cardinal do such a thing?"

"It cures passion. Many priests must take the cure." Serafina's smile deepened, as she stared at me. "On Sundays, when the families visit, we hear all the gossip. You, Angelica Voglia, excited all the princes of Rome, even the pope's own nephew. Coaches filled the piazza day and night, and still you sang with your shutters thrown wide. His Holiness would have sent you to a convent for wayward women had the priest not placed you here."

"*Bugie*...Lies!" Bianca exclaimed. "My sister sang for suitors who came by invitation."

But I held my tongue. I stared at Serafina until our eyes locked.

"If I were you"—she leaned closer—"I would be careful. There are those inside this convent who live to sing in church on Sundays. They fear that you will take their place and sing the solos."

"But I am not permitted to sing!"

Serafina smiled. "These choir mistresses will do anything to better the other. Believe me, one of them will find a way to put your talent to use."

My mind raced with questions, but as the bell rang, Serafina took Bianca's arm and quickly led us toward the dining room. There I was met by a wall of glaring eyes, as the novices made their scornful whispers heard. "She's the one...the *devil's breath*!"

I felt their judging eyes and shivered. Even in here, enclosed by walls, I didn't feel safe.

⟳

There are girls who might find happiness in such a life. Girls who prefer to be told how to dress, what to do, what to think. Girls who might find the life restful—freed from decisions, choices, responsibilities—who wish to learn only what the church deems proper.

But I wasn't one of them.

I tried to observe the spiritual exercises—prayers, chores, silence—hours of the same routine until I lost all sense of time, until the days blurred together. The other nuns kept their distance. Only Bianca sat beside me at meals, with Serafina on her other side. The other novices watched me, and at first I smiled, hoping to find a friend. But seeing their cold eyes, their tight mouths, I grew defiant. I raised my chin and stared back. I had no choice but to pull away, to hold myself apart.

Soon enough I understood why I was placed on the top floor. Here were the women who had no religious calling but were enclosed for their own safety. One suffered delusions; another had not spoken since her husband had killed her lover. These women rarely left their rooms, except to stroll in the garden, and lived off the baskets that arrived daily from their fami-

124
∽

lies, filled with roasted chicken, dark breads, and fresh fruit. Often, at night, I heard them weeping. The cardinal's niece, Anna de Cabrera, was also in this wing. She refused to eat anything besides the communion wafers dipped in holy wine and was said to be starving.

At night I thought of Theodon. I had snuck the piece of marble into the convent, and now I rubbed it, dreaming of his skin, his hands, his strong arms. I thought of it as a charm and convinced myself that when I touched the marble, I could make him think of me. Rubbing the marble, I hummed the songs I would sing to him if he were standing outside my window. But one of the nuns complained that I wasn't observing the vow of silence, and the abbess chided me, "We have rooms in the basement for those who refuse to try."

During those first days when my heart was still clinging to the past, I missed Lucia, her sturdy voice urging me to hold on to my own truths. I hoped she would come with my family to visit on Sunday. I counted the days—the hours—until I would see them. But Sunday, after mass, the abbess called me away from the grille, where I sat waiting. "We don't allow visits the first month, not until we're certain you've adjusted."

❧

Right away, I felt caged inside the convent. Never before had I been forbidden to sing. Bianca and I spent our mornings training young girls in music, and when I tried to pull my sister aside, to whisper my frustration over all the rules, she put her finger to her lips to silence me. She observed the rules so strictly, we had no opportunity to be alone, to pour out our hearts. At first I told myself that this was the life she had always wanted—just as I had found my strength in song, Bianca found her strength in prayer. But as the days passed and Bianca continued to refuse my secrets and to cling to Serafina like a shadow, I began to feel abandoned.

Each morning, my sister taught the novices to read notes while I took each girl aside and trained her voice. Twelve years of age, the girls sat on a bench, dull-eyed and sleepy, their shoulders slumped, their hands twisting nervously in their laps. They weren't here to sing. They were here until a proper husband might be found; and if no husband could be arranged, these girls would spend their lives enclosed in convent walls. To keep their spirits lifted, their parents sent baskets of marmalade, dark breads, smoked fish, and biscuits. One morning, when one of the novices arrived with crumbs on her mouth and fishy breath, I lost my patience. "How dare you come to lessons with crumbs creasing your lips!"

"*Mi dispiace*...I'm sorry." Her chin dimpled as one tear, then another, rolled down her rosy cheeks.

"Crying will cloud your voice. Now swallow your tears and try again."

But hearing my sharp tone, she burst into tears.

"Go to your room, Carmela." Bianca lifted the girl by the shoulders, then nodded at the others. "The rest of you go, too. I must speak with my sister alone."

As soon as the girls had left, Bianca vented her anger. "How can you be so cruel, Angelica?"

"I teach them simple songs, and still they refuse to concentrate."

"They try their hardest." Bianca breathed in deeply. "These girls are separated from their families. Can't you see how they long for your approval?"

"Why are you so kind to them and so cruel to me?" I blurted. "You never speak to me anymore. You're always with Serafina, laughing and whispering."

"Would you deny me a friend?" Bianca raised her voice like a shield. "You didn't confide in me when Lucia filled your ears with secrets."

I reached for my sister's hand. "Don't you miss our old life?"

But she pulled away. "Our mother's pinches? Your suitors lined up with their gifts?"

"Papa, Franco, Pietro?"

"Of course, but I'm happier here." Then her eyes filled with a certainty I'd never seen before as she said, "Truly happy."

I stepped forward and tried to embrace my sister. "If I stay here, Bianca, I'll lose my talent, the only thing that sets me apart in this world."

But she did not return my hug and said in a chiding voice, "Perhaps God doesn't wish you to set yourself apart. Talent is a virtue only when it serves the church, Angelica. It's prayer, not the admiration of suitors, that gives life meaning."

I felt the sting of her words, felt her contempt. It frightened me. I knew that if my sister might change so quickly, then I, too, could change—I could disappear inside these walls.

∞

The following night, I was awakened by Sister Benedetta, one of the choir mistresses, who stood in my room, shaking me awake. "Our soprano has lost her voice," she whispered. "You must sing in her place the day after tomorrow, for the Feast of Saint Agnes." She handed me sheets of music. "Study this well."

I took the music. "Will I rehearse with the choir tomorrow?"

"No!" Her eyes flashed. "You must not speak of this with anyone."

"But they will find out when they hear me."

"Hopefully not before," Sister Benedetta whispered, before hurrying from the room.

I told no one, not even my sister, that I would sing on the Feast Day of Saint Agnes. Nevertheless, word of the soprano's illness made its way through the hallways, as did the rumors about who would replace her. The next day, as we sat for the midday meal, Bianca handed me a hard-boiled egg. "A girl who fasts on the Eve of Saint Agnes, then eats a hard-boiled egg before she goes to bed, will dream of her future husband. Eat this, Angelica, and if you dream of your Frenchman, perhaps it is God's will."

We had not spoken since our argument two days before, and now I smiled, thinking she meant to make up to me. "But you have always scorned Theodon."

"You *must* fast," she insisted, still pressing the egg into my hand. "Eat *nothing* but this egg if you wish to dream of your future husband."

But I was hungry, and as the nun served me a bowl of soup, I took up my wooden spoon. "I will only sip the broth."

But before the spoon touched my mouth, Bianca hit my arm and spilled the soup across my lap. At first I thought she was still angry and had meant to make a fool of me, but then I saw it—*argento vivo*, live mercury—swimming in the bowl. *Someone tried to poison me!* Mopping up my lap, Bianca whispered, "Serafina heard a rumor that you will sing tomorrow at the Feast of Saint Agnes, *if* you survive today's soup. You mustn't sing, Angelica. Serafina told me the choir mistresses will stop at nothing. The soprano who was supposed to sing tomorrow missed several notes at yesterday's practice. Last night she fell ill after eating her soup. If you sing, you will never be safe inside these walls."

I did not sleep that night. Fear kept me wide awake, listening for sounds outside my door. The following morning, I refused to leave my bed and complained of a sore throat. When Sister Benedetta came to my room, I shook my head and pretended I had no voice to speak.

Eighteen days, eighteen nights. That was how long we had been enclosed inside these walls.

And yet it felt like eighteen years.

Two mornings later, I was awakened by the portress, summoning me to the abbess's apartment. When I arrived and saw Mother standing beside the abbess, with Bianca weeping at her side, my heart stopped. "Mother, what is it?"

"Father Zachary." Mother rushed toward me and took me in her arms. "He is dead."

I stood back. "When?"

"Last night," she whispered. "Chest pains took him."

I longed to release the knot in my throat, the dryness coating my mouth, but seeing Mother's firm gaze, I choked back my feeling. *My blood father is dead.*

The abbess stood in front of the door. "The priest has not yet paid what he promised."

"That is not my concern," Mother replied.

"Three weeks' worth of food and lodging is owed." The abbess blocked the door.

Impatient to leave, Mother took a coral bracelet from her wrist. "I dare say this is generous for the watery soup and stale bread you've fed them." Then, turning toward us, she said, "Go on, get your things, Angelica. You, too, Bianca."

But the abbess continued, "Without a dowry paid in full, your daughters cannot return after the funeral."

Mother smiled bitterly. "Whatever money Father Zachary has left to my daughter will not find its way into your pockets, Abbess."

Bianca spoke softly. "Mother, I wish to stay."

"Go and pack your things," the abbess told her. "We have no room for girls without dowries."

The portress made a great noise with her keys, slamming the door on our backs. Bianca wept, even as Franco and Pietro hugged us and Mother looked us over. "I see you're none the worse for your stay here. Perhaps the rest was good for you."

Then, taking my arm, she led the way. "We must hurry to Father Zachary's apartment before the cook steals his belongings. As your patron, he told me he would leave a sum of money in the bank to provide for your future."

I listened with a great sadness inside. And maybe a little anger, too. Even now the lies continued. As long as Mother pretended he was nothing more than a generous priest who'd believed in my talent, I could not vent my grief, could not say the thoughts piling on top of my heart. He was my father... *my blood father!*

It was the Day of Cripples, and all around us, we saw the parade of crutches and stretchers making their way to Saint Peter's Basilica for the pope's blessing. Those with twisted arms, missing fingers, humped backs—all of them moved slowly in one direction. Mother, wishing to get away from them, led us across the bridge. It was my first time crossing a bridge, and any other day, I would've been excited to see the city. Pietro grabbed my arm, pointing to a boat weighted with crates. On the deck was a donkey with a parrot sitting on its back. I smiled as Pietro waved, but Mother grabbed his arm. "Don't call attention to your sister."

We entered a piazza where several women sat in chairs, sewing long curtains that hung from the second-story windows. There Mother pulled me inside a gate and knocked on the large wooden door. When an elderly bishop opened the door, Mother pushed me forward. "This is my daughter, Angelica Voglia. Father Zachary was her patron."

The bishop frowned at me. "I know who you are." Then, breathing heavily, he gestured for us to follow him up the stairs. I'd always imagined that Father Zachary lived in lavish surroundings, filled with books and fine furniture. And yet when the bishop opened the door and showed us the priest's small room, we were all shocked. There was only a simple bed, desk, and chair.

"This is where Father Zachary lived? *Our* Father Zachary?" Mother eyed the bishop suspiciously. "Not even a rug on his floor? No paintings? No silver candleholders?"

"What you see is the extent of his fortune," the bishop told her.

Straightening herself, Mother faced the bishop. "He assured me of a sum of money in the bank, intended for my daughter—"

"Frozen by creditors this morning," the bishop said, "to cover his debts."

"Debts!" Mother gasped. "Impossible!"

"Dressmakers, tutors, musical instruments, even a harpsichord...all summoned to your address, Signora Voglia. He kept tidy records." The bishop glanced at me, then turned his stern gaze on Mother. "He must have felt a great responsibility for your daughter. He spared no expense, yet his own salary couldn't come close to his expenditures."

Mother's voice rose in pitch. "Your Holiness knows well enough, a girl born with talent has no chance in this city without a priest as her patron."

Walking home, I felt a great heaviness in my chest. My mind raced with memories of Father Zachary—I would never again see his black cossack blowing in the wind as he arrived in the morning, his broad hands holding out a gift for me. Nor would I hear his loud voice as he set Mother straight on my future. Whenever Mother mentioned something I needed—sheets of music, ink to copy the librettos, stockings, a new pair of gloves— Father Zachary supplied them. Now, as I recalled his small, bare bedroom, my throat tightened. *He gave me everything I needed to improve my talent, and I never thanked him properly. Grazie, Father is all I said, and never with a hug or straight gaze. I was always in a hurry to practice my music. If only I had known how much he'd sacrificed, I would have said more...*

Now it was too late. *I had never once spoken true to him.* And knowing that, I felt tears spring into my eyes. Pietro saw the tears running down my cheeks and offered me his scarf, even though it meant baring his chin in public.

As we crossed the city, Mother kept silent, her face lowered in thought. I worried that without Father Zachary to intervene, Mother would marry me off to the first rich suitor to make an offer. That, too, I had taken for granted—how the priest had always questioned Mother's ambitions, taking the part of my happiness. Now, as she walked fast, I could see that Mother, too, was grieved over Father Zachary's death, but her sadness vented itself in anger. "How dare he leave us before you are married," she muttered. "Now is when you need him most."

I had needed him! Someone had tried to poison me, and now, in some strange way, his death had saved me. It was a strange moment—I felt deep grief over the priest's death, but I also felt great relief to be free of the convent. I no longer had to starve myself at meals, fearing another attack of poison. And now I could sing…at least in the privacy of my own room. Although Papa always said we should pray on our knees, I prayed as I walked. I thanked God for giving me two loving fathers.

Weaving our way through the market stands, I smelled the baskets of fresh apples. The cheese-seller's daughter winked at Franco and held a slice out to him. But as he drew close, she let it drop down her shirt, then laughed. "You'll have to find it later, Franco."

Turning the corner, I saw Lucia standing in our doorway, and my heart nearly burst—I was home.

CHAPTER TWELVE

As soon as we were alone together, Lucia stared at me with a grim face. "I hate to add one grief to another, Miss. Theodon has left, gone to France." She dug into her pocket. "He left you this letter."

My hands shook as I opened the paper.

> *Dearest Angelica,*
>
> *How pleased I was to receive your note and to know that while I am away you will be safe in a convent. Monsieur Errard, the director of the French Academy, grows sicker by the day, and I must leave this night for France. I am pleased to tell you that King Louis XIV wishes to approve my appointment as the new director. I must better my position so that your talents are well served, and this journey will no doubt benefit my career. How your voice has inspired me! Upon my word, I shall return to you with better prospects for our future together, and*

> *perhaps with my new title as director, your mother*
> *will permit me to court you.*
>
> *With deep respect and fondness,*
> *Theodon*

My throat knotted. "How long will he be gone?"

"It's a long journey, Miss." Lucia's eyes fell. "But there's worse to tell."

And here she sat beside me, squeezing my hands. "Now that Father Zachary is gone and cannot broker your future, your mother means to marry you off quick and has laid a plan."

Lucia's words planted such a weight inside me, I found it hard to breathe.

"I never saw a mother so taken by ambitions, Miss, as your own is, and yet, it is also plain to me that she believes herself acting on your behalf. But if I may speak my mind, Miss, the Duke of Mantua is a deceiving sort, and no husband for you. Even in your absence, he visits often. He stops at nothing to take you to his court in the north, and he persuades your mother with gifts and promises—"

"What promises?"

"That you'll sing for the best composers in all the world, Miss. He tells her there is no future for you here, in the pope's city. He says he is a great patron of opera and guarantees that nobles will come from all over the world to hear you sing during the Carnevale season. He tells your mother there is plenty of room for all your family, and he's offered her a huge sum...two thousand scudi!"

Two thousand scudi! I clasped my hands over my mouth.

Lucia gave me a somber nod. "Enough to last a lifetime, Miss."

I thought of Theodon and how much I missed him. "When? When does the duke wish to take me to his court?"

"Your mother does not waste any opportunity. The queen offered a hefty sum for your performance, and your mother was much grieved that you should miss the grand event. She has just sent word that you are home from the convent and might still sing for the English ambassador—"

"But we're in mourning. I cannot sing—"

"Your mother wishes all of Rome to know of your talent before you leave—"

"Leave!"

Lucia nodded. "After your performance at the queen's palace, the duke and his guards will escort you outside the city, away from the pope's laws, and take you to his palace in the north, where you will become a court singer. He makes a pretense of marrying you, Miss, saying that his dying wife will leave him soon, and only a woman so beautiful and talented as you could ease his grief."

"Ridiculous! The Duke of Mantua will not marry me...I'm a glazier's daughter. You've seen the way he looks at me when I sing, Lucia. He'll have his way with me, I know it. The duke tells Mother what she wishes to hear, and she believes him because it suits her own ambitions."

"I should tell you plain, your mother is most pleased to join you in the north."

I was shaken. "Does Papa know?"

Lucia gave me a weary nod. "He knows your mother schemes with the duke. When he learned that the duke visited even in your absence, he raised his voice on the subject of your future. They had a terrible row, Miss. Your papa said your future happiness was not worth any sum of money, and he would not agree to such a marriage unless you yourself wished it."

"And what did Mother say to that?"

"She said that your papa had no right to speak on your future." Lucia paused. "Since then, your mother and Papa do not speak…unless it is about coal or coins."

"So Papa doesn't know about the duke's plans to take me to the north?"

She shook her head. "No one knows. I heard your mother tell the duke that it would be best to keep their agreement a secret until you are safely out of Rome."

"If I tell Papa, he will surely stop her, but then Mother will make his life miserable. I don't want to be the cause of their arguments." Looking up, my throat knotted. "What can I do, Lucia?"

"I've thought hard on it, Miss." She leaned close. "I can make you a drink, curdled goat's milk mixed with burning nettles. It fogs your sound, at least for a bit…long enough to convince your mother you've lost your voice."

Hearing Mother's footsteps, Lucia quickly took up my soiled clothes, leaving through the door as Mother entered, carrying a tray of soup and bread. Thinking my tears were meant for Father Zachary, Mother lit the candle and forced the bowl of soup onto my lap. "Enough moping about. Drink this broth and then practice your songs. The Duke of Mantua grows bored in this rain, and tomorrow he's bringing a guest to hear you sing."

"Mother, I can't sing. We're in mourning." I stared at the moonlike shapes of fat floating on the broth.

"Do you think the priest buried himself in debt so that you could sit in bed and mourn him?" Mother gripped my chin, held it high. "I am thinking of you, Angelica. The Duke of Mantua wishes to marry you. He has a great court in the north, where you will have many opportunities to perform."

I pulled back. "I care nothing for him."

"Think of your talent. Now that the pope calls your voice the devil's breath, the suitors will be afraid to come. I admit it was my mistake; I didn't judge the risk. Your reputation is damaged. But we're fortunate, and the duke has made a firm offer—a very generous offer."

I threw my arms around her, pleading, "I don't want to leave you and Papa."

Here she smiled. "We will join you in the north."

"What about Papa's workshop? He'll never leave this neighborhood."

Leaning close, Mother whispered, "You will not speak of this to him, or anyone else, unless you wish to divide our family. With the money the duke offers, your papa can open three workshops in the north. I am certain that once he sees you made content as the duke's wife and realizes that all of us will benefit by such a marriage, he will change his mind."

"But the duke is so old, Mother."

"All the better. You'll not have to suffer him the whole of your life."

I stared at her, wondering at her hardness. For the first time, I saw the truth: Mother did not care about my happiness. She used my talent to further her own dreams, to guarantee her own future. If she truly cared for me, as a mother should, she wouldn't offer me up to the duke with no regard for my own feelings, my own wishes.

"You're too young to understand that your fate can change overnight, Angelica. You're at the age when an honorable girl marries. Soon the nobles will look past you to next season's flowers."

"I won't miss the attentions of the nobles."

"You don't know what you'll miss! None of us does, until it's too late. Once you marry the duke, you'll have his title as duchess. Your future will be secure."

I thought of Theodon and my eyes filled with tears.

Mother wiped my cheek with a kerchief. "I know you, Angelica, better than you know yourself. This feeling you have for the Frenchman is a passing affection. But your talent will never leave you. You must sing—it's in your blood...your bones. This is your choice, Angelica. Marry the duke and sing for the world; or wait and risk your whole future."

❧

"What if she's right?" I said to Lucia, when we were alone.

"Oh, Miss." Lucia shook her head. "No one can see deep enough into your heart or far enough into the future to know what's best for you."

"What're you saying, Lucia?"

"It's fine to listen to others, but you must trust yourself." She sat beside me. "I could try to find a noble family to serve, and I might wear a fine linen frock instead of this scratchy sackcloth." She giggled at the smock Mother had given her. "But this feeling for Franco; it makes your mother's harsh ways tolerable. It is true you've got your talent, and I don't. And maybe if I did, I'd feel different. But the way I see it, Miss, if you go to the duke's court, your talent will always depend on him. Pardon me for speaking plain, but you'll be a commoner marrying up. That seems a great risk to me." Lucia squeezed my hands. "I do believe that Theodon will come back to you, Miss, if you can find a way to wait for him."

"But how?"

"There's always a way, Miss, even if it means drinking a brew of stinging nettles."

"But Theodon may not be back for months." I felt desperate now, saying out loud what I knew to be the truth. "Mother won't be swayed from her purpose for that long, not if she's bent on marrying me quickly."

Lucia hugged me fiercely, having nothing else to offer up as comfort. When she left, I crawled beneath the bedcovers. I listened to the rain pelting against the roof. A month ago the world had seemed a game. Now I couldn't see a way to my own happiness. When Bianca came into the room, I was glad for her company and offered her the soup. "Bianca, are you hungry?"

But now that we were home, she tried to maintain the same routine that had consumed our days inside the convent—prayer and silence. She knelt in the corner, ignoring me.

"Please, Bianca, talk to me."

"Leave me alone. Do you think you're the only one to lose your dream?"

"Sometimes I think you no longer care for me as your sister."

She prayed louder, as if to shut me out. I closed my eyes. Perhaps Bianca had always used her prayers to hold a space between us, to mark our differences, to hold our lives apart. *God's will. God's plan. God's love.* That was her life, her future. But just as Mother had pinched my arms for singing too freely, Bianca's prayers pinched my heart.

I slept fitfully and woke the next morning knowing I had to escape Mother's plan. The question was not whether to leave the city with the duke. I knew I couldn't. But I was torn about which course to take—whether to drink nettle juice, run away during the night, or confess my feeling to Papa, knowing he would take my side. All morning my thoughts raced as I waited to speak to Lucia, but Mother had sent her on errands to buy pastries and wine before the duke arrived.

I was desperate. Call it luck or fate or sheer determination, but that afternoon, when the opportunity showed itself, I acted without pause. For the first time in my life, I made a decision on my own, without confiding in anyone.

It happened when the duke arrived with his friend, Marquis-blah-di-blah, whose name was lost on me because he announced himself while holding back a belch. They arrived in high spirits, reeking of wine and tobacco. But what was most noticeable, especially because the duke kept crimping his neck to balance it, was his extravagant red wig and large blue hat, white feathers swooping to one side. As I curtsied, the duke's smile deepened, making his chins crease. I smiled, remembering the nickname, Duke of Dobble-chins.

Then, I glanced at the marquis' face, draped by a brown wig of coiled locks. I thought him familiar and I tried not to stare at his moles—tried, but failed. From ear to neck brown islands popped up on his sea of pink flesh. Marquis of Moles, I anointed him.

"Signorina Angelica is the finest sight in all of Rome." Tossing back his curls, the duke draped a swath of purple silk around my shoulders. "I look forward to seeing you in a gown made of this silk. You will captivate my entire court."

Mother touched the shiny fabric. "Venetian silk…the finest."

As Lucia served coffee and cakes, and Mother made polite conversation about the weather, the duke rubbed his hands on his thighs, as if to tempt me. Smiling, winking, he breathed excitedly. I kept my gaze lowered.

When I thought of marrying him, my throat tightened and my heart pounded. *Impossible! I'd prefer the pope's prison to the duke's paunchy face and wrinkled hands!* Pulling my sister to her feet, I began singing an opera, *Lagrime d' Erminia*. I knew I was disobeying the pope's laws, and part of me wished his police would come and arrest me.

"Brava…an opera!" The marquis applauded when we'd finished. "You're as independent as my daughter claims."

"Your daughter?"

"Mariuccia. You sang with her at Palazzo Pamphili. Perhaps you didn't recognize me with this new wig." He bowed. "Marquis del Monte, first gentleman to Queen Christina."

Mariuccia's father…Of course, that is why he looked familiar.

"Mariuccia sends her highest regards and looks forward to performing with you in two days' time for the English ambassador's arrival. I'm in charge of the event, and you will sing with a choir of one hundred singers and an orchestra of fifty. There will be fireworks, dancers, theater…"

As he described at length all the preparations, I felt the first glimmer of hope. My heart quickened as I thought how I might escape the future Mother planned. Never before had I taken such a risk. I had no time to ponder, no time to hesitate. Raising my eyes, I dared to ask, "Might I send a greeting to Mariuccia in writing?"

The marquis nodded. "Of course. I'll deliver it myself."

Mother's lips grew tight: *Since when do you send letters to ladies in the queen's court!*

Ignoring her icy stare, I lifted my skirts and rushed up the stairs. Alone in the bedroom, I wrote:

> *Dearest Mariuccia,*
> *Might my voice still find a place in Queen Christina's court, before my mother marries me to a man I do not love? As you know, we sing together at Queen Christina's gala, which would allow certain opportunities to occur without inviting suspicions. You are my last, my only hope.*
>
> *Your friend,*
> *Angelica*

After sealing it with candle wax, I flew down the stairs and handed the envelope to the marquis. "I'm most grateful for your kindness."

As soon as the two nobles left the house, Mother cornered me. "What message did you send to the marquis' daughter?"

"Only a greeting."

"You should not presume a friendship with a nobleman's daughter. You overstep your place in the world—"

"Isn't that what you wish"—I faced Mother squarely—"to overstep this life we lead?"

A smile crept across her face. "Does the duke please you? He is rich and powerful, and when you marry him, Angelica, you will be saved. You will escape the pope's laws and secure yourself and our family a future."

Mother's words, her excitement, made my heart ache. I was betraying her dreams, and yet what choice did she leave me? Queen Christina's court was my only hope, the only place where I might still perform and wait for Theodon's return, while living protected from the pope's police.

It was a risk, a great risk. My whole future hung on the note I'd written to Mariuccia—scribblings to a woman I'd sung with once. I told no one except Lucia, and she hugged me fiercely. "Oh, I'll miss you! But you did right, I'm sure of it."

⌘

The following morning, a page arrived with a note from Mariuccia, informing me that a coach would come early the next day to take me to Palazzo Riario and that she was looking forward to singing beside me. I ran upstairs and wept, believing I was saved. I thought it a good sign that she made no mention of my request, knowing well enough that Mother would insist on reading her note.

Seeing me weep and thinking it nerves, Mother brought me a cup of tea. She sat beside me on the bed, hugging me and offering up the most tender voice. "You've done well, Angelica. How proud you make me."

I couldn't meet her eye, couldn't hug her back. From that

moment on, I knew there was no turning back. In saving myself, I would hurt those I loved most.

That night, as I lay next to my sister, I realized how betrayed she would feel the following morning when she discovered that I had left without confiding in her or saying good-bye. As my sister's breathing slowed to the airy rhythms of sleep, I took the end of her black braid as if it were an artist's paintbrush and touched it to my cheek, nose, lips, painting my face as I'd done when we were children. Even though we had not spoken our hearts in a long time, I would miss her. And now, listening to her soft sighs, I thought of all that I would leave behind. Mother's belief in me, Papa's patience, Franco's teasing, Pietro's curiosity, Bianca's pious spirit, and Lucia's friendship. Tossing and turning, I wondered, *Who is the Saint of Endings? Saint of Beginnings? Who do I pray to now?*

CHAPTER THIRTEEN

Never were my nerves so fraught as they were the next morning.

Already, as Papa and my brothers left the house, I was close to unraveled. I wasn't made for lies, nor for high emotions of the kind that might bring pain to others. Had Lucia not urged me upstairs to prepare myself, I might've wept in the open, confessing my scheme.

Even worse, Mother acted so loving toward me. In the coach, she stroked my hand, speaking in the same tender voice I'd heard as a child. "Never was a mother so blessed by a daughter as I have been by you, Angelica."

I was much relieved when we finally arrived at Queen Christina's palace and the *maestro di casa,* the head of the household, greeted me warmly, "Signorina Angelica, we've been expecting you."

But then he glanced at Mother, as if confused. "Madam?"

"I am Signora Voglia, the soprano's mother," Mother announced herself.

Searching his scroll, the *maestro di casa* shook his head. "I beg your pardon, Madam, but your name is not on our list of guests, and we have strict orders to adhere to this list." He tapped his scroll. "Your daughter's escort is Mariuccia Landini, lady to the queen."

"I will not leave my daughter's side." Mother's shrill voice did not inspire sympathy, and I saw the guards turn away to hide their smiles. The *maestro di casa* sent a valet up the stairs, and when the boy returned and whispered something in his ear, he apologized. "I am very sorry, Signora Voglia. We have no place for you to rest. All our rooms are occupied. Our guest list is so numerous, we are told no exceptions. The queen's ladies shall be at your daughter's side every moment, and I guarantee the queen spares no effort to protect her ladies. Shall I have the coach return you home?" He hesitated, lowering his voice. "Or, if you still wish to stay, Madam, we can put you in the maids' chamber, where the laundry girls eat and rest. You may wait there."

Mother's face reddened. "I shall not sit with the laundry girls." For the first time, Mother didn't know how to put her ambitions to action. I couldn't bear her humiliation and reached out to hold her arm, but she shrugged me off.

"Signora Voglia," the *maestro di casa* spoke softly as he opened the coach door, "you have my word your daughter shall come to no harm. I am deeply sorry for this misunderstanding." Then he took Mother's hand and helped her step inside. "Good day, Madam."

"Mother?" I stared through the window, awaiting Mother's advice and encouragement. But she refused me and stared straight ahead, even as the coachman whipped the horses into a trot.

"Mother!"

Still she offered no farewell wave, no good-luck wish, no good-bye…nothing. In that moment, I understood that Mother's love could not be separated from her own ambitions. Always before, my success had been her success. Now, for the first time, I'd been welcomed while she'd been turned away. And not even the prospect of having me carried away by the duke this evening, as she believed I would be, could soften her own humiliation. I felt the truth then—Mother could withstand a life of hardship, but she couldn't rise above her own defeated pride.

Mariuccia appeared at the top of the marble steps and hurried to greet me. "I was sorry to refuse your mother, but how can you enter the queen's service if your mother is here, laying her own plan?"

I threw my arms around her. "Oh, Mariuccia, it is true, then? The queen will take me into her service?"

She linked her arm through mine. "She was very pleased by your request. And so was I. What fun we'll have singing together." She led me up the steps. "First I'll give you the grand tour, and then we must rehearse."

Using a small, hidden stairwell, we climbed to the top floor. "While most of the staff lives outside the palace, in housing provided by the queen, she prefers her ladies to have their own chambers on the top floor, where we might be better protected." Mariuccia showed me my own room and, drawing back the curtains, nodded at the immense garden that stretched as far as the eye could see. "It is the queen's prize, this garden. Over three hundred orange and lemon trees imported from Sicily, and every type of flower blooms here in the spring."

My chamber was next to the dining room shared by all the queen's ladies, and Mariuccia showed me how a small lift was used to bring up food from the kitchen. She whispered that Octavia lived with her husband and children but often dined with the ladies. "So would I," she whispered, "if I had such a frightfully boring husband."

Next Mariuccia showed me the queen's library, filled with books in six languages. Across the hallway stood a locked door. "This is the *guardaroba*, where the queen's wardrobe and jewels are kept. Only the queen and her dresser have keys to this door."

"What kind of queen is she?"

"*Very* strong in her opinions. It is the queen's manner that starts tongues wagging. Some say she is mannish in her demeanor." Mariuccia leaned close. "But I'll tell you, never was a queen so kind to her domestics. Nor so fierce when it comes to loyalty. If she's crossed, Her Highness will punish those who betray her."

Mio Dio! I followed Mariuccia down another private staircase, to the kitchen on the ground floor. The most wonderful smells came from meats roasting on spits over a huge fire and pots steaming on the cooking counter. One cook sliced potatoes, another rolled dough, still another iced tiny cakes. Above one of the fireplaces, there was a large loft where the kitchen boys slept. It made me think of Franco and Pietro...and I missed them already.

Mariuccia then led me through the audience halls on the first floor. Opening a hidden door, she pulled me into a dark, secret passageway and pointed to the small holes drilled in the wall. "This is where the queen spies on visitors who come to admire her art collection. Go ahead!"

Peeking through the row of holes, I couldn't believe my eyes—sword smiths polishing swords for the dancers; tailors pinning costumes and sewing gloves for the servers; scene painters preparing a cloth with paint, the smell of oil and enamel piercing our noses; the harpsichord tuner tapping keys; a wig maker combing wigs.

"She must be the wealthiest queen in the world," I whispered. "So many people work for her."

"That's how the queen exerts her power, by sparing no expense on tonight's gala. If the world believes her wealthy and powerful, they will leave her alone to rule this quarter as she likes." She leaned close. "The truth is that the pope has cut her stipend because she refuses to give up control of her quarter, and now she throws this lavish celebration to prove his efforts futile. But I tell you frankly, Angelica, the queen is often in debt, and sometimes we do not receive the whole of our allowances. We must be careful, though, speaking on such topics. The pope's spies are everywhere."

"Here? In the queen's own palace?"

Nodding, Mariuccia put her finger to her lips and led me to the rehearsal room.

∞

Later, when it was time to perform, my old tutor, Gasparini, greeted me warmly. "The audience has heard that the famous girl with the miracle voice will perform. See how they crowd into the prime viewing spots?"

I stared at a sea of satin gowns, velvet waistcoats, ruffled shirts, fans, gloves, jewels, and wigs. Mariuccia took my hand. "Tonight you sing as the queen's soprano."

I was brought very close to nerves then, but I had no time to crumple under the pressure. Taking deep breaths, I prepared myself. As the orchestra took up a military march and the horns joined from the balcony, Mariuccia led me onstage. I admit my heart was pounding, but I refused to let my mind fill with doubts. We opened with a song by Caccini, one of Queen Christina's favorites. *"Ardi, cor mio...How ardent my love...that has never seen flames more beautiful."* Right away new freedom climbed inside my voice—a fearlessness, perhaps—as if the music were drawing a thread right through my heart. For the first time, I need not worry about the pope's laws or my mother's rules. For the first time, I could sing absolutely as I wished, letting my voice fill the hall. I closed my eyes and sang to Theodon on his journey north...and to a future of my own choosing. I soared as if the notes were wings carrying me higher and higher. I bared my heart. I *was* the song.

Afterward, the gentlemen stood, waving their silk kerchiefs, and the women dabbed at their eyes. Even Queen Christina, sitting next to England's ambassador, rose and smiled her approval.

We sang two more songs with an orchestra and chorus, and even after we'd curtsied, the applause would not stop. Finally, Maestro Corelli came over to us and kissed our hands. "Go quickly or they will beg for more."

"*Bravissime*, Angelica and Mariuccia." The voices followed us backstage.

"Sing more…more from the sopranos!"

But as Mariuccia led me toward the stairs, I pulled her back. "Look…the Duke of Mantua and his guards are waiting there!"

Without a word, Mariuccia led me to a secret door. She knew every door, hallway, and staircase inside the queen's palace, and soon enough we were safe upstairs in our own apartment.

That's when I collapsed on a chair and wept.

"Aren't you happy?"

"I am relieved and terrified." I wiped my eyes. "It's the first decision I've ever made on my own."

"You made the right decision, Angelica." Mariuccia poured us each a glass of wine from the bottle on the table. Then she uncovered a tray sent up from the kitchen: soup, bread, cheese, and fresh figs. "The duke has the worst reputation as a seducer of women. And if I might speak frankly, it is highly unlikely he would have married a tradesman's daughter, even one so talented as you." She served me a plate and refilled my wineglass but remained standing. "With the duke waiting below, you must stay here with your door locked." Then she tucked a coil of hair behind a ribbon and offered up a coy smile. "But if you won't feel abandoned, I'll return to the party. I have an admirer waiting to dance with me."

I didn't mind. Indeed, after she left I breathed a sigh of relief, glad for a moment alone. I stared at my new home—marble floors, a high bed with a mountain of pillows, a silk nightgown folded on the blanket. I pulled back the drapes so the stars were visible, and after dressing for bed, I climbed between the silk sheets. Staring at the night sky, I set my hand on the empty place beside me, where my sister had always slept. My whole future lay ahead of me, wider and more uncertain than ever before.

I didn't know myself inside this palace, didn't know what was expected of me. My life felt small without Mother's voice planning my future, without Lucia telling me who I was, who I might be. Listening to the laughter and music float up from below, I wondered if I could ever feel at home in such a grand palace.

CHAPTER FOURTEEN

S "Never stare at the queen's shoes, though they are the size of ships." Portia giggled the next morning as she powdered my face. "Nor her waistcoat. She often wears a man's jacket to hide the curve of her right shoulder."

Portia, Octavia, and Mariuccia were preparing me for my first audience with the queen, and now they gathered around the dressing table, offering advice.

"Never stammer," Octavia told me. "The queen has no patience with slow speech."

"Answer honestly or not at all." Mariuccia sprinkled perfumed water on my shoulders. "She prefers her ladies to speak their minds."

"Unless she reads to you from the book she is writing, her book of maxims"—Octavia rolled her eyes—"then it's best to say you find her ideas most enlightening."

After they'd pinned my curls five ways—loose, twined, divided, braided, and wound into a knot—they decided wound was best and pulled out two long curls on each side of my face. Portia painted my lips the color of ripe plums, then dusted my cheeks with a piece of fur sewn around a stick. When they pronounced me ready, Mariuccia took my hand and led me down the main stairs to the *piano nobile*, the floor where the queen's apartments were situated—one for winter, facing the river; the other for summer, overlooking the garden.

When I heard the guard announce my name, Mariuccia pushed me through the doors, and I curtsied, keeping my gaze low.

"Up with you, let me see your face," the queen commanded. Sitting on an elevated chair under a *baldacchino*—a large canopy of red velvet—Her Majesty sat between her two white poodles, tall regal dogs with their fur fluffed into clouds and their long noses stretching toward me. "Meet Anthony and Cleopatra, my two greatest treasures."

The poodles pressed their noses to my skirts and licked my hands.

"Do you lace your hands with meat fat?" The queen clapped with delight. "They never lick strangers!"

I smiled and tried not to let my eyes wander, but it was difficult not to stare at the intricate green and blue frescoed ceilings and marble floors. Behind the queen was an aviary with at least a dozen blue cages, each covered with a gold jacket. In the corner stood a hand-painted harpsichord, the most beautiful I'd ever seen. The queen followed my gaze. "I hope you'll play it often, Angelica."

"It would be my pleasure, Your Majesty."

The queen observed me steadily. "As a child I was only

allowed four hours sleep, so to maintain my studies. Now I cannot break the habit. Often, music calms me in the night. But since my poor Giovanniana passed away, I have no voice that puts me to sleep so well."

"I'll be honored to sing, as Your Majesty wishes."

"I expect absolute secrecy and loyalty from those who serve my inner chambers. Do you understand?"

"Yes, Your Highness."

The queen drew herself up and spoke in a solemn voice. "I have risked much in my decision to take you into my palace. I am sure by no fault of your own, your reputation for inciting scandal has grown. I know the pope intended to put an end to your singing in public. I also know that you were hidden in a convent, because of the posters placed on the gate of my dear friend Cardinal de Cabrera." She laughed heartily. "Though he wears a cardinal's red berretta, he cannot resist a talented soprano, so great is his passion for music."

My face turned hot as I kept my hands folded in front of me, my chin tucked, my eyes lowered.

"I also know that the pope's nephew caused a great scene outside your house," she said in a playful tone. "Our dear Mignon must have lost sleep that night."

I would soon learn that *Mignon* was the queen's nickname for the pope, by which she meant her *pet*.

"I also know you asked for a position in my palace because you wished to avoid leaving the city with the Duke of Mantua."

I didn't know how to read the queen's tone, but I looked up and saw that her eyes were twinkling. "And I've heard rumors of a Frenchman...a sculptor?"

How can she know?

"Don't look so surprised. I make it my business to know who rises and falls in this city. I am told that your Frenchman is on his way to Paris and will soon be appointed as the new director of the French Academy."

"Yes, Your Majesty."

"A promising future, then." The queen adjusted the belt around her waist. "Your singing pleases *me* immensely, Angelica. You shall perform often, but in a way that does not provoke the pope. I prefer small, private gatherings."

Just then there came a knock, and Mariuccia entered the room and curtsied. "Queen Christina, a boy named Pietro waits below. He claims to be Angelica's brother and brings urgent news."

I looked at Mariuccia. "How does he look?"

"His chin is quite prominent."

"It is my brother, Your Highness."

"Go and see him. Then come directly and bring me word of this urgent news."

∽✇∾

As soon as Pietro saw me, he rushed into my arms. "Angelica," he cried. But such great sobs escaped his throat, he could barely continue. "Papa...Franco!"

I pulled him close, feeling my own heart pound. "What... what's happened?"

"The Duke of Mantua...He went to the workshop early this morning." Pietro's great chin trembled. "Papa saw only their shadows. He believed they were nobles coming to place an order. Franco was stirring the molten lead, getting ready to pour it into the frames, and I was in the courtyard, filling buckets of water." Tears sprang to his eyes. "Before we sensed danger, the duke ordered his guards to block the entrance, then removed his knife from its shaft. The duke cried out, 'This is a message for your wife, who double-crossed me—that she may suffer all her days looking at your face.' Then he sliced Papa's face, drawing a blade down both cheeks."

"Does he live?" I cried out.

Nodding, Pietro swallowed his tears. "Franco rushed to help Papa, but the guards overpowered him, and the duke sliced off part of Franco's ear."

"No!" I clasped my hands over my mouth.

"I tried to warn Mother...I ran through the back alleys," Pietro continued in a hoarse whisper, "but the duke arrived just as I got there. He demanded his payment back and yelled at Mother that she didn't know her daughter as well as a mother should."

I winced. Even across this distance, I could feel Mother's fury.

Pietro wiped his tears with a bloody sleeve. "Mother gave him the pouch of money, crying out that he'd made a great mistake in doing violence against her family, for she knew nothing of your plan and had also been betrayed. The duke tossed her the handkerchief with Franco's ear wrapped inside it, and when Mother opened it, she fainted."

"I must go to them!" Not knowing what condition Papa and Franco might be in, I had no time to waste. "Wait here—I must ask the queen's permission to return home."

The queen took one look at my swollen eyes and told me to speak what I had heard. When I'd explained what had happened, her eyes filled with sympathy. "I'm deeply sorry for the harm done to your family, Angelica." Then her shoulders grew tall, and she ordered a coach, with two guards alongside for protection. "And the sibyl will accompany you, too," the queen told me. "No one is more skilled in healing."

I hadn't expected such kindness, and tears sprang to my eyes. "*Grazie,* Your Highness."

"I shall also send word to the Duke of Mantua that you are under my protection, and if he dares to hurt anyone else in your family, he'll answer to me. I fear, however, that he is far from Rome by now."

⚭

It had always been Pietro's dream to ride in a coach, but that day, he did not even glance out the window. I think he was ashamed that he'd hidden himself from the duke instead of defending Papa and Franco, and as we bounced along the cobbled streets, he covered his chin with one hand, his eyes with the other. The sibyl sat beside me. Dark eyed, dark skinned, her rough hands clutched a basket that contained a wooden spoon, a clamshell, two jars of powder—one white, one yellow—and a glass bottle marked with an X, filled with a dark copper liquid. When she saw me looking, she picked that bottle up in her hand and whispered, "Too much can kill a person, but a few drops can ease pain and put a person to sleep. With certain wounds, it's best to sleep through the first days."

I nodded, squeezing back tears. I was glad she didn't try to speak words of comfort. We didn't know each other, and I didn't want to pretend that she eased my heart, which beat faster the closer we drew to my home. It was my fault the duke had taken his knife to Papa and Franco...my fault they lay in pain. And now I didn't know how I could face my family.

As we stepped from the coach at the end of our street, I could hear Franco's cries and groans coming through the upstairs shutters. A crowd had gathered outside our door, and as I approached with the sibyl at my side, they stared at me, shaking their heads. The neighbors who had once stood below my window, admiring my talent, now judged me. Echoing the pope's words, they whispered, "The devil's breath is in her songs. See what bad luck she brings to her family?"

The sibyl took my arm, pulling me toward the house. Inside we were met by the heavy stench of blood—bloody towels soaked with lye in pails. Mother stood with her back to the door, stoking the coals to keep them hot, to keep the water boiling while she bobbed the towels. When she heard our footsteps, she turned and then narrowed her eyes as she lifted a handful of bloody rags. "Look what you have done!"

I rushed toward her to offer her comfort, but she dropped the rags and raised her fists. "How dare you come inside this house. You abandoned this family."

"Mother, please!"

"A disgrace—that is what you are—a thankless, ungrateful girl. No thought to anyone but yourself! Get out...get out!" Her mouth foamed as she picked up the stick she used to bob the bloody rags and jabbed it at me. "Out...out...out!"

I took two steps back. Shaking, I stared at her hair, matted with blood.

"You've broken my heart." She seethed. "You've ruined this family. Get away—"

"Please, Mother, I must see Papa and Franco." I nodded at the sibyl, who stood behind me, holding her basket. "I've brought the queen's healer. She brings medicines to ease their pain."

"Go and see them." She spit her words at me. "See how they suffer because of you! Then leave this house and never come back. I want you gone! Do you hear me? *Vattene*...Leave!"

The sibyl took my arm and pulled me up the stairs, where heavier scents filled the air—sage, camphor, eucalyptus, brandy. Inside the room I'd shared with my sister, Lucia and Bianca worked side by side, Bianca pressing a towel against my brother's ear to stop the flow of blood, while Lucia pinned his arms so he couldn't turn over and cause more blood to flow. I had never imagined an ear could spill so much blood, staining their hands and aprons. When I entered, only Lucia looked up, nodding. My sister ignored me and prayed out loud, in her low, murmuring way.

I introduced the sibyl, who stood by my brother's side, checking his pulse. "This is the queen's healer." She nodded at Bianca and Lucia.

"You've done well by him. His pulse is still strong." Pointing at a strip of white flesh, exposed through the wound, she whispered, "First I'll give him this medicine to ease the pain, and then I'll sew the wound closed. We must change his compresses often to keep him from infection." Taking out her bottle, she told me to open his lips and not to let him bite down. Then, using the dropper, she put five drops of the copper liquid on his tongue. After a short time, his body relaxed and there was no need to pin his arms.

Only then did I turn to my sister. "Bianca, I'm sorry—"

But her prayers grew louder until I grabbed her arm. "Bianca, I did not tell you because I didn't want you to have to lie for me."

But she turned away, still praying. She prayed out loud for Papa and Franco and Mother and Pietro. She even prayed for Lucia. But she didn't pray for me.

When the sibyl returned, she whispered, "Your papa will be fine. The knife will leave scars, but the wounds were not deep." I hurried to Papa's side and knelt by his bed. His face was covered with rags except for holes over his eyes, nose, and mouth. Already the sibyl's elixir had begun to do its work, and Papa was starting to breathe deeply, sinking into sleep. I knelt and squeezed his hand, begging his forgiveness.

"He doesn't hear you." The sibyl pulled me up. "You should leave soon, Angelica. It won't help your brother or papa to hear your mother cursing you downstairs."

Lucia waited in the hallway, and I threw my arms around her. "Will you still love him, Lucia? Even with half his ear gone?"

"Shhh!" Her finger shot to her lips as she leaned close. "What's a bit of an ear, Miss? Maybe now he won't be able to hear the cheese-seller's daughter offering him slices of her biggest, ripest cheeses." She pretended to stuff cheese down her shirt, as the cheese-seller's daughter did when Franco walked by.

Even in the midst of so much sadness, she made me smile.

"Just so you know, Miss, when word came last night that you

had found a position with the queen instead of going off with the duke, your papa was proud. And your brothers wolfed down your portion of the soup and toasted your generosity. Even your sister was pleased that you would stay nearby in Rome rather than be carried off to the north. Only your mother took it hard—"

Tears sprang to my eyes. "Oh, Lucia, if I'd known—"

She shook her head. "Give it a bit of time, and your mother will come around. Once you invite her to visit you at the palace and send her a coin or two from your allowance, she'll boast your talent all over again."

The sibyl came up the stairs with a pile of clean rags. "I have asked your mother if I might stay, and seeing that my medicine has eased their pain, she has agreed. But you must go now, Angelica. I will bring you word tomorrow."

∞

As I rode in the coach back to the palace, I trembled and wept. Trying to calm myself, I repeated Lucia's words. *Give it time, Miss.* But I knew Mother better than anyone—her strengths and weaknesses. Like me, Mother was driven by her dreams. And like me, she could be unforgiving.

When I arrived at the palace, Mariuccia met the coach and, taking one look at me, put her hand on my forehead. "Do you have a fever? You're trembling."

"It was a great shock." I burst into tears. "Oh, Mariuccia, I didn't mean to cause so much suffering. My mother will never forgive me...never!"

Mariuccia led me to my bedroom. "You have nothing to fear, Angelica. Your mother can do nothing to harm you while you live in the queen's palace. The queen protects us."

But Mariuccia didn't understand. It wasn't Mother's fists I feared. It was something deeper. Mother had always been strong for me, for all of us. Her expectations had ruled my life—my hopes, my dreams, and now my fears. Without her, I couldn't imagine the future. Everything became smaller...less important. *Even this palace, even my talent, even Theodon.* And for the first time, I wondered how much of my choice to come here had been born to resist Mother...to carve out my own future.

"What is it you're thinking?" Mariuccia searched my face.

"I don't want the queen to protect me from my own mother."

"This will surely lift your spirits." Mariuccia opened the *Gazzetta* and read aloud, *"Last night, under the reign of Queen Christina, never has Rome witnessed such a spectacle of beauty as was shown to England's ambassador, Lord Castlemaine. The highlight of the evening came in the performance of Angelica Voglia and Mariuccia Landini, whose stunning voices charmed the audience to an extreme. There was such sweetness and purity in the performance of the queen's new soprano, it is clear she has no equal..."* Mariuccia held up the paper. "Perhaps we should have a copy of the *Gazzetta* delivered to your mother. Then she would see the wisdom of your choice."

"She placed her hope in me...And I failed her."

"You're the queen's soprano," Mariuccia protested. "I see no failure in that!"

But words couldn't comfort me, and I told Mariuccia I needed to rest.

Much later I listened as the doorkeeper rang the bell twenty-five times, signaling the closing of the palace. The doors were locked, and no one was allowed to move about except by order of the queen. I heard footsteps below—guards extinguishing torches, preparing their makeshift beds in the hallway near the queen's chambers. An owl hooted outside the window. I prayed for Papa and Franco's health. I prayed for Mother's forgiveness. I prayed that Theodon's feeling for me was true and that the suffering I had caused was not in vain...that one day I might make it up to my family.

CHAPTER FIFTEEN

The following morning, Queen Christina summoned me. "Come here, Angelica, and sit beside the sibyl. She has just returned from your home and brings news."

I could see by the dark shadows under the sibyl's eyes that she hadn't slept.

"The worst is over, and your father is recovering," the sibyl said calmly. "Your brother is also improving. His fever is almost gone, and I have left him in the care of the maid, Lucia, who seems determined to nurse him back to good health."

"How relieved I am...and grateful!"

The sibyl's smile faded then, and only when the queen nodded to her to tell me the rest did she continue. "Your mother sent a trunk with your belongings. She said she has no use for your things now."

I covered my face to hide my grief.

"You must be strong, Angelica." Queen Christina regarded me with soft eyes, but her voice remained firm. "You have a new home now. What has happened to your father and brother cannot be undone. My spies tell me that the Duke of Mantua has left the city, with the pope's blessing. His Holiness sees the violence done to your family as proper punishment for the scandals you have caused."

The sibyl offered me a kerchief, and I wiped away my tears.

Queen Christina said, "I welcomed you into my service because I admire your talent and respect your courage. It's not easy to make a life different from the one your family chooses for you. I, too, had to make such a choice. I gave up my throne for a future of my own choosing." The queen sat tall and spoke forcefully. "I shall offer you every opportunity to sing. As you probably already know, I have founded an academy of music, and I have acted as patron to many famous composers. Scarlatti resided here until he left for Naples four years ago. Maestro Corelli resided here until last year, when he left for Cardinal Pamphili's palace, but he returns often to conduct my music events. Some of Rome's finest singers have found a home here. Do you know the name Cicciolino…a castrato who died last year? Cicci broke chandeliers! And sweet Giovanniana…poor girl." The queen stared at me, breathing deeply. "But you, Angelica…you have the greatest gift of all."

"I am honored by your praise, Your Majesty."

"I do not wish to burden you with duties, but Maestro Corelli will be coming today to rehearse for a small dinner I am hosting this evening. It is your decision…if you wish to sing—"

"I would like to begin right away, Your Majesty. It will take my mind off my family's suffering." I saw she was pleased by my reply.

As I backed to the door, the queen raised her voice once more. "Angelica, I am certain my generosity will be well-rewarded."

I believe she meant her words as encouragement, but they sat inside me like a warning. Octavia was waiting outside the queen's chamber, and as she led me through a long corridor, I whispered, "Who was Giovanniana?"

Octavia spun around. "My own, dear sister. She was once the queen's favorite soprano, but a wicked man corrupted her and she died in childbirth." Gripping my arm, she pulled me close. "We don't say his name in this palace, though he once resided here. The queen herself has made him her enemy and has banished him from her palace. But I'll tell you, so no one forgets—Bishop Vanini!"

Bishop Wet Lips! "But my own mother welcomed him!"

"Don't let him near you. He'll stop at nothing to ruin a woman's reputation." Octavia descended the circular stairs, stopping once more. "I'll tell you another gentleman you must avoid—the Marquis del Monte—"

"Mariuccia's father?"

"The scourge on this palace."

"But why does the queen make him first gentleman?"

"Because our queen, though wise in most ways, has a weakness for hearing herself praised, and the Marquis del Monte showers her with compliments."

⁂

That first day was the hardest. I was plagued by uncertainty, so that each step I took, each word I uttered, was followed by a cloud of doubt. I hadn't imagined that a single decision could change the whole of my life. And nowhere did I feel it more than in the music room.

Gasparini welcomed me with a warm embrace as Maestro Corelli passed out sheets of handwritten music to each of us. Then, with Mariuccia at my side, we waited. Maestro Corelli stared with furrowed brow at his own composition until the room fell silent, then raised his baton, signaling Pasquini, the harpsichordist, to begin playing softly.

But almost at once, the maestro silenced us. "Who is stomping? Which one of you is interrupting me?"

As the sound of marching grew and the marble floor shook, Maestro Corelli realized the sound came from outside, and he hurried to the windows, throwing them open. "The pope's soldiers are marching below."

We joined him at the window and stared at the battalion of soldiers marching outside the queen's palace.

"It's a warning." Pasquini fixed his eyes on me. "If the queen continues to offer refuge to the pope's enemies, the pope will stop at nothing to take over this quarter."

I glanced at Mariuccia, who rolled her eyes. "Look at the way they swagger with their swords."

Gasparini pointed at a small dog, confused and circling within their ranks. "Poor beast."

"We'll all be poor beasts if the pope does battle with our queen," Pasquini muttered.

"I don't think it will come to that." Maestro Corelli waved us away from the window. "Back to your positions."

"And if the pope does take control?" I dared to ask. "What would happen to those of us under the queen's protection?"

"We're musicians, not politicians," Maestro Corelli answered brusquely.

As our rehearsal continued, I tried to sing the words on the page. *"A gentle heart, a gentle soul... seeks but one love. Lord, divine ruler..."* But as my voice rose, fear gripped my throat.

Maestro Corelli drew his baton to silence the ensemble. "Angelica, your voice is wound so tightly, it drags behind the violin. Are you ill?"

"No, Maestro." My voice quavered.

"Now that you're the queen's soprano, you must prove yourself worthy of such an honor."

"Yes, Maestro."

As Maestro Corelli raised his baton, I tried to focus on the music, but I couldn't control my thoughts... *Who am I to think my voice might protect me? This is the life I chose for myself—soldiers marching... Papa and Franco suffering... my mother's anger turned against me.*

Outside, the soldiers thundered past Palazzo Riario, rattling the windows, the chandeliers, the doors. Maestro Corelli's forehead beaded with sweat. Reading the music as I sang, I raised my voice, first leaping, then trilling. But I was too controlled. I heard it, and I knew the maestro heard it, too.

Lowering his baton, Maestro Corelli lifted the sheet of music in front of me. "Learn this music before tonight." Then, dismissing the others, he took his music and left the room.

Gasparini remained behind, his brow furrowed, "The soldiers scared you?"

I blinked back tears. "Is it true the pope sent his soldiers because of me?"

"It's true the queen provokes His Holiness by taking you into her service after the pope banned women from performing outside convents." He took my hands, squeezing them gently. "But there are many cardinals who would side with the queen. You're a gifted soprano, Angelica. You must concern yourself with music. Let others decide what happens to this city."

I looked him in the eye. "Could the queen lose her power?"

"It's possible."

"What would happen to those of us in her service?"

Gasparini shrugged. "Who knows? We're all living on edge these days."

"I chose this life and now my family is suffering. If the queen loses her power, I can no longer go home."

Gasparini had already heard what had happened to my papa and brother, and he kindly handed me a handkerchief. "You mustn't blame yourself, Angelica. Nobles think nothing of taking justice into their own hands."

"The pope calls my voice the devil's breath." My voice trembled. "If His Holiness takes control of the queen's palace, surely I'll be sent to a convent for wayward women or placed in his prison."

Gasparini did not counter my words, and I could see by the way his gaze dropped that he didn't know how to comfort me. I handed back his kerchief, thanked him for his kindness, then quickly hurried away.

Alone in my room, I lay down on my bed, with the curtains drawn. Never before had so much depended on my talent. Each time I studied the music, my throat grew tight and my heart raced. Late in the afternoon, a breeze wafted the drapes, and the guard dogs howled whenever a carriage passed the gate. I missed Lucia. Mariuccia was a friend, too, but already I could see that she used her knowledge of life to play games, and I feared being part of something I didn't yet understand.

When the bell tolled at the end of evening vespers, I knew it was time to prepare myself for the evening concert. I stared at myself in the looking glass, recalling Lucia's wise words: *No one can see deep enough into your heart or far enough into the future to know what's best for you. You must trust yourself.*

And that is what I did. I told myself I was singing for Lucia, and that I would not let her down. And singing for her was different than performing for the queen and her guests, who did not yet know me. I sang the same song I had stumbled over this morning, only now my voice rose from a truer place inside me.

The queen herself mopped her eyes, while Cardinal Azzolino, the queen's guest, stood and bowed to me. Even Maestro Corelli turned and kissed my hand...high praise, indeed.

CHAPTER SIXTEEN

My second morning in the palace, the queen requested a private recital. I confess my heart fluttered fiercely to have an audience of one, and her the famous queen. But my purpose was to sing for the queen, *day or night, as Her Majesty wishes.* And now when I arrived, most punctual as I was warned to be, she was waiting expectantly. Nodding toward the maids who were packing her clothes, she announced, "Today I shall move to my apartment overlooking the garden. I wish to hear a song that welcomes in the spring."

I sat at the harpsichord and took a deep breath, deciding on a composition by Scarlatti, since he had once resided in the queen's palace. *"Da sventura a sventura…passo, passo l'ore…a maturità…From suffering, I pass…pass the hours…to wisdom."*

Sometimes the songs took me beyond myself, beyond what I knew about life. Songs can do that. They reach higher than the roofs, the horizon, the sky. They claim a life of their own. And that day when I sang for the queen, I saw the admiration in her eyes and found myself singing in ways I'd never sung before. Afterward, when the room fell quiet and it was just the two of us, the queen stared at me. "Your voice, Angelica, it is like a star in the midst of growing darkness."

From that day forward, every morning, every night, the queen summoned me. I would hear the bell, and then the guard's voice through the turnstile, *Her Majesty wishes a song*.

Being new to the palace, I liked to be needed, to feel useful. It did not matter if it was before dawn, I would leap from bed, put on a simple gown, drape a shawl around my shoulders, then hurry down the hidden staircase to the queen's inner chamber.

At first I sang softly, and between songs, remained quiet.

"Louder," the queen commanded.

I let my voice rise. My songs filled the queen's chamber. Outside her door, the guards slept on pallets—and once in a while they would snore so loudly, she could not hear my voice in a proper way, so she ordered them to wake up. Her Highness lay propped on silk pillows, silver hair cascading over her shoulders. Sometimes her eyes remained closed, her skin pale in the candlelight. She preferred opera at night, religious songs in the morning. I learned quickly and grew to know her tastes by the expressions on her face and the way her hands clutched the blanket.

Loose fingers, opera. Tight fingers, religious songs.

Her Highness was known to suffer from terrible bouts of cramping. Some said it was the lack of a husband, her body rebelling from disuse. Others said it was her disdain of wine. Others claimed it was her passion for scandal. Whatever its causes, the doctor came each Monday and bled her, despite the sibyl's warnings that bleeding would do no good and might worsen her condition.

If the pain was very great, she didn't say a word to me, but sighed, her eyebrows knit and lips pursed, as she raised her hand to command another song. Occasionally she would groan, releasing a dull hum into the air. "Your voice takes my mind off the pain. Sing softly until I fall asleep, will you, my dear?"

Yes, that is how she spoke to me. Not as her lady, not as her maid. But, *my dear.*

Me...*MY DEAR!*

∞

Everything about the queen amazed me: the queen's clock, *her very own time machine,* a gift from Louis XIV, chiming the passing of hours. Her gardenia perfume, sent from Paris, kept in a Venetian bottle. Her telescope, poised in a window of the library, used to spy on the French ambassador's palace across the river. The box of marzipan at the queen's bedside, each shaped like a different spring flower. The sun through the tall windows, reflecting off the marble floors so that each room filled with light in the morning, softening to blue shadows in the afternoon before the candles and fireplaces were lit.

I noticed everything—even the scents of her favorite dinner, pork roasted in apples and onions. She did not drink wine but preferred fresh nectars—apricot, orange, pear—squeezed from the fruits of her garden. And there was nothing the queen did not do well—reading, writing, horseback riding. Most of all, she was adept at conversation, no matter who came to visit. Cardinals, nobles, ambassadors, even the nuns and priests begging charity—the queen could shift her tone to suit any occasion.

One night, when thunder rolled and rain fell hard on the window panes, the queen interrupted my song. "You and I are alike, Angelica."

Then she patted the side of her bed and asked me to take a cup of tea with her. "We have been born into lives that separate us from other people. I, by my title as queen and heir to my father's throne. And you, by your talent. You have an angel's voice, too pure for this world, I fear."

"*Grazie*, Your Majesty."

"Do not thank me. We did not choose this life. It chose us. Both of us carry a burden. I must live up to my title, and you must live up to your talent." She sat up, eyes wide. Her hair, though combed, always seemed in disarray, as if she had just come inside from a heavy wind. "Come, sit here for a moment. Talk to me…talk to me as you might to the other ladies. How did your voice come to be discovered?"

I could see she wanted to be entertained with stories…*my stories*. But it wasn't in my nature to speak of my past. All my life, Mother had cautioned me, "The less said, the better."

Seeing me hesitate, the queen said softly, "I ask only out of curiosity. I am impressed by those who do not stay condemned to the life they have been given. I was the queen of Sweden, born to lead the Protestant countries in their battle against Catholicism. But I, like you, escaped the future chosen for me."

Yes, I thought, *but unlike me, Your Majesty had power and money to guarantee your choices*. And yet perhaps because she was a queen, and perhaps because her eyes were so kind, I whispered, "As a child, I was an *orecchiante*...I learned music by ear. A priest, Father Zachary, became my benefactor. He provided tutors. They taught me how to read music."

The queen nodded as if to encourage me to keep talking.

But I didn't trust myself to speak. I was still too new to the palace, and although I found the rules of the palace life easy to follow, I didn't understand *this part*, all the unspoken affections and loyalties that were never discussed openly but bared themselves in whispers and secrets. Now I wondered, *Am I obliged to tell the queen my past?*

Seeing my reluctance to open up, the queen sighed. "I, too, was saved by a man of the church. My dearest friend, Cardinal Azzolino." Leaning close, the queen whispered, "Though I find most wives frightfully boring, he is the only man I might have married. I tell no one this but you, Angelica. Without Cardinal Azzolino's counsel, I would have lost my power. Yes, it is true. I would have ended up bankrupt. I have not always been wise with money, but the good Cardinal Azzolino has helped me greatly in these matters." Then she asked, "Do you hear from your mother?"

"No, Your Majesty." I kept my eyes lowered.

"Oh, Angelica, I would not want your beauty and talent. It silences those who are modest and makes bold those who would corrupt. The Duke of Mantua should be punished for the wrong he has done to your family. Your mother should blame *him*, not you."

I curtsied, not knowing what else to do, which caused the queen to smile. Though she wished me to speak freely, I couldn't. *Not to a queen.*

"I, too, suffered from my own mother's disappointment. What a dour woman! She was French and never got over leaving her country behind. She adored jewels, paintings, lavish surroundings. She was always trying to make me wear pretty clothes. She wanted me to cultivate what she called feminine graces. My father's family was strict and frugal, as are the people of the northern countries. I was a great disappointment to her. She refused to touch me. As her queen, I was above her in rank, which angered her greatly. She went to live in a castle far away, where she surrounded herself with dwarves." Closing her eyes, the queen reached over, resting her hand on my arm. "Now that you are a queen's lady, you, too, have risen above your mother in rank. Perhaps you must reach out to your mother, invite her to the palace."

I was amazed by her words. I had never considered myself *above* my mother, and it pained me to think of it.

"You are at the beginning of your life, Angelica. I am reaching the end of mine." The queen squeezed my arm gently. "I see the fear in your eyes. You have become a lady by your own choice, and now you see that a lady's life has its own rules and obligations. Isn't that true?"

I nodded.

She gripped my hands tightly. "Do not confuse ambition for love, Angelica. Do not make every situation into an opportunity. That is *not* how God would have us live. The desire for power is what keeps us from knowing happiness. It has taken me sixty years to understand that. Most of us cannot see our way. But you, my dear child, sing as if you have already discovered the deeper truths. Never betray your gift!"

∞

When I was not singing for the queen, my time was free to use how I pleased. I often sat with the other ladies, listening to their gossip. Whole mornings, whole afternoons, they sat at the table arguing, laughing, whispering. Right away I saw that the queen's ladies talked about everything, especially the men in the queen's service. "Have you noticed Paolo, the new guard?" Mariuccia smiled coyly. "I should like to polish his sword. And then I should like to make it dull again."

Laughter filled the room, and often these conversations came around to me. "And your Frenchman, Angelica...does he, too, boast a sharp sword?" They loved to embarrass me with questions. "Tell us about him. Sculptors are known for their sturdy arms...all that stone they lift and chisel—"

"He has black curls," I told them. "His dark eyes sparkle, especially when he smiles."

"When he speaks to you of love, is it in French or Italian?" Octavia asked.

"I have never once spoken to him, except in church, when he kept me from tripping, and even then I was hidden behind a veil."

Octavia's mouth dropped open. "You wait for a man you do not know?"

"I do know him." My face grew warm. "We sent messages to

each other, and by his passion for art and mine for music, I believe we share a true regard for each other."

"A true regard," Octavia gently mocked. "My, how innocent!"

Mariuccia sighed dreamily. "I should prefer a husband who does not speak to me directly, but sends me secret messages. That way, married life would not become too dull."

"You would grow bored by any husband," Octavia whispered. "Unless he was married to another woman."

We all laughed heartily then, even Mariuccia, who seemed to enjoy the other women's teasing. But I soon learned that all their conversations, both idle and serious, ended the same way, with their voices lowering as they spoke about the rising tensions between the pope and the queen.

"Now that the French ambassador has died, the queen's power is threatened more than ever," Octavia whispered one day, not long after I had arrived.

"Of course it will come to a battle." Mariuccia always spoke her mind. "Our queen is the last noble in Rome who rules her own quarter and defies the pope's strictness, and unless the French king sends his troops quickly, the pope will surely try to take control of the French quarter first, and *then* the queen's quarter." Mariuccia glanced at me. "That will be the end of our singing in Rome, Angelica. We will all need a French husband then, to carry us off to Paris, where we can perform as we wish!"

I had studied Mariuccia enough to know she used her playful tone to mask her fears.

"'Suffering accepted, power respected,' that is our pope's motto," Mariuccia exclaimed. "They call *him* the poor man's pope, for he disdains excesses of any kind—unwashed children, wordy questions, spicy sauces. But his own tastes are often frivolous. Sachets of lavender in his drawers, underclothes sewn of Venetian silk, *only in red!* He adores figs—fig bread, fig pudding, stewed figs." She laughed. "And his favorite slippers are lined with mink."

"How do you know what fur lines his slippers?" I asked.

"She pays any number of kisses for the right information," Octavia teased.

In that way, my days passed. I learned much by listening to the ladies talk, but I also came to see how they always stuck to the same topics. Before long, I could predict their words before they said them, and I grew weary of their chatter. I realized that life could still feel small, even inside a grand palace.

I was glad when spring arrived and the garden burst with orange blossoms. It put the queen in the highest spirits, and she wished me by her side each day so that I could offer a song whenever her heart desired. And that made me feel as if I belonged there.

But at night, I missed home. It only took the smallest thing— the scent of broth, a pigeon cooing, the sound of boys laughing—and I would think of my family, what they were doing just then. It didn't get easier, that part of it. I couldn't reconcile myself to Mother's anger or the silence grown between us, and each Monday, I sent the coins paid me by the queen, along with a note, inviting my family to visit me the following Sunday.

Each Monday afternoon, the page named Pascal returned with the same answer. "Your mother says she is overly occupied."

"Did she say anything else?"

"That working long days to feed her family leaves her no time to visit palaces."

❧

Then, one Sunday, just when I had stopped expecting a visitor, Lucia surprised me. "I found one of your invitations thrown in the fire and decided to come on my own." She glanced down, smoothing her smock. "I couldn't dress too proper in my church clothes, Miss, without your mother growing suspicious. I told her I was off to pick flowers along the river."

Holding her hands, I stared at her hair, plaited into two neat braids, her best apron cleaned and ironed. I was near to bursting, I was so happy to see her smiling face. "Tell me everything, Lucia." I pulled her to a marble bench surrounded by hedges, so we could be alone.

"I can only stay a moment, but I had to see for myself that you really are a lady. And here you are, dressed in a gown in the middle of a palace garden."

Listening to her, I felt a great longing to go home and could not stop myself from turning misty eyed.

"Oh, my, did I say something? Are you treated badly, Miss?"

"No, no, the queen treats me with every kindness. It's just that with you, I speak my heart. We always have, Lucia. And there's no one else in the world who is so dear a friend to me."

"I miss you, too." She threw her arms around me then. "We all do."

"Even Mother?"

But here she could not bring herself to lie. She sighed deeply and didn't speak, for fear of hurting me.

"I'm glad you don't pretend with me, Lucia. I know Mother may never find it in her heart to forgive me."

"I can say, Miss, she doesn't speak against you, as she did before, but holds her feeling inside her. Your papa put her straight on that, saying whatever she felt was partly of her own making and she had no right to turn your brothers and sister against you, too."

Then Lucia looked me up and down and offered up a big grin. "I dare say, Miss, if your mother could see you here, dressed so fine, surrounded by a garden, she would change her mind and boast to all the world that her daughter is the queen's own soprano." Leaning close, she giggled. "And do you piss in a pot on silver legs, as my duchess did?"

I laughed. "The queen has been generous—gowns, a velvet cloak, even a pearl necklace and earrings to wear when I perform. But all the trimmings mean little to me, as you once said they would, Lucia. What pleases me most is singing, and I perform often for the queen and her guests."

"I expect she's pleased by your voice?"

I nodded, embarrassed.

Lucia squeezed my hands, telling me all about my family— how Franco's ear had healed enough so that if he cupped his hand behind it, he could hear nearly as well as before; how Papa had begun training Pietro in the skills of a glazier, and Pietro, feeling older, no longer hid his chin behind his hand. She told me Bianca had planted the garden in the courtyard, which was a good thing, because she'd taken to praying so much her knees were stuck with slivers from the wood floor. She'd not heard any news about Theodon, but his friend Lucien had fallen in love with the cheese-seller's daughter. She laughed boisterously. "I guess that fits, him being French."

Then shifting in her mood, she searched my face. "Do you still care for Theodon, Miss, now that you are a lady?"

"Yes...I believe so."

"Hardly convincing, that reply," she told me in her frank way.

Here, the words came flooding out of me, and I told her what I'd not yet admitted to myself. "I do not know Theodon... not really. Not in the way a girl who is deciding her future must know a man. Is he a man of his word? How am I to know if he is the sort to be content as a husband? Secrets, notes, and sketches...that is all I know of him."

Lucia started to speak, but I cut her off. "And yet I've used what little I know of him to chart my own course."

Lucia smiled. "Sometimes, Miss, I think you expect to know the future before you live it. You can be sure he's a risk, but not so much of one as the nobles and gents who have made a game of your talent. Has he once given you a sign he's not to be trusted?"

I shook my head.

"Has he made your heart brim with happiness until it spilled into your songs?"

I nodded.

"What's to be done, then, Miss, by turning your heart cold to *him*? You'll not win back your mother's love, if that's what fills your mind, not unless you are also willing to marry the husband she chooses. That's the bargain she'll make of your future, and, you can be sure, your mother could outbargain the devil. I don't think waiting for the Frenchman is near so great a gamble."

"Oh, Lucia, I wish you lived with me in the palace. You always put my mind right."

Satisfied by my reply that I hadn't changed too much, she asked me what filled my days and how I found the other ladies. But just then, the church bells tolled evening vespers, and Lucia leaped to her feet. "Your mother's sure to scold me now."

"Will you come again, Lucia?" I hugged her close.

"I will, Miss, but not so soon as to draw your mother's suspicions. Sundays she expects me at the house."

My life felt bigger then. By coming to visit me, Lucia had built a bridge between my past and my present, and now the two halves made a whole. At least that is how it felt to me.

CHAPTER SEVENTEEN

It is hard to be good in this world. That is what I discovered the day after Lucia's visit. Even when you put your heart to it and do your best, there are those who will find fault in your goodness, as if it were but a ploy.

Returning from rehearsals that afternoon, I heard my name mentioned through the door to the ladies' apartment. "I don't think Angelica's voice is so perfect," Octavia was saying. "It is the knowledge that she can be lifted from her background and made into something—that is what the queen loves...A commoner, so easy to mold, so willing to listen, so grateful for the smallest morsel of sweetness."

Even if I'd words to speak, I couldn't have spoken them. Not then, not after her harsh words had taken my breath away.

"Stop your jealous whispers," Mariuccia scolded. "She's not to blame for the queen's affections."

I stepped away from the door, then made my footsteps loud. Entering, I tried to hide my feelings, but the ladies busied themselves, surrounding me with hard silences and downcast eyes. And when Octavia did speak, it was not so much what she said but how she said it that unnerved me…as if I had much to learn. "Now that the weather turns warmer, Angelica, the queen will not call you to sing so often. Her Majesty prefers to ride her horse, Azzurro, in the hills."

"How are your children, Octavia?" I switched to her favorite topic.

"The queen prefers I send them to the country, where they cannot make noise and disrupt your songs."

My mouth fell open as I realized the reason for her anger. "Surely you cannot blame me for the queen's decision."

"These days"—Octavia lifted her gaze to me—"the queen cares only for her favorite soprano."

"That is not true!" I felt my face turn hot. "You are her first lady. It is you she calls on for advice about her staff. It is Portia who powders her face and styles her hair. And it is Mariuccia who reads the gossip papers to the queen and makes her laugh out loud. We are all her favorites, in one way or another. I sing for the queen, as is *my* duty." Then I hurried to my room.

But that afternoon, Mariuccia pulled me into the garden. "You were right to speak up this morning, Angelica, yet it's also important to make allies of the other ladies. You never know when you will need them. And I must warn you—"

"Warn me of what?"

"The queen is known for her shifts in mood, and her favorites are often abandoned like broken wheels in a ditch. I caution you—soon enough, you may lose favor with the queen."

"Have you heard the queen complain about my songs?"

She glanced around, then whispered, "Though she is our queen, you must be careful."

"In what way, careful?"

"There are things you don't know." She put her lips to my ear. "The queen was born with a birth caul, a thin layer of skin over her privates."

Horrified, I drew away. "What does this have to do with me?"

"At her birth, she was declared a boy, and all the palace rejoiced. But when the caul was removed, the midwives saw the truth, only no one dared tell the king. Not until the following day, when the baby's aunt came to visit. She saw that the baby was a girl and laid the child naked on the king's bed, so that he would see for himself—his heir was a daughter."

"Why do you tell me this?" I asked.

"Such confusion left its mark. The queen is not consistent in her affections."

I stared at Mariuccia—her dark, coiled hair and red lips. Now, in the sunlight, she looked older.

"I see you doubt my words. You probably think I'm telling you these things because I'm jealous. But you're wrong."

"Then, why?"

"As a friend, Angelica. I mean only to warn you that the queen is both more and less than she seems. You must be careful not to presume you are her friend... *her equal*. No matter how much she confides."

"She treats me well. Isn't that enough?"

"Her Majesty always has a favorite, to keep by her side like a pretty doll. Someone to entertain her. But her affections are only as deep as her needs. I warn you." Mariuccia held her voice low.

"Those Her Majesty favors most often become her greatest enemies. Just be careful."

"Please," I whispered. "Say no more." Already my loyalty to the queen was so great that I hurried away. But Mariuccia's words clung to my heart. I walked briskly through the herb garden, fragrant with wild rosemary, trying to breathe myself free from her secrets.

❧

That evening, after dining with Cardinal Azzolino, the queen called me to her chamber and commanded a love song. "Something sweet, Angelica. Something that stirs the heart."

Breathing deeply, I let my voice rise as I accompanied myself on the harpsichord, *"Allegro con il discorso dell'amore... Joyful with the discourse of Love, a brilliant clear flame has been kindled that generously spreads happiness with its bright burning..."*

But beneath the notes, beneath my voice, my doubts and fears had been kindled by Mariuccia's secrets. *Was the queen fickle in her affections? Would I soon be cast aside?*

The queen immediately interrupted my song. "Angelica, your voice rises like windless sails. Please, begin again."

I did as she commanded, playing the opening stanzas, and yet my sound was tight and heavy, even as I tried to spring it loose. The queen sat against her pillows and smiled thinly. "What ails you?"

It was as if Mariuccia had planted new eyes in my head: I noticed the queen's eyes lit like smoldering coals, her fingers posed like spiders upon her blanket. I lowered my eyes.

"Your sound is faltering this evening, Angelica. Are you tired?"

I shook my head. "No, Your Highness."

"Is it the Frenchman...his absence sours your notes?"

"No, Your Highness."

"As your queen, I command you to tell me what bothers you." She softened her voice. "And as your friend, I ask you to tell me."

I met the queen's stern gaze. I was beneath her, *far beneath her,* and yet she expected me to speak to her as an equal. *It isn't fair!*

As if the queen could read my mind, she said softly, "It is the other ladies? They're growing jealous of my fondness for your songs? Tell you stories about me? Tell you that I am hot and cold in my affections?" The queen nodded. "It is always the same."

When my gaze dropped to the marble floor, the queen sighed impatiently. "Go, then. But come back tomorrow prepared to sing. And do not listen to everything you hear, Angelica."

Keeping my head low, I backed toward the doorway.

"Angelica?"

I glanced up. "Yes, Your Majesty."

"Do you know what those of us with power long for most?"

"No, Your Majesty."

"The ability to trust one's own heart. To hear it, to know it, to live by it."

"Yes, Your Majesty."

"Do not let others fill your heart with their truths. Find your own. Do you understand?"

The queen was famous for her blue eyes—sometimes cold as ice, sometimes raging as the sea, sometimes twinkling playfully like sunlight on water. But in her eyes, one could always see the truth of her feeling.

I looked up now and met her gaze. I saw only kindness .. wisdom…affection. My heart grew tight…ashamed.

❧

I knew what I had to do. That evening, after the candles had been extinguished, I sat in the ladies' sitting room, waiting in darkness. It was late, well past the hour when all the queen's ladies were expected to be safely in their rooms. Portia and Octavia had long since gone to sleep. The bells had rung twenty-five times, and the doors had been locked. No one was supposed to be moving about. Yet Mariuccia had not returned.

Then I heard the sound of a door opening and heels clicking across the floor. The moonlight was bright through the window, and as Mariuccia approached, she asked, "Who's there?"

"Angelica."

"What keeps you awake at this hour?" She giggled. "*Lalalalalaaaaa…*Why aren't you singing for the queen?"

"I'm waiting for you, Mariuccia. I must speak my heart."

"Oh, yes, *do* speak your heart. Tell me about this Frenchman you wait for." And before I could stop her, she carried on. "Do you love him? Oh, yes, it is easy to love someone far away…far away and handsome…far away and the director of the French Academy. Far away is easy." Swaying, she waved a finger at me. "It's like loving the clouds, the stars, the moon—"

"That is not what I mean to discuss." And before she could interrupt, I blurted, "It is most difficult to stay loyal to our queen without offending her other ladies. You must never speak rumors of Her Majesty again in my presence. I can't endure the shame such rumors cast on Her Majesty, and myself for listening. I want to remain worthy of the queen's trust."

"Brava…wonderful speech." Mariuccia feigned a yawn. "And now, if you're finished, I'd like to go to bed."

I hadn't expected her mockery. I pulled her down next to me on the window seat. "Please understand me. I don't mean to sound ungrateful." I took Mariuccia's hands in my own. "I have you to thank for this new life. But I do not wish to be torn between loyalties…You are a dear friend, but she is my queen— *our* queen!"

She pulled her hands away and applauded. "I almost suspect it is true what the others say—that you act as the queen's spy."

I shook my head. "I sing as she wishes. That is all."

"That is not all." Shedding her smile, Mariuccia lowered her voice. "How quickly innocence becomes ignorance if one pretends not to see the truth of this life we lead."

"What do you mean?"

"Do you know what power is?"

"Wealth…rank."

"There are many with wealth and rank." She spoke in a callous tone. "But few with so much power as the queen. Power is the ability to decide for yourself and live by your decisions. You and I will never have that power, Angelica. You believe that your talent is power, but that's not true. You might even think that by your gifted voice, you can decide your own future, but you are wrong. The queen decides for us. Never forget that. Your loyalty to the queen is honorable, Angelica, but you must serve the queen with open eyes. Queen Christina uses everyone to one purpose or another. She uses you."

"Say no more."

Mariuccia ignored me. "For now, you have earned your place as the queen's favorite. No doubt Her Majesty praises you, makes you feel chosen by your talent. But your talent earns you enemies. Queen Christina is your patron, not your friend. I am your friend. Remember that. And mark my words, these are difficult times. The pope is growing impatient to control this quarter. You'll need a friend someday."

Then, standing quickly, Mariuccia slipped into her room, leaving me alone. As I stared into the darkness, I trembled from her words. I could see already that there was room in this world for more than one truth. And I could also see that I *would* have to be careful. I passed a fretful night, kept wide awake thinking on a future that offered up no certainty.

CHAPTER EIGHTEEN

Rumor: The queen ordered Pascal to employ all the French-men he could find to withstand the pope's armies. Her Majesty wishes to stave off the pope until the French king sends his troops.

I felt it. Heard it. Tasted it in the air—gunpowder, sword polish, newly laundered uniforms. French guards, their brothers and cousins, multiplying on the first floor, drinking the giant kegs the queen ordered to keep them happy. *Mais oui...mais non...Voilà!*

Ten Sundays had passed since I'd moved into the queen's palace. French soldiers now lived on the ground floor, next to the stable, and flies buzzed around the makeshift reed fences that circled their pails. Only human, but oh, the smells! Though the weather had turned warm, the stench was so strong we were forced to keep our windows closed.

Those days before Easter, the queen was busy, too busy for my songs.

Upstairs, we listened through walls, floors, stairwells. I sat with the other ladies, waiting for the familiar knock at the door, the guard summoning me to sing. I suffered the ladies' told-you-so smiles. "You do not sing for the queen this morning?" Octavia *tsk-tsk*ed as she knit a small sock dangling on a line of yarn. "How long has it been...three days?"

"Yes. And what of it?"

"And still no word from your Frenchman?" Mariuccia tried to shift the conversation.

I shook my head sadly.

"Surely you will hear soon." She smiled. "I'm told the letters sent to the queen from France take months to arrive." Since our discussion two nights before, Mariuccia and I had been gentle with each other.

"You hardly know him," Octavia told me. "Perhaps he has decided to stay in Paris."

She spoke my own doubts. I hadn't yet come close enough to Theodon to know his failings. In my mind he was perfection. He was everything I *might* love if I had the chance. And yet I worried. Two nights past, I'd had a strange dream. Theodon had arrived from France and stood outside the palace, calling to me. I heard his voice, but when I descended the stairs, there were no doors, no windows—no way for us to greet each other. I woke with a terrible panic inside, glad that it was daylight and I could hear the doors below opening and closing.

We all lacked sleep. In this palace of over a hundred rooms, we all felt trapped by this battle between our queen and the pope. I grew impatient. All around us were secrets, brewing like a thick tea. And yet their meaning was kept from us, as if we were children.

One floor below, inside the queen's innermost chamber, urgent voices rose—Queen Christina, Cardinal Azzolino, and Captain Caponi argued late into the night. The queen remained closed off; only Cardinal Azzolino and her captains were given audience. Pages delivered maps and messages. Maids delivered trays of food. Tempers flared. Late one night, we heard the queen cry out, "Enough patience! Mignon has pushed me too far this time."

By orders of the queen, no one was to leave or enter the palace without the queen's permission. Only Mariuccia disobeyed. She snuck away after the other ladies had gone to their rooms at night. She did not speak of it. None of us knew.

But one night she returned late, after the gates and doors had been locked. It was well past midnight when I heard a pebble thrown against my window. I lay still, listening. Then another pebble landed. I rose quickly and, looking down at the garden, saw Mariuccia standing below. Even in the darkness, I recognized her hat—the extravagant broad brim and swoop of feathers. Without a word, she stepped into the moonlight and used her arms to gesture—telling me to come down the circular stairs used by the piss-pot maids and let her in through the laundry room windows.

I'd never taken these stairs before and had to hold my nose against the foul stench. The stairs were so tight and steep, I saw how impossible it would be not to spill the pots. Even worse, I'd worn no shoes for fear of making noise. Now, judging by the wet, clammy wood under my feet, I was stepping in the slop of human waste and so hurried doubly to be done with my task.

Only when we were safe upstairs did Mariuccia see my feet. "Oh no, you didn't go barefoot on those stairs!"

"I didn't want to make noise."

She doubled over, muffling her laughter so as not to wake the others. Then, still giggling, she filled a bowl with perfumed water and put it at my feet so I could soak them clean.

It was then I dared to ask, "Is he married, then? Is that why you must meet in secret?"

Her eyes twinkled, but she did not respond except to pull back her sleeve and show me the bracelet he'd given her. "Twelve pearls, one for each time we've met."

∞

With Easter fast approaching, I had sent my family a basket of sweets and a note asking them to join us in the garden for tea on Easter day:

> *Dear Mother,*
> *Let us put the past behind us. I wish only to mend*
> *the rift that puts this distance between us.*

I received no response, yet held out hope that at least Lucia would come to visit me.

Easter morning I woke to shouting voices. I wrapped myself in a shawl and hurried to the window. Below on the street, the queen's footmen and stable boys surrounded the pope's soldiers, who were holding Pascal, the queen's favorite page, by force.

"Leave him alone," the footmen cried out. "Let him go!"

But the pope's corporal yelled, "By orders of His Holiness the pope, we arrest him."

Mariuccia burst through the door and joined me at the window. "The pope's soldiers arrested Pascal on his way to church

They claim he stole a shipment of brandy, then sold it on the black market. The queen is greatly vexed. Her domestics have managed to block the soldiers until the queen's guards arrive. Come, get dressed." She pulled a day frock from the wardrobe and handed it to me. "Octavia's husband leads the queen's soldiers. She's sorely worried."

Mariuccia hurried out the door, and after pulling on the smock, I followed. At the table in the dining room, Portia sat in silence, while Octavia wept, her eyes swollen and red. "He is not a courageous man, my husband. He lacks a soldier's character."

"I am certain the pope sends his soldiers merely as provocation," Mariuccia said. "Surely they will not go to battle on Easter morning."

"Whatever the pope's reasons," Octavia cried out, "I do not wish my husband to die for them."

On the street below, gates opened, horses clomped, and crowds lining the street cheered, "Long live the queen!" As the queen's guards rode out in uniform, swords at their sides, Mariuccia stood at the window and threw her handkerchief, calling, *"Viva la Regina Christina!"* Then sighing, she turned back. "Soldiers are so handsome in their battle uniforms."

Octavia cursed. "Have you no shame? My husband goes to battle, and you stand there admiring the soldiers' uniforms?"

We sat in silence then, each of us lost in our prayers, our thoughts, our worries.

When I could sit no longer, I joined Mariuccia at the window. We stared at the crowds cheering the queen's guards— there was no denying that the queen's quarter had its fill of orphans, courtesans, beggars, and thieves. No street was free of them. And yet, they raised their voices loudly, *"Viva la regina!"*

"Where does His Holiness think all those thieves and swindlers will go if the pope takes over this quarter?" Mariuccia whispered. "Where will the courtesans conduct their business? Does His Holiness really want them spread throughout his city? The pope should thank our queen, who is compassionate and willing to overlook those who have no place else to live."

We watched as the queen's guards surrounded the pope's soldiers. Then, all at once, the pope's corporal raised his sword and called on his men to release Pascal. In the time it takes to sing a hymn, the confrontation was over, and cheers rose from the street. "Long live Your Majesty!" Leaning out the window, we watched as the crowd separated on either side of the Lungara, the long street that stretched from the queen's palace to Saint Peter's, and the queen's guards returned on horseback. At the head was Pascal, waving to the cheering crowd.

"It's over...We won!" Mariuccia pulled Octavia to the window. "Just as I said. The pope would never risk a battle on Easter morning."

Then Mariuccia popped the cork of a champagne bottle, poured it into four glasses, and raised a toast. "Here's to our queen and her brave captain!"

Octavia pushed her glass away. "This is no time for celebration. Today is hardly a victory. The queen's health worsens, and the pope readies his army. This is not the ending, it is only the beginning."

ন্তঔ

Octavia was right.

That night, I lay awake listening to all the sounds—the stable doors opening and closing, horses pounding the cobbled street outside the palace, guards moving about inside the palace, their boots clomping on the marble floors.

The following morning, the queen summoned me for the first time in days. When I entered her inner chamber, she requested a hymn. "I have not slept in two nights, Angelica. Please sing a hymn, something hopeful, asking God's guidance." She sat on her chair, eyes closed, her hands resting on her Bible.

Just as I had begun playing the opening chords, there came a loud knock, and Captain Caponi, looking greatly distressed, entered and bowed. "Terrible news, Your Majesty. Dozens of placards with the pope's seal have been posted on the queen's palace gates." Trembling, he handed a placard to the queen. "They claim that yesterday the queen's guards committed violence to the pope and his laws. The placards condemn myself and ten of Your Majesty's guards to death."

"To death!" The queen drew herself up, becoming wholly *The Queen*. Chin high, shoulders raised, she commanded, "Take your leave, Angelica, I must speak with Captain Caponi alone."

I gathered my skirts, curtsied, and backed from the room. Upstairs, the ladies were still in their nightdresses, drinking coffee. Seeing my stricken face, they gathered around me. "What has happened?"

As soon as I confided the news, Octavia clutched her heart, sinking into a chair. "My own dear husband…condemned to death!"

Mariuccia whispered, "The queen will call in Merula."

"Merula?" I asked.

"Sshhhh." Octavia's eyes flashed. "We do not speak of him."

"Crude and brutal, Merula kills with a lust that pleases Her Highness," Mariuccia said. "Do not look so shocked, Angelica. It's true. He is head of a group of Neapolitans in the queen's service. You will never see him, and he leaves no trace of his violence. He lives outside the palace walls and is summoned at night, then led up the back stairs. He holds a knife to his face, scratches lines across his cheek, a scar for each man he kills for the queen, proof that he is willing to risk all in service to Her Majesty."

I did not want to believe her. I couldn't imagine Queen Christina hiring such a man. Moments later, the bell rang, and a guard summoned us to the queen's chambers. As Mariuccia led me down the stairs, she took my hand, and said, "Just wait and see…Merula will do in private what the queen's soldiers cannot do in public."

Dressed in a white muslin gown, hair falling over her shoulders, Queen Christina looked like a peasant grandmother. She sat on her bed, fingering a necklace she wore, lace spun of gold around a silver cross. She held up a placard. "No doubt you have enjoyed this morning's entertainment. The pope, my dear Mignon, tries to humiliate me in public, but I shall call his bluff. Dress yourselves properly. We are going to pay His Holiness a formal visit this morning."

Our mouths fell open.

"Does Your Highness speak in jest?" Octavia cried out.

"Don't look so shocked. It is the Jesuit's Feast at Saint Peter's, and you shall join me. You have heard my captains are *Wanted Men*. Well, I mean to brave the pope's threats and call his hand.

I want the condemned guards, including your husband, Octavia, at the sides of my coach and the rest of my guards, well-armed, in a train behind me. We will take five coaches—everyone looking merry, of course. We shall see if His Holiness dares to arrest my men from under my nose."

"Your Majesty, if—if the soldiers take my husband, they will put him to death," Octavia stammered.

"Don't look so fearful, Octavia. Your husband will be under my protection."

"If I might speak, Your Highness." I swallowed. "The pope has called my voice the devil's breath. Am I to attend as well?"

"Of course." The queen laughed. "Perhaps I shall even call on you to sing for His Holiness, Angelica."

I shivered. *How the queen loves to exert her power!*

"Prepare yourselves at once." Waving us away, the queen smiled mischievously. "And wear pins in your hair for protection!"

Her laughter echoed behind us as we hurried up the stairs.

While dressing, Octavia fretted. "Why must we go? The queen uses us to provoke the pope. What if he calls her bluff?"

Outside the palace, we could hear the queen's pages on the street, calling out, "Move aside. Get your carts off the street; the queen takes a large train to visit the pope this Feast Day!"

Shops closed. Men and women lined the street to see the queen's coaches pass along the Lungara.

As we descended the stairs, Mariuccia and I were ordered inside the queen's coach, while the other ladies would ride in the second coach. When the queen arrived, I was amazed to see her dressed so elegantly, in a green gown with matching green satin slippers. Her Highness almost always wore flat black shoes.

202

Mariuccia nudged me. "The pope disdains the way the queen dresses as if she were a man, always in a black waistcoat. Today she means to impress him."

As the queen entered the coach, to sit across from us, she spoke cheerfully. "At least if we are to be arrested, we shall go to our prison cells looking our best."

How can she laugh at a time like this! And yet, I knew why: Her laughter put us at ease.

Mariuccia had said Merula was never seen in daylight, but there he was—scars across his face—riding alongside the queen's coach. Making a great show of their bravado, the queen's soldiers waved their swords, encouraging the crowds' chants. *"Viva la regina!"*

The queen herself waved and seemed not to be at all afraid. "Smile, show your lovely faces," she commanded. "We are paying Mignon a friendly visit!"

By the time we reached the end of the Lungara, Captain Caponi, riding his horse in front of the queen's coach, trembled so fiercely that he could not sit upright. Merula leaned his head inside the queen's coach. "This will not do, Your Majesty. We cannot arrive at Saint Peter's with your captain fainting from fear." I stared at the scars covering Merula's cheeks—*could he really have killed so many men for the queen?*

"Bring Captain Caponi here," the queen commanded. "He will ride with me, as a show of protection."

"Captain Coward," Mariuccia whispered. "A show indeed!"

Captain Caponi sat beside us in the queen's coach for the remainder of the journey. Humiliated, he remained silent, holding his sword and staring out the window. I kept glancing at the queen to see if she might grow nervous as we neared Saint Peter's, but she seemed to draw strength from the crowds who cheered her on. Seeing her unwavering smile, I felt bolstered by her courage.

We entered the Piazza San Pietro to the sound of drums. The pope had ordered his Swiss Guard to greet us, and as soon as they saluted us, Mariuccia smiled. "Aren't they magnificent? His Holiness has only northerners in his inner guard, unmarried, under twenty-five, and forced to live in solitary confinement. How I should like to take a feather to their chins and force a smile to those stern faces."

The queen, overhearing, laughed out loud. When the train of coaches came to a stop inside the Vatican grounds, the pope and the attending cardinals received the queen at the top of the steps. Taking our escorts' arms, we followed the queen and His Holiness to the main audience room of the Vatican palace. In truth, I could not believe my eyes—His Holiness treated the queen with every sign of respect. Whatever battle simmered behind closed doors, their conflicts seemed hidden behind smiles on this day.

Our eyes searched nervously to read the placement of seats. "*Grazie a Dio*, the queen sits beside the pope on a lower level, as she has always sat," Mariuccia whispered. "Now we know we are safe and shall be treated with full honors."

According to Mariuccia, the seating placement was a map of social relations, revealing politics, power, loyalty, and love. Queen Christina, she'd explained, was the only woman to ever receive the distinction of sitting beside His Holiness, though always at a lower elevation. Years before, when Her Highness had first arrived in Rome, this seating arrangement—how to honor a queen, without dishonoring a pope—had been given many hours of diplomatic meetings. Four days' worth, to be exact, when pages were sent back and forth with the questions and responses between the parties.

After the pope raised his glass to welcome the queen, he remarked, "I have heard, Your Majesty, that your garden has over three hundred orange trees imported from Sicily. How do they fare after this harsh winter?"

"Never better! I shall send you carts of sweet oranges." The queen's voice rose for all to hear. "To keep His Holiness in good health!"

Good health...hardly! I had always imagined the pope tall and robust, a physical presence that would equal his power. But now I saw how thin and frail he was, his robes billowing, tiny wrists peeking out from his sleeves. His face, delicate and pointy, remained concentrated.

The queen took a bunch of green grapes from the tray, a great rarity in Rome this time of year, and, holding them up, teased His Holiness. "Is this how your foreign princes gain an audience with His Holiness, by bringing exotic foods from faraway places?"

The pope laughed freely, seemingly amused by the queen's wit. "I order exotic foods to honor Your Majesty."

Indeed, he had ordered a great feast: black mushrooms from the north, trout on a bed of oranges and fennel, polenta with truffle sauce, biscuits soaked in amaretto, a blackberry torte from France (the queen's favorite sweet), wines from Venice.

Glancing at the other ladies—all of us sitting among the queen's captains, all of us making a great show of enjoying ourselves—I was amazed. *How is it possible that after condemning her captain and guards to death, His Holiness could pretend to be on such good terms with Her Majesty?*

When dessert was cleared and coffee served, the papal choir arrived to perform for us. The papal choir was well-known for recruiting castrati and paying them well for their talents. As the boys' voices rose in perfect pitch, reaching even the highest notes, I looked away. I had seen boys dragged into the barbershop by a poor mother, determined to gain by her son's voice even if it meant sacrificing his manhood. I had heard the boys' terrified screams, and afterward, I had seen them leave, pale and weak, carried away by family members. I only hoped the boys singing before me this day had chosen this life for themselves.

Just as the choir had finished singing and had begun to file out, the doors flew open and in walked Cardinal de Cabrera in a mud-splattered robe, his red berretta soaked and unevenly placed on his head, his shoes caked with sludge, as if he'd ridden through a flood. Quickly he knelt and kissed the pope's ring, and then the cardinal's eyes were drawn to the queen, and though he tried to compose himself, his face could not hide his surprise.

He bowed deeply. "Queen Christina."

"Cardinal de Cabrera." The queen kissed the cardinal's ring.

I was glad to be sitting far away, at the opposite end of the long table. The cardinal's distress seemed too great, and I didn't want to add to his feeling. Leaning over, he murmured something urgent in the pope's ear, while the pope's face stiffened. When Cardinal de Cabrera had finished speaking, the pope turned toward our queen and spoke loudly. "Queen Christina, I apologize for this interruption, but Cardinal de Cabrera delivers disturbing news. A coach carrying the French cardinal has been attacked on its return from Paris."

"You speak of Cardinal de Bouillon?"

"Yes." Cardinal de Cabrera nodded. "Fortunately, he escaped unharmed. But we're not certain about the others. The cardinal was returning to Rome with the new director of the French Academy—"

Theodon! As my hands flew to my mouth, the queen's eyes lifted, meeting mine with a fierce gaze, a warning: *Keep still, Angelica.*

From that moment on, I heard only the pounding of my heart.

I was told afterward that Her Majesty bid farewell with a great flourish of gratitude. But I have no memory of this. No memory of the queen standing, and us following. Apparently I, too, knelt and kissed the pope's hand. I, too, curtsied and thanked the cardinals. I, too, backed from the room, holding a smile to my lips, *as Her Majesty wished.*

Then we left—*merrily, merrily*—as the queen commanded. As soon as we were in the coach, Her Highness took my hand and squeezed it. "If the cardinal escaped, surely your Frenchman did, too. Now breathe and smile and wave."

Breathe, smile, and wave. The queen herself smiled and waved, though her voice was filled with anger. "Look how Mignon surrounds my coaches with his own escort. This pope means to vex me further. He wishes to show the citizens lining the streets that he, too, can put on a parade."

Whatever the pope's reasons for sending us home surrounded by marching guards, the queen did not try to speak through the thunderous *stomp, stomp, stomp*ing, in front and behind, all the way back to the palace.

As soon as we arrived, I hurried to my room and closed the door. There, I wept, realizing that Theodon might not return. As long as I could dream of a future with him, I had something to hold on to—the possibility of our future together. It didn't matter that I'd only known Theodon a short time. It didn't matter that my desire for him was mostly a dream, an imagined life. What mattered was the future. If the queen were to lose her power, I no longer had my family to return to, and now, if I lost Theodon, I would have nothing.

Early evening, Mariuccia knocked on my door. "Angelica?"

"Please, I want to be alone."

"The queen wishes you to come to her chamber."

"Please, tell Her Majesty I am ill."

"She insists you come to her at once, Angelica."

Opening the door, I muttered, "Must we always be at her beck and call?"

Mariuccia caught my arm. "Calm yourself before you enter Her Majesty's chamber. It will not do to vent your grief on the queen. You are in service to her."

The queen was sitting up in bed and spoke softly as I entered. "Do not curtsy. Come sit next to me. I wish to know how you are feeling."

I did as she commanded, but I didn't lift my gaze.

The queen held my wrist, patting it. "I did not call you here to entertain me. I wish to confide in you. I have news, and it regards your Frenchman. I have just had a private visit from Cardinal de Cabrera, but you are the only one to hear of it. He told me that he suspects the pope's own infantry disguised themselves as French peasants and attacked the cardinal's coach, meaning to kill the cardinal and your Frenchman."

Astonished, I raised my eyes. "Why would the pope try to kill one of his own cardinals?"

"Cardinal de Bouillon was delivering a message to the pope, declaring the king's intent to take back the French quarter, even if it means a battle," the queen explained. "The pope did not want this message to arrive…not before he had time to send his troops into my quarter and take it over. The cardinal also told me there were French guards planted inside the coach, so I expect your Frenchman escaped, though I cannot speak with certainty."

I took no comfort from her words, still not knowing if Theodon were dead or alive.

"Make no mistake"—the queen lowered her voice—"the pope's actions will not go unpunished."

⚮

I admit that always before, I'd welcomed the queen's confidences, feeling they were a sign of her trust in me. But the next morning, as Octavia broke the news, I wished myself free of the queen's words.

"A corporal, one of the pope's most trusted soldiers and a father to seven children, was stabbed last night inside the queen's quarter." Octavia stared at us grimly. "This morning, the pope pours his soldiers into this neighborhood."

"Merula murdered him." Mariuccia put her finger to my cheek and drew a slash.

I looked away. I didn't want to believe the queen would go so far to use her power.

"Cardinal Azzolino arrived early this morning," Octavia told us. "The pope blames the queen for his corporal's death and proposes to banish the queen from Rome and the Ecclesiastic States."

We had no time to react. The bell of the turnstile rang and a guard announced, "Her Majesty commands her ladies and domestics to appear immediately in the *Grande Salone.*"

"What does it mean?" I asked.

No one answered my question. Mariuccia took my hand, and for the first time, she did not smile or joke but clutched my fingers tightly as we descended the stairs.

We were all there, over a hundred of us, filling the ballroom—laundry girls, cooks, kitchen boys, coachmen, even the queen's royal antiquarian, Pietro Bellori, who rarely left the stacks of books in the library. The stable lads stood at the back of the ballroom, wringing their hands, their boots smelling of manure.

Her Highness stood on a platform, her face gripped by emotion. "Gentlemen, ladies, and all you others, my domestics, I have brought you together to tell you that the pope is coming to sword's point with me. He seeks to take my guards into the hands of his justice. I am resolved not to forsake them. Therefore, those of you in my service must prepare yourselves to be courageous. I will be at your head, and exposed to the same perils as you. You know me and understand by the actions of my life that I am not fearful. Let those who have not the courage to serve me, declare it, for I will force no one. I know the pope is your sovereign, and if you desire to retire from my service, you may do it freely. I would rather have ten courageous men, who are willing and faithful, than a thousand cowards. Though he be the pope, I will make him remember that I am queen!"

I felt the chandeliers shake as the queen's domestics applauded. I, too, clapped, but my heart was not in it. Glancing around, I saw that many of the queen's servants pretended to be courageous, and yet, by their worried eyes and sideways glances, I knew they wished themselves far away. Even I worried the queen's pride would push the pope too far.

That night, lying awake, I could hear doors opening and closing. I shivered, knowing there were those who would leave rather than do battle against the pope. Before dawn, the queen called me to her chamber and asked for a song. But halfway through, she interrupted. "Stop your singing. I am too vexed for a song, Angelica. Under the cover of darkness, twenty-four domestics left my service this night."

My mouth fell open.

"A pastry chef, three gardeners, six footmen, five laundry girls, four chambermaids, and a handful of stable lads." The queen sighed deeply. "I do not blame them. Most who left have relatives in service to a cardinal or bishop and do not wish to see their families torn apart." Now the queen searched my face. "And you, Angelica?"

"And I?"

"Where do you stand if we should go to battle against His Holiness, the pope?"

"By your side, Your Highness."

"Good." Then, with another heavy sigh, she offered up a faint smile. "You may go. I have no time for songs today."

CHAPTER NINETEEN

We were all on edge, fearing the pope's army might attack at any moment. The other ladies seemed to know exactly what to do and began plotting the fastest escape through the palace. They also discussed which noble families outside of Rome might be inclined to take them into their service.

We were all made foolish by our fears, and I no less than the others. I'm not proud to admit that I, too, was driven to schemes. I wanted to know if Theodon was alive, and I was not willing to take the queen's word on it. Twice she had assured me he was safe, and then, like an afterthought, admitted she had no certainty on the subject.

I had it in my mind that if the queen should go to battle and lose, Theodon was my only hope, and I could not bear to plant my hopes on a man who might already be dead. I had prayed often for his return, but the uncertainty of it kept me awake at night. And so I decided to send Pascal, the queen's valet, to the French workshop. Paying my week's wage, I asked him to arrange for Lucien to meet me in the garden, late afternoon. I wished it to be kept a secret and was willing to pay the price. I knew the queen would be displeased, having already assured me my Frenchman would return.

Earlier the queen had decided to give a concert to raise the spirits of the French soldiers she'd hired to protect her quarter. She had sent word to Mariuccia and me that Maestro Corelli would hold a rehearsal that morning. I was late, having met with Pascal, and when I raised my voice to sing, Maestro Corelli scowled. "Your voice stirs the hairs inside the ear…nothing more."

"I am doing my best."

"I have heard your best, Angelica. You can do better. I am told by the queen that your voice suffers of late because of bad news—something to do with a Frenchman. If you do not have the heart to sing, then I will find another soprano."

Stung by his words, I blurted, "Perhaps you ask of a singer what God asks of saints!"

The musicians stared at me—*no one ever spoke back to Maestro Corelli.*

Corelli fixed his eyes on me. "You are no *saint*, Angelica."

"And you are not God," I muttered.

"If only your boldness took its form in music instead of this insipid sweetness," Corelli replied sharply. "Perhaps it is time to forget the Frenchman. Perhaps he prefers the king's court, where the sopranos know how to do more than tickle the ear."

Tears sprang to my eyes, and all I could do was flee—most *unladylike,* but I lifted my skirts and ran—out the door, down the hallway. I took the stairs two at a time.

Behind me the maestro's voice rose angrily. "Angelica! You cannot leave rehearsal until I dismiss you."

Yet I did leave—*up, up, up, the stairs...but where to?* I could not risk strolling the garden, for the French soldiers were too numerous. Nor to the ladies' chamber, only to hear their bickering and endless worries. Hearing footsteps, I stepped into the servants' privy next to the laundry room and was, for the moment, entertained by the laundress's gossip.

"Look at the Marquis del Monte's shirt...lipstick marks along the collar."

"A brute is he. I don't know why the queen makes him first gentleman in her court."

"They say he's a great opinionator."

"And has as many hairs as opinions. Like a pig, little curlies sticking to his pantaloons."

"God bless our queen, trusting whoever plumps her cushions."

*Such impertinence...*Cracking the door open, I saw the women holding up pieces of laundry, reading them for clues— a torn petticoat, a muddy stocking, lipstick and wine stains. By the scent and stain of our clothing, they knew us all.

"Who do you think Her Majesty prefers—the soprano or Cardinal Azzolino?"

"One soothes the soul; the other balances the books."

How dare they! I clasped my hands over my mouth, listening to their raucous laughter. I might have come out of hiding and scolded them, but the doors flew open and Captain Caponi bellowed, "Have you seen the queen's soprano?"

My heart nearly stopped. Maestro Corelli must have complained about my behavior, and the queen wished to reprimand me. Why else would Her Majesty send her guards to find me?

The laundresses stood back while the guards stomped from one end of the room to the other before leaving. When their footsteps grew faint, I peeked from the privy. The women were busy carrying the bins of wet laundry outside, to hang the clothes on a line.

I made a fast exit and tiptoed up the circular stairwell. As soon as I entered the ladies' chamber, Mariuccia cried, "Where have you been? The queen's guards are searching for you everywhere. Pascal was caught bringing a stranger into the queen's garden. He claims you paid him to arrange a meeting."

"And what of it?"

"With so many spies about, the queen forbids such meetings," Octavia said. "You know that—"

"But I did nothing to betray the queen."

"You didn't ask the queen's permission," Octavia replied. Then, ringing the bell, she told a page to bring her husband.

When he arrived, Captain Caponi bowed nervously, then led me into the queen's formal receiving room. "Lady Angelica arrives, Your Majesty."

The queen did not speak but held her chin high. Dressed in a new riding habit—long tails, a pleated skirt—the queen looked prepared for a hunt. *A good sign,* I thought. When Her Majesty felt robust, she spent long hours riding her favorite horse, Azzurro, through the wooded hills behind the palace garden.

Good health, perhaps, but an icy stare. I curtsied. "The queen wishes a song?"

"No, the queen does *not* wish a song!"

I caught my breath. Never had the queen used this tone with me.

Sweeping the pleated sides of her new riding coat back in a grand gesture, the queen took her seat, roaring, "Where have you been? I demand to know!"

"I...I rehearsed in the music room with Maestro Corelli, Your Majesty." My voice trembled.

"He left this palace before tea, very displeased with your behavior. As am I!" The queen's eyes flashed. "I demand to know if you left the palace secretly."

I could not admit that I had hidden in the servants' privy without making it seem as if I'd sneaked about and spied on the queen's domestics. I looked up but couldn't find the words to explain myself. I would sound guilty if I told the truth, and so I remained quiet.

Startled by my silence, the queen's voice grew harsh. "I see you have secrets that you hide from your queen. Do not think me so bewitched by your talent, Angelica, that I will not take action if I find that you have betrayed me."

Holding the queen's gaze, I said, "I have never betrayed you, Your Majesty."

"Then where have you been?" The queen's cane pounded the marble floor with each word. "My ladies do not leave the palace without my permission!"

"Your Majesty, I was in the privy by the laundry room," I confessed.

The queen's eyes widened. "Doing what?"

"I rehearsed badly. I needed time alone."

She leaned forward. "The garden doesn't please you? Isn't large enough? Colorful enough?"

My face grew hot. "The French soldiers are too numerous."

Again her eyes searched my face. "You cannot take refuge in the ladies' apartment? In your own chamber?"

I looked at the floor.

"I command you to speak the truth, Angelica!"

"The truth, Your Highness, is that the other ladies speak of nothing but the rising tensions between Your Majesty and the pope. They speak to me of this matter more than I can tolerate."

"I see." Chin lowering, eyes steady, the queen breathed deeply. "You speak the whole truth?"

I nodded.

Heaving a great sigh, she waved her hand at Captain Caponi. He opened a door at the side of the queen's chamber, and four guards dragged Lucien and Pascal into the center of the room, their feet and hands bound. Heads hanging, eyes swollen and bruised, they had no strength to walk on their own.

I gasped, lurching toward them, but Captain Caponi gripped my arm.

"No stranger enters my garden without permission," the queen said. "At first they were reluctant to explain. Finally, after much persuasion, Pascal claimed you arranged this meeting."

Pascal, lacking the strength to raise his head, whispered, "I beg your pardon, Signorina Angelica."

"It is all my fault," I cried out. "Your Majesty, please let them go!"

The queen stared at me coldly. "Do you know the Frenchman?"

I looked at Lucien—blood ran from his mouth. "Yes, his name is Lucien," I told her. "He is an artist, a member of the French Academy, friend to Theodon."

The queen nodded again, and the guards lowered the men to their knees.

"I know very well that the pope plants French spies among my troops. And your secrecy plants suspicions, Angelica. Your friend, Lucien, and Pascal, my own valet, tried to bribe one of my guards so that they might enter the garden unseen." The queen held a large envelope toward the flame of a candle. "The Frenchman carried this letter in his pocket. He tells me it comes from the king's court in France. It is addressed to you."

As the queen stared at me with a coldness I had never seen before, I remembered Mariuccia's warning: *Those Her Majesty favors most often become her greatest enemies.*

"If you scheme behind my back or act as a spy, it is better to say the truth before I read it for myself."

"I do not know the contents of this letter, Your Highness."

Taking a knife, the queen cut the envelope open and read in silence. As I watched her read, my heart raced. *Is it news of Theodon's death or a promise of his return?*

Then, slowly, she folded the note and nodded at the guards. "Release these men. Have the sibyl tend to their wounds, then feed them well. I see their words are true."

As the guards carried them away, I whispered, "Pascal...Lucien, forgive me—"

But the queen cut me off. "Though I am liberal in my views, Angelica, my ladies do not invite strangers into this palace without my permission. Especially now, with the pope's soldiers everywhere. Your protection is my responsibility. A scandal would give the pope reason to send in his soldiers and take over my quarter. Don't ever repeat this mistake. By arranging such meetings, you compromise my own safety and that of my other ladies. Do you understand?"

"Yes, Your Highness."

Sighing deeply, the queen handed me the letter. Seeing the envelope addressed in Theodon's own handwriting, my heart leaped, and I quickly backed toward the door.

"I have not dismissed you," the queen said. "Read it here, out loud."

I flushed. I didn't want to read Theodon's letter in front of the queen and her guards. But I also understood why she commanded me to do so. This was my punishment. By humiliating me, the queen sent a clear message: *No one—not even those I favor most—is above the rules of my court!*

My hands shook as I opened the envelope. With a trembling voice, I read: "*Dearest Angelica, I hope you have not forgotten me during these recent months. It is by no fault of my own that I have not written, for my journey back to Rome was fraught with danger. I was accompanied by a cardinal and two bishops, appointed by His Majesty, King Louis XIV. The bishops seemed overly fearful as we rode south from Paris, and when I asked why they did not sleep but kept watch, they asked if I had heard about the rebellions in the countryside. They told me about bands of peasants who kill the king's men and disappear into the woods. In truth, my dearest, the bishops seemed so beastly I did not think them suitable as clergymen. We were indeed ambushed as we came to a halt near the river. I shall spare you the gory details, though I hasten to add that the* bishops were really the king's guards in clerics' clothing. They fought well, and I was fortunate to escape. I fled into the woods and did not look back, though I believe the cardinal, too, escaped.

"I was forced to go over the mountains, and given the bitter cold, I took ill with a brutish cough that racked my body and took away my hearing. Grazie a Dio, I was nursed back to health by an old goatherd and his wife, who gave me the most amazing medicine, which I dare not name by its contents for it contained the blood of birds. I was so sick I did not care what I drank. By their kind care, I was revived and made stronger. They gave me a pack with goat's cheese and dark roots, along with two loaves of black bread. I made my way to the nearest village, a difficult trek, but arrived safely and was able to send word to the king.

"As the king's men brought me to the French court, I suffered a relapse of illness and, missing the wisdom of the goatherd, was bled by the king's doctors until I barely had a pulse. During these past months, I have lived between life and death, in a small attic room at the court. Were it not for the gardener, who brought me the best of his stewed fruits, and a knowledgeable apothecary, I should be dead. Through the spring and summer, I have thought of you as my reason to live, Angelica. The king makes plans to send a new ambassador to Rome and an army to take back the French quarter. I shall return safely, surrounded by the king's ranks. Believe me when I tell you there is no singer who compares to you in all the world. Of that, I am certain. My heart aches for the day when I might sit beside you. Your faithful admirer, Jean Theodon."

When I finished the letter, I stood still, staring at his handwriting. I was so relieved to hear from him that I wanted to laugh and cry all at once. But with the queen so angry, I didn't want to

221

show how moved I was by his tender words, so I kept my eyes lowered.

"This letter confirms my own hope that the king of France sends his army soon." The queen's anger seemed to have lifted, and now her face softened. "Angelica?"

"Yes, Your Highness?"

"We shall have no more secrets."

"No, Your Majesty."

"Come here, then."

I made my way to her chair and kneeled before her on the sweep of rug. She laid her hand on my hair and sighed, as if she wished to say more. Silence stilled the room. Then Her Majesty took a jeweled pin from her own hair and clasped it to my bun, her fingers fumbling. I reached up to touch the jeweled pin. I knew it by its shape—a gold leaf with a stem of emeralds.

The queen's hand covered my own. "There are no hiding places...You understand?"

"Yes, Your Highness."

"Not even in our hearts."

CHAPTER TWENTY

Autumn was a time of waiting. Waiting for the French ambassador to arrive with his army...waiting for Theodon. I fingered Theodon's letter until it became soft as skin. Read it so often, I could recite it out loud. As Theodon's return neared, my heart grew lighter.

It was the beginning of November, eight months since I had come to live under the queen's protection. The truffles had been picked, the olives crushed to oil, and the oranges boiled to marmalade, filling the palace with a sweet orange scent. Three seasons I had strolled the garden, and now I watched as the leaves turned yellow. A cold wind bit my cheeks.

Yes, I missed my family. But I no longer held out hope that they would visit. And I no longer permitted myself to ask, *Who am I without my mother? Why won't she forgive me?* Instead, I planted other thoughts in my mind. *Theodon returns. I am the queen's favored lady. I am proud of this life I have chosen.*

Lucia came to visit when she could. One such visit, right

after the first frost, she began by telling me about each member of my family. I was both comforted and grieved to see how little had changed. "Their lives are the same," I told her. "But my life changes so quickly, it's all a jumble in my heart. The more I see, the less I know."

"Are you speaking of *him,* Miss?" she asked of Theodon.

I was. But I was also speaking of my family and my own purpose in life, for I'd come to realize that I could never separate the two. I'd started out a glazier's daughter and was marked by it, in good ways and bad. Whatever future shaped itself, I would always be seen as rising above my station in life. Because of that, more was expected of me.

"In truth, Lucia, to be a queen's lady is a limiting role, indeed, for we are silenced on most topics, except to whisper, and then we must do so with great caution."

"Limiting, indeed!" Lucia made gentle fun of my new way of talking, but then her smile faded and her eyes lowered, as if she had something more to say but thought better of it.

"Lucia, have I said something to put you off?"

Lucia could not lie. "It is your mother, Miss. She is but a shell of herself these days. But I know you will want to know why, and then I must say what pains you, and I do not wish to burden you."

"Go on," I whispered.

"All the hope she planted on your future, Miss, it has all turned hard inside her." Lucia buried her face in her hands and wept, which was not a common thing for her to do.

"What has happened?"

"Your brother and I hope to marry, but she says she has already been abandoned by her eldest daughter and threatens to poison herself if her eldest son abandons her, too, especially to marry the servant girl."

"She would never do such a thing."

Lucia raised her watery eyes to me. "She has never come completely right, Miss, since your leaving. She is the same in her doings, but I do not think she cares much to go on about life, having no future ahead to lift her burden. Your brother says it is best to give her time"—and here her chin trembled—"but it hurts that he thinks more to please her than me."

I wished to comfort her, as she had always comforted me, but I had been away so long, I did not know the truth of my brother's feelings. I could only hug her close and offer her my handkerchief.

❧

I thought on Lucia's words with a heavy heart but was made glad again when the queen announced, "Your Frenchman arrives soon, my dear." The queen explained that the new French ambassador and his army were but a two-day journey from Rome. And with him came eight hundred soldiers, three hundred wagons, and enough victuals to withstand a siege of eight months. It put the queen in the highest spirits. "Finally I will have an ally with an army!"

Then she told us how the pope had sent his pages throughout the city, warning all the citizens faithful to the church to refrain from parades or festivities marking the ambassador's arrival, unless the ambassador renounced his rights to govern the French quarter.

"Poor Mignon," the queen mocked. "He does not know his own citizens very well if he thinks they shall turn their backs on a parade."

The queen herself had ordered several of her guards, including Octavia's husband, to disguise themselves as spies during the ambassador's arrival. "If you wish Captain Caponi to deliver a note to Theodon," the queen offered, "he will carry it for you."

I hurried to my room and quickly wrote:

> Dearest Theodon,
> I am now a lady to Queen Christina, at Palazzo Ri-
> ario. Waste no time, my beloved, and come to me
> at first opportunity. Announce yourself, for the
> queen knows you by name and has given permis-
> sion for your visit.

I sprinkled the paper with perfume and pressed the envelope with red wax, but I did not sign my name, in case the note fell into the wrong hands.

I was always careful now. Never again would I give the queen reason to doubt me.

I hardly slept that night. And when I awoke in the morning, I smelled smoke. Joining the other ladies, I learned that the smoke came from the pope's army. They'd built hundreds of fires to stay warm in their camps at the edge of the city, where they planned to defend it by holding the king's army outside the gates.

At first no one spoke. Although we sat at the same table, we waited separately, suffering our nerves alone. Each of us felt our lives would change by that day. Each of us believed a battle was shaping around us. Listening to the winds blow fiercely from the sea, bringing torrents of rain and howling in the chimneys, we waited for the sounds of cannons and guns.

We inhaled, exhaled, filled the room with our sighs. We tapped our fingers and poured coffee. Our voices grew sharp, impatient.

"The coffee is bitter," Portia said.

"Then have the maids bring a fresh pot," Octavia snapped.

Mariuccia stood by the window. "Such dark clouds."

All at once, we heard drums rolling in the distance. Then, as if on cue, thunder clapped and rain fell in a heavy downpour, bringing Octavia to tears.

Mariuccia called us all to the window. "Come, see…the sun peeks through the clouds." We stood in awe, watching as the rain died, the clouds parted, and a brilliant sun poured through our window, arching a dense rainbow over the queen's garden. *Surely,* I thought, *this is a sign from God.*

"A miracle," Her Majesty declared, after summoning us to her chamber. "Captain Caponi has just returned, and he tells me that the very moment the ambassador's coach entered the gates, their swords drawn and their armor glittering, the sun shown upon him and his men and the rain ceased, so that even the pope was amazed and called back his men."

Now the queen commanded a toast, and French champagne was poured. "Surely God means to welcome the French ambassador to our city." She raised her glass to us.

As we sipped our champagne, Captain Caponi whispered to me, "Your Frenchman comes directly."

I had already instructed the guards to show Theodon to a marble bench where I would be waiting. Now I sat restlessly—dogs barked, horses galloped by on the cobbled street, the gate opened and closed. With each sound, my heart beat faster until finally I heard the rustle of leaves as someone approached. I rushed to the break in the hedge and gasped as Theodon stepped toward me, smiling bashfully.

Gesummaria. I stood still, trying to hide my shock. "Theodon?"

"I know." His eyes fell. "The journey was long, and I am still recovering from my illness."

Is this my Theodon? The ridiculous wig? The hawkish face? The sunken eyes?

His clothes hung as if he were a beggar boy who'd stolen a noble's fashions: full breeches, a coat of embroidered silk, buttoned only to the middle, where it opened over his narrow hips, displaying a billowing white silk shirt that fell to his knees. The clothes were so big, he swam inside the seams. But what seemed most absurd was the wig of brown ringlets, mocking his delicate features. And at the ends, green ribbons tied into bows to match the wide-brimmed hat, sprouting green-tinted ostrich feathers. *How ridiculous!*

I tried to control my voice. "You wear a wig?"

His smile faded. "My hair was so snarled from the time I spent with the goatherd, the king's barber shaved it off. Now it grows back, but slowly." As he stepped forward and kissed my gloved hand, I could not stop myself from pulling back.

I am certain he noticed. I could not hide my feeling, which turned my voice cold and my eyes hard. And yet I could be no other way.

228

Theodon reached into his leather bag and drew out a beautiful crocheted shawl. "For you."

"My favorite red, the color of ripened plums." I touched the soft shawl. "How did you know?"

He pulled a small ribbon from his pocket. "You tied a note with this ribbon. I carried it with me, searching for something of the same color."

"*Grazie.*" I draped the shawl around my shoulders. "It is beautiful."

"To keep you warm when we meet, for I intend to see you often to make up for the time apart." His eyes were black, with the same flickering light at the middle. They stared at me now, searching my face.

I lowered my gaze and fingered the shawl, searching its weave for words, and yet I could think of nothing to say.

"You are even more beautiful than I remembered," he whispered.

His words only filled me with shame. *You are not what I remembered.* I raised my eyes, then glanced away. Again we fell into a silence, and again he pulled from his bag a leather pouch and emptied its contents onto the bench. Dead grass…handfuls of it.

I stared at the pile of grass, thinking something was hidden—perhaps a glass egg cushioned in the grass? Perhaps this was a special grass from the French court?

"I picked a blade of grass for each day we were apart." He scattered it on the ground, at our feet. "Now I am freed of counting." He took my gloved hands in his own.

Where was the wild artist with long curls and a steady smile? Where was the man whose eyes stirred my blood? Had I built my future on a dream…and now I was forced to wake up? "Tell me of your travels." I withdrew my hands. "And of the king's court. Is it true the French sopranos choose what they sing without fear of losing their reputations?"

"It's true, they are not bound so much by rules of the church." But as he spoke, he began coughing, and the coughs spread through his body. He removed a flask from his bag, took a long drink.

Seeing how weakened he was, I looked away. I found him pitiful.

But he took my gloved hand again and spoke softly. "French women are more forthright, but they do not laugh so easily as Italian women. Tell me of your life here in the palace."

"Queen Christina is the kindest of patrons. I have all the comforts I would choose. I sing often with Maestro Corelli conducting." But as I spoke, my voice tiptoed, circling, circling, but never stepping inside true feelings. "I live with the other ladies-in-waiting. We are like a thick spicy soup within one bowl. The Italian guards distrust the French, and each suspects the other of spying for the pope. One always has the feeling of being watched. And yet, I belong here. The queen has been like a mother to me, now that my own mother shuns me." Tears sprang to my eyes.

"What is it? What is the matter, Angelica?" He leaned toward me, put his arm around my shoulder. "Has your feeling changed? Is there another gentleman you prefer?"

"No." On that topic, I could look him in the eye. "There is no one else."

"What, then?" He moved closer. His breath smelled sweet.

He took off one of my gloves and touched each of my fingers. "I have missed your songs."

I closed my eyes, squeezing back tears. I drew my hand away. I felt nothing... *nothing!*

Reaching for my other hand, he held it so tightly I could not draw away. "Close your eyes." He brushed away my tears. "All I want is a bit of time to get better and prove myself worthy of you. Whatever you feel... it is all right. I am a patient man."

I kept my eyes closed, let his lips tickle my ear.

"Je t'adore, cherie. Je t'adore."

And yet, when I opened my eyes, I pulled back. "I must go. The queen often wishes me to sing this time of day."

"May I come tomorrow?"

Nodding, I stood up, gathering my shawl around my shoulders.

"And the day after?" he called out.

I turned quickly and did not look back. I didn't want him to see how my eyes filled with tears as I ran toward the servants' entrance.

CHAPTER TWENTY-ONE

*S*There is no better fit for sadness than a feather pillow, and now, alone in my room, I buried my head, muffled my weeping. How guilty I felt...guilty for caring too much about the wrong things—his clothes, his hair, his pathetic hat. Guilty for preferring dreams to the truth...the truth of my thin, sickly Theodon—I hardly knew him! Something Mother once said echoed in my mind: *You're in love with longing, not with the man himself. Courtship is not a game, Angelica.*

Perhaps she was right.

Mariuccia had been watching through a window as I fled the garden, and now she knocked at the door. When I didn't answer, she tiptoed into my room and, seeing my face buried in a pillow, handed me a dry handkerchief. "Tell me what happened."

I turned over. "He's so thin, so worn down by illness. He looks hideous...and dresses like a fop. I wish never to see him again—"

"Oh, Angelica." Mariuccia looked at me solemnly. "You demand perfection of yourself, first, and then you expect it from everyone else. Do you expect a life without disappointment?" Then, taking my hands, she shook her head at me. "You are no longer a child, and only a child runs from one dream to another. You pin all your hopes on the future, and yet when the future arrives, it is never what you hoped, and then you see your own disappointments as if they were the truth, as if you had chosen wrongly."

"But he has changed so much—"

"So have you," she said. "You are no longer the wide-eyed innocent you were when you arrived here."

I sat up, dried my eyes.

"I am older than you, and I know that we can't wait forever for the perfect life to embrace us. How often I've scorned a man for being too short, too poor, or too dull, hoping for better prospects. Now it is too late. I'm well past the marrying age." She observed me sadly. "Don't make the same mistake that I've made, Angelica. We have to take our life and make of it what we want. If I were you, I wouldn't run so quickly from Theodon. Perhaps in time, your feelings will grow back and become stronger than before."

I couldn't deny the wisdom of her words, but I needed time to think through my own feelings. "*Grazie*, Mariuccia. You've been a great comfort to me."

After she left, I lay beneath my covers until the queen summoned me for a song.

"So, your Frenchman has returned," she said cheerily. "In his honor, I should like to hear a love song this evening."

I sat at the harpsichord and began to play. *"O cessate di pia-garmi, o lasciatemi morir…Oh stop wounding me…leave me to die…"*

"Oh, no, such a gloomy song. You sound as if you are sere-nading a funeral march." The queen stared at me. "What sadness plants itself in your face, Angelica?" She patted the side of her bed. "Come, speak to me. Here, have a pastry filled with nuts and honey…fried. I must sneak them or the sibyl chides me."

I sat, as the queen wished.

"Has Theodon betrayed you in some way?"

"No, Your Majesty."

"Then, what? You must tell me."

"My heart no longer yearns for him." I sighed. "He has suf-fered. His demeanor is greatly changed."

"Oh, Angelica." The queen reached over and took my hand. "But that is the nature of the heart…affections always change. One day Cardinal Azzolino refuses to speak to me. The next day we cannot cease talking. You must be patient. Your Frenchman has only just arrived."

"Yes, I know, but—"

"But what?" She gripped my arm. "Do you think that be-cause I have chosen not to marry, I do not understand the heart?"

"No, Your Majesty."

"Do you remember when I said we were alike, you and I?"

I nodded.

"As queen, I am expected to be strong, forthright, firm in my understandings of the world. That is the *role* I must play. And you, as Rome's beloved soprano, you are expected to know the truths of the heart. You sing with such passion." She smiled

234

kindly. "And yet, if I might be entirely honest, you know nothing of what you sing."

My face fell, and the queen laughed. "By that I mean you are only a girl…so innocent, and no doubt afraid."

My cheeks burned. "I feel *nothing* in his presence."

"Love is not a jewel that can be encased in gold, Angelica. It is a flame that needs air. It grows over time, casts a different light moment to moment, as you do. Every love comes from risking something deep inside the heart."

It was, I am sure, my own need that drove me to forget myself. If ever I'd needed a mother it was now, and here was the queen herself speaking in a soft tone, with her eyes all shiny, and her voice warm as a blanket, and her hand patting my hand. It seemed most natural to throw my arms around the queen's neck, planting a kiss on her cheek. And, then, realizing myself, I jerked back. "Queen Christina, I beg your pardon."

"Oh, my child." The queen laughed and embraced me with a forceful hug—lasting a good, long moment—before she sat back, rubbing the tops of my hands. "I do not know if I would choose to be young again. And so hopeful."

It was the queen who listened and understood, better than my own mother ever had, and I would be lying to myself if I didn't admit that I loved the queen as well as my own mother, and maybe more.

❧

The next day, I stood in the library window, watching Theodon. I studied his hands, black from charcoal as he sketched the queen's statues while he waited for me. He had worn a wig again, but I was glad that at least he did not dress in fancy clothes. He wore his white billowy shirt under a blue jacket, his breeches tucked inside his leather boots that rose and folded above the knee. Once he glanced at the window where I stood, as if he sensed I was watching.

When I arrived, holding my skirts above the soggy ground, Theodon pulled more gifts from his pouch—blue silk ribbons, French lace, Chinese tea the color of emeralds.

I'd waited months to see him, but now I felt shy.

"Do the chocolates please you?"

I smiled. "They are delicious… *grazie.*"

But his gifts made me uneasy. Mother had once told me that every gift equals a song. *You must give something in return, Angelica. That is the nature of gifts.* And now I couldn't shake the feeling that each gift equaled more of myself. Besides, he'd confided that money from the king of France was scarce. "He spends great sums on soldiers and uniforms, but pays his artists nothing. I cannot think what will happen to our stipends if the king does battle against the pope. Does your queen speak of a battle?"

Even though I trusted Theodon, I held my tongue. "I sing for Her Majesty, that is all. I'm not privy to her secrets."

"A lady who doesn't gossip of her queen?" He smiled. "Yet another admirable quality."

I looked away. His compliments made me fearful. Perhaps because I had no compliments to offer in return.

The days passed, and Theodon came to visit every afternoon, but my heart remained a mystery. Some days, as he wooed me, I felt my feelings grow stronger. Other days I thought him too eager to please. Still other moments I found him so well-spoken, so passionate about his work, that I felt myself unworthy.

And yet... when we parted, I had constant thoughts of him. I often lay awake at night, listing his good and bad qualities in my mind. Good qualities: *kind, talented, intelligent, wise, sincere.* Bad qualities: *too thin, badly dressed, overly ambitious about his work.*

Such foolery!

And yet, I couldn't erase my doubts. I'd always believed that when I found true love, I would be certain of it. I'd imagined love was like singing. Just as I could be swept away by songs, I wanted to feel the same about a man.

One afternoon, not long after Theodon had arrived, the queen remarked, "I am told he comes each day to see you."

"Yes, Your Highness."

"Make him sit where I might see him. I would like a good peek."

"Of course, Your Highness."

"I have heard he draws my garden, Angelica?"

"Only to capture its natural beauty, Your Majesty."

"I should like a sketch, if he would be so kind."

"He will be glad of your interest."

The next day, I told Theodon of the queen's request.

He raised his sketch pad, his eyes focused on the distance. "Who is that?"

"The sibyl, the queen's healer."

Working his charcoal, he drew the folds of her apron, her fingers digging the earth for roots, her glass bottles organized at her feet. With a few lines, he captured the sibyl, crouched on her heels, her dark skirt spread over her knees. When he had finished, he rolled up the sketch and handed it to me. "Tell the queen I am honored."

His breath smelled of onions and herring, and I couldn't help noticing the mustard at the crease of his lips. Moments like this, I felt ashamed.

"How is the queen?" he asked. "How are the other ladies?"

But as I opened my mouth to speak, his eyes grew sleepy, and he yawned. Feeling a heat climb my cheeks, I turned away. "Am I so dull that I deserve your yawns?"

He laughed. "You are hardly boring."

"But my life is not so interesting as your own. I have not lived in other cities, nor have I the freedom to leave this palace."

"You sing like an angel. You study under Corelli. Your mind is that of an artist, not a queen's lady-in-waiting."

"And what is wrong with the queen's ladies-in-waiting?"

"You're not like the others. They seek to fill their minds with idle thoughts so as not to outwit a future husband."

"You don't know the other ladies," I objected.

"I know they are well protected in these walls."

"Would you wish *me* unprotected?"

"Protection is one thing, ignorance another."

I stared at him. "Tell me, how can one remain protected without becoming ignorant?"

"When I was in France," he said softly, "I met a duchess from Lyons who had given birth to a daughter whose body lay twisted

238

and could not grow to standing. She told me she could not sustain such *unpleasantness*. That is the word she used for her child. She gave the girl to the nuns, for she could not bear to look at her. She told me she wished to avoid *unpleasantness* of all sorts."

He nodded. "That is ignorance. To avoid all suffering. To wish only for what pleases."

"Why did she confide in you"—my cheeks burned—"unless you led her to believe you cared for her words?"

"She thought me her confessor." He laughed. "My illness made me a great listener."

I felt a rush of anger. "She visited you in the attic room where you slept?"

"She brought me bread and soup. I couldn't move from my bed." Then, smiling, he whispered, "Are you jealous of the lady I scorn?"

Indeed, almost driven to tears. He reached for my hand, but I drew it away. "I do not believe this woman deserves your harsh judgment. She tried to help you."

Laughing, Theodon grabbed my gloved hand. "You're the only woman I wish to scorn," he teased, "and then I'll make up to you."

◈

I turned eighteen on the Feast Day of Saint Cecilia, but I told no one it was my birthday. That day, I was brought low by thoughts of Mother. I wondered if my family ever missed me, if they even remembered me on my birthday. Just as the bells rang evening vespers, Mariuccia told me there was a maid to see me in the garden. I knew it was Lucia and hurried down the stairs.

"It's but a token, Miss." She handed me a new ribbon. "But I wished you to know we are all thinking on you today."

I hugged her close. "I thought myself forgotten."

"I didn't tell your mother where I was going; I just snuck off. And being it's your birthday, she might suspect, so I can't stay long."

I pulled her inside the servants' door so she could warm herself before heading back. She chuckled, "I see your Frenchman often now, Miss, and with a broad smile to his face, as he goes to and from the workshop."

"He visits me each afternoon," I told her.

"And is he your own true love, Miss?"

"Sometimes, Lucia, I think I don't know love at all. For every sweet feeling, a doubt follows."

"It's a common enough feeling, I believe, to want something well until it comes, and then be frightened by it."

"When I first came to know Theodon, we had to hide our feelings, and my songs were the only way to show him how I felt. The passion I felt for him flooded my songs."

"And is it not true now, Miss?"

"Now my songs swell with more than passion—jealousy, anger, fear." I touched my chest. "It's like a storm inside."

"Because of him?"

I nodded.

She laughed. "Then he is your own true love, Miss."

I smiled and nudged her gently. "And you, Lucia?"

"I'm the same, Miss, vexed by your mother as always. But

your brother and I, we mean to marry next summer. We've not told your mother, but your papa has given us his blessing."

"Oh, Lucia, I'm so glad." I embraced her.

"Now I must get back," she whispered.

I watched her bundle herself and hurry off. I was always lifted during our conversations, but, afterward, made melancholy by her leaving.

One afternoon in early December, Theodon didn't arrive for his usual visit. The wind was blustery, and I hadn't dressed for the chill. Theodon was always prompt, and I worried that he'd taken ill again. Just as I was about to go inside, I heard his voice. "Angelica...wait!"

He hurried toward me and pulled me behind the hedge. "Great news, Angelica. I've been given a commission at Saint Peter's workshop." Theodon squeezed my hands. "I am the first Frenchman to receive such an honor."

I pulled him to the bench. "The pope has given you—a *Frenchman*—a commission?"

"Not the pope," he told me. "Cardinal de Cabrera, head of Cultural Affairs, he chose my work—a sculpture of Cardinal Altieri." He opened his sketch pad and showed me his drawings.

"Cardinal de Cabrera chose you?"

Seeing my shocked expression, Theodon closed his sketch pad. "Do you know this cardinal?"

My face grew hot. I'd never told Theodon about Cardinal de Cabrera. "He's the same cardinal who neglected his duties and spent his mornings sitting in his coach listening to my songs. The very same cardinal who had *cartelli infamanti* stuck to his gates, showing my likeness." I stared at Theodon. "He once told me he would do *anything* to further my talent—"

Theodon paled. "You believe he chose my work because I court you?"

I spoke carefully. "With such high tension between the pope and the French king, doesn't it seem strange that Cardinal de Cabrera would choose a Frenchman for this commission?"

"I am an artist, and this cardinal respects my work." Theodon's voice sputtered with fury. "Though you've made it plain that you think me unworthy of this commission." Then, without another word, he gathered his sketches and hurried away from me.

∾

The following afternoon, when Theodon did not return, I told myself calmly: *Let him resolve his anger.*

The second day, I sat on the bench, stroking the queen's dogs. *Perhaps he is busy with his commission.*

The third day, I stared at the trees that had lost their leaves. *How dare he stay away, without sending any message.*

The fourth day, I bit my nails. *What if he never returns?*

The fifth day, I did not go into the garden but stared from the window, in case he should come. *I miss him.*

The sixth day, I crawled under my covers. *Theodon will not return.*

December's rains fell. Fires burned in every fireplace. The

palace halls were filled with evergreen boughs, a tradition the queen had brought from her home in Sweden. Each morning, Mariuccia and I rehearsed religious songs, preparing music for Nativity.

"Your mood thins." Mariuccia nudged me. "Is it Theodon?"

My eyes welled. "I fear I've driven him away."

"Passion is a ship anchored in harbor, waiting a destination." She sang the words to one of our songs, then whispered, "You must make your feelings clear to him."

Just then, a guard arrived. "You have a visitor, Signorina Angelica."

Thinking it Theodon, my heart soared.

"Your mother waits below."

CHAPTER TWENTY-TWO

Nearly ten months had passed since Mother and I had last laid eyes on each other. Now, as I descended the stairs, my heart raced. I'd grown a habit of missing Mother, thinking her a softer sort of person from this distance. Now I was thrown into confusion, wondering what we could say to each other after so much time apart. It crossed my mind that with Nativity approaching, Papa had pleaded with Mother to welcome me home for the holiday, and I hoped it was true. I couldn't abide a future without my mother being part of it. Until now I'd not admitted so much to myself.

But the moment I saw Lucia, standing beside Mother, and realized she would not raise her eyes to greet me, I knew something was wrong. I took her downcast gaze as a warning.

Mother stood still, waiting for me to come to her, and I knew I was meant to act the part of a daughter and not a queen's lady. I stepped toward her, kissed her on each cheek, and then we stood apart. She looked older—white hair fanning from her temples, gray shadows draping her eyes. Fearing myself the cause, I wished to make it up to her, but then I grew wary. I didn't want to be returned to my former self—made into a dutiful child, with no mind of my own.

"Has something happened?" I whispered.

Mother breathed in deeply. "I bring news that concerns *you*, Angelica."

Thinking it might be news of my family, perhaps even news of Franco and Lucia's marriage, I lowered my guard a bit. We were all shivering, and I nodded toward the door. "It's too cold out here. Please come inside." I led Mother and Lucia up the stairs into a small sitting room, where the ladies served tea to their families on Sunday, and asked the maid to bring coffee and something sweet to eat.

When Mother removed her cloak, I took a deep breath. She looked as if she were attending a ball—overly ruffled and overly ribboned for a morning tea. She glanced around the room but did not remark on the high ceilings, the marble floor, the lovely flowers on the table. Instead, she remained silent.

My heart sank. As I served Mother a slice of cake and a cup of coffee, I realized she refused to say what I longed to hear— *You've done well, daughter. I can see you made the right choice.* She tasted the cake, then grimaced. "Is this what the queen serves the mother of her soprano...stale cake?" She pushed her plate away and leaned toward me. "I have come about a serious matter, Angelica."

Again I glanced at Lucia, and again she refused my gaze. Her lips stayed in a tight frown, her shoulders rigid, as if she'd been pressed to come here and wished herself far away.

"I know your Frenchman has returned." Mother leaned toward me. "I shall speak plainly, even if what I have to say is painful. Do you know why your Frenchman was given the new commission?"

"You know of Theodon's commission?" My mouth fell open.

"We live across from the French workshop. The whole neighborhood speaks of it." And here Mother sat tall, her chin lifting. "Your Frenchman has another woman…courts another woman."

I couldn't breathe. Staring at Mother, her rueful smile and prideful gaze, I saw that she was glad for my pain. "Please, Mother, don't be cruel."

"I knew you wouldn't believe me." Mother nudged Lucia, urging her to speak. "Go on, tell her what you heard at the fountain."

Lucia wore such a sad expression that I knew what she'd be forced to say if I gave her the chance.

"False gossip and lies." My voice rose shrilly. "I don't care what they say at the fountain. You wish to hurt me, Mother, because I chose to come here instead of marrying one of the suitors you preferred."

"Sometimes the truth *is* cruel, Angelica." Mother shook her head. "This Frenchman shames you and our family. The woman's name is Rosanna. She is the daughter of the shipping agent who handles all the orders for Saint Peter's workshop. That is how your Frenchman got his new commission, courting the daughter of a powerful man. He goes to her father's house and dines with the family every evening. He will marry this girl to further his career."

My throat tightened. I wished to turn and run, and yet my feet would not let me.

"You are still my daughter, Angelica." Mother softened her tone. "I have come to help you. I can still arrange for you to marry a nobleman. Bishop Vanini has offered to help me."

In that moment, I saw by her crazed smile that she was beyond her own reason. "Speak on this topic no more," I demanded. "You're no mother to me if you mean to always use me to your own advantage."

Instinctively Mother raised her hand, ready to unleash her fury, but I was quicker and gripped her wrist until she cried out, "How dare you raise a hand to me. I am your mother!"

"Might I remind you, Mother"—I released my grip—"I am a lady and above you in rank. I could have you arrested for raising your hand to me."

Proof—these words. Proof of my rank, my title, my power over Mother. And yet I took no delight in my power.

Mother's voice fell low as her eyes narrowed. "I've wasted my life on you."

"I command you to leave!"

Gasping, she spun around, grabbed her cloak, and hurried toward the door.

"Oh, Miss." Lucia squeezed my hand. "I'm sorry." Then, she followed after Mother, down the stairs.

❧

A feather pillow, damp with tears, smells of geese—their endless journeys north and south. I wept hard into my pillow, grieving my own journey. I was tired of being strong, tired of being independent, tired of believing in myself. I wanted someone to lean on, someone to believe in me even when I wasn't singing. *I wanted Theodon.* And now, it seemed, I had lost him.

That afternoon, after my mother's visit, I sent word to Her Majesty that I could not sing. I should've known better. Immediately the queen sent for me, insisting I come alone to her inner chambers.

"Are you ill? Tell me what is wrong. I can see by your eyes, you have been crying." The queen's long nose lowered, as her eyebrows lifted. "I am told your Frenchman does not visit these days. Obviously, you have quarreled."

"Yes, Your Majesty."

"Over the future?"

"No, Your Majesty."

"Angelica, speak up and tell me what has happened!" It was not a question, it was a command.

I raised my eyes. "I didn't celebrate his new commission."

"Why not?" She patted a place beside her on the bed, gestured for me to sit.

I rested beside her. "It's a commission at Saint Peter's workshop. With so much tension between the pope and the king of France, I didn't think Cardinal de Cabrera would hire a Frenchman without there being some other reason. Theodon took my doubt to mean I didn't respect his talent."

"You should have spoken to me first. By hiring your Frenchman, Cardinal de Cabrera sends a message to the pope to make allies of the French." The queen breathed in. "Have you not learned anything from me, Angelica? That is how the powers in this city make their voices heard—every concert, every sculpture, every parade. It is all to a purpose."

I kept my eyes lowered.

But the queen sat tall. "Don't fret. I shall send Theodon a note. I shall praise his sketch of the sibyl and command him to come pay his respects. Then you shall be here, and he will have to see you."

Horrified, I drew back.

"Ah." She observed me. "You do not speak the whole truth. What else, Angelica? I am growing impatient."

"My mother came this morning."

"Your mother visited?" The queen looked very pleased. "Why was I not told?"

My voice quavered. "She told me that Theodon courts another woman."

"Who?"

"The daughter of the shipping agent for Saint Peter's workshop, where he received the commission."

The queen laughed heartily. "Of course he visits this daughter. He's no fool! How else could he secure his new commission? Don't believe another woman can steal his heart, Angelica, unless you discard it first. You are the queen's soprano! You sing for Rome! Believe in yourself, my dear, and he will never leave you!" The queen nodded at her desk. "Now go and write to him this moment. That is my command!"

❧

The following afternoon, I waited in the garden. The air was brisk, the birds silent. Only the great grove of cypress at the top of the hill swayed against a gray sky.

When I heard Theodon's footsteps, I hurried around the hedge, nearly knocking him over. "Forgive me, Theodon." Then I buried my face in his soft scarf and leaned against his chest. I would not let go, not until he laughed and, taking my hands, pulled me to the bench. "With this commission, Angelica, I hope to be worthy of our future together."

By his words, I knew Mother was wrong. He didn't court the woman named Rosanna; he courted her father and her father's connections. The queen was right. He was no fool!

Theodon removed my glove, kissing my fingers. For a long time his mouth remained against my bare hand, kissing me softly, his warm breath sending shivers through me.

The only way I could return his tenderness was to sing for him. And that day, I poured my feeling into a song. When I finished, he took my hand and reached it beneath his coat, beneath his shirt, where I could feel his heart beating. "Do you see what I feel? What your songs do to me?"

CHAPTER TWENTY-THREE

Everyone knew. Everyone poked fun at me. They called him *the Frenchman.*

The ladies blew kisses in the air and cooed, *"Ma cherie… mon amour."*

Maestro Corelli praised my voice. "Vigor returns to your songs, a shrewd sound, a delightful wickedness. I shall have to personally thank *the Frenchman.*"

The queen, too, made her feelings known. "You no longer sing for me but to your Frenchman. I hear it in your voice, the way you sing to the distance. Does he listen from beneath my window?"

"I shall tell him not to, if it displeases Your Highness."

The queen gave a forceful sigh. "I shall speak plainly, Angelica. I don't care a pigeon's wing if he sits in the garden. It is meant to be sat in. I encouraged these feelings of love, so I do not say you are at fault. But you must be careful not to betray your gift. Love can teach, but it can also destroy. You must re-member you are the queen's soprano. You must always keep one foot planted *firmly* in your own future, then the other can step into all sorts of murky puddles without your losing balance."

That morning, as the queen offered advice, I noticed no heavy sighs or gulps of breath, so common when the queen suf-fered her stomach pain. Indeed, I was much surprised later in the day to hear that Her Highness had taken to her bed with severe stomach cramps. When I asked the sibyl if I might sit with her, I was told the queen wished no visitors. I made nothing of it, for the queen was known to drive herself to exhaustion, sleeping as little as three hours a night for weeks on end, whereupon she stayed in bed for a day and was revived.

But when I returned the following day and the sibyl again turned me away, I worried. "Perhaps if I sing for her, it might soothe her and ease the pain."

"I, myself, think so," said the sibyl. "But the doctor says she must refrain from all excitement. He is of the opinion that music leaves its mark upon the body, stirring up the vapors in our blood. If he hears that you've sung for the queen, Angelica, I'm afraid it will drive the doctor to bleed her more, to release the vapors. And she's already too weak to rise."

For two days, we prayed for the queen to regain her health.

Then, on the Eve of Nativity, the queen summoned us, her ladies and gentleman, to make a toast. You can be sure we were all greatly pleased by her recovery.

As we entered the queen's inner chamber, bowing and curt-sying, the queen stood silently in front of a tall mirror, dressed in a beautiful white gown. At first I was greatly relieved to see the queen looking so well and back on her feet.

But the queen did not greet us and, instead, remained silent as she took many turns displaying the dress with its stitched flowers, gold threads, and French lace. She walked back and forth in front of her mirror, wearing white satin shoes...the only sound being the soft *swish, swish* of Her Majesty's crinoline. Still we waited for Her Highness to speak first, which was the rule in the queen's presence.

Finally the door opened and the sibyl entered. She was called often now to the queen's side, as Cardinal Azzolino did not trust the queen's doctor, Bandiere, and often sent for the sibyl to countercheck the doctor's prescriptions.

"Sybil"—the queen nodded—"I am glad you are here."

"What a magnificent gown," exclaimed the sibyl. "And so well suited to Your Majesty."

"You come very luckily, Sybil," said Captain Caponi, "for the rest of us are acting as mutes."

"It is true. Nobody has said a word, nor I myself." The queen stopped pacing and glanced at us with a private look on her face. "But this dress makes me think of the future. I believe I shall wear it in one of the greatest functions that can be. Sybil, you are able to divine my meaning?"

"Dare I speak of it?" The sibyl's voice trembled.

"Yes." The queen's sturdy gaze held the sibyl's eyes. "I wish you to say what your mind reads."

"Your Majesty thinks you shall be buried in this dress."

"No...*no!*" My voice filled the room.

But the queen raised her hand to silence me.

"And I have no doubt," the Marquis del Monte said in a jovial way, "the queen will wear this dress to wish the pope a happy new year."

The queen refrained from smiling and made her voice firm. "The sibyl speaks the truth. She says my own thought, though it be in the hand of God, for we are all mortal. I, as well as another."

The dressmaker, Signor Leopaldi, was also standing silently, in the corner of the room, and now he tried to shift this sad conversation. "Perhaps I should prepare a covering for this garment?"

"Why a cover?" asked the queen.

"If it be used as a burial gown, then let it stand waiting twenty more years without the worms eating away at it."

At this the queen fell to laughing, and we all joined her, as the marquis toasted Her Highness. "Twenty more years!"

Taking only a sip of her champagne, the queen then lowered her glass and smiled, waving us to the door. "I wish to be alone now. Go and celebrate... I wish you all a *Buon Natale*."

I lingered, hoping the queen might ask for a song.

"You, too, Angelica. I will not ask for a song tonight. Go with the other ladies."

I stared at her long nose, steady eyes.

Seeing my reluctance to leave, the queen sighed. "I do not wish the world to think me frail. If my ladies do not leave my side, then the world suspects that my days are numbered, and nothing would please the pope more. Tomorrow, you must sing at the Christmas tea."

"You will be there, Your Majesty?"

A groan. That was the queen's answer as she clutched her blanket.

"Are you sure the queen would not like a song?" My voice clouded. "To take your mind off the pain?"

"Oh, Angelica." The queen waved me away. "You are *dear* to me, as you well know. But I wish to be alone."

Outside the doors, the marquis was scolding the sibyl. "You should not speak of death while Her Majesty still recovers from her illness."

"You mistake my words," said the sibyl. "I have not foretold the queen's death, only what I found in her own mind. She believes her end is near."

Cardinal Azzolino was just arriving and, when he heard what had happened, grew very angry. "How dare you speak to the queen of such melancholy visions!"

"Believe me," the sibyl said, "no one shall suffer more than I from the queen's death."

"What do you mean to say, Sybil?" Cardinal Azzolino towered over her. "If you know something, then speak."

The sibyl spoke calmly, her eyes locked on the cardinal's stern gaze. "In the queen's absence, crosses and persecutions will inflict great pain on me and many others. God preserve us, Cardinal, but you shall not be long after Her Majesty. The pope will die in the same year, and all our lives will change."

The cardinal was speechless. Flushed with anger, he gathered himself upright before he entered the queen's chamber.

After the sibyl left, we hurried upstairs to the warmth of our own apartment. Mariuccia poured champagne, handing us each a glass, but instead of toasting the holiday, she quickly drank her own empty and poured herself another. "If the queen dies, none of us is protected. The pope has banned noble families from taking in the queen's ladies. We'll be on the streets."

I excused myself and went to the queen's chapel. There I lit a candle and prayed. *Please, God, let Her Majesty live...Let the new year bring peace to Rome.*

⚬⚬⚬

The morning of Nativity, I rose early and found Pascal sitting with the stable boys. Wearing heavy sheepskin vests, they sat on barrels, warming themselves with bowls of hot coffee. I handed Pascal a large basket, filled with marzipan, wine, fruit, cakes, and nuts. Wrapped in a small cloth were a few coins. "Take this to my family in Trastevere," I told him. "But make sure you give it to my father and be clear in your words, saying it's a gift from Angelica, who wishes them a joyous Christmas."

Upstairs, Octavia met me at the door of the queen's apartment. "Her health has worsened."

I hurried to the queen's inner chamber, hoping a song might raise her spirits. But when I arrived, the room was dark and filled with the scent of eucalyptus. The sibyl stood beside the queen's bed, mopping her face with a cool cloth.

As the sibyl peeled back the wool blanket, I stared at the queen's swollen legs. "Would the queen like a song?"

But the queen didn't open her eyes. She groaned and twisted with pain.

256

The sibyl led me to the door. "Angelica, speak to no one of the queen's condition."

I had made the queen a gift for Nativity, a poem embroidered on a silk handkerchief.

My song will find you,
From now until then,
My heart beating true,
In every wind.

It was such a simple gift, I feared it might drive the queen to pity me. And yet, having sent my allowance to my family, it was all I had to give. Embarrassed, I thrust the small package into the sibyl's hands. "A small gift for such a great queen."

Later in the day, after we attended mass at the Church of Seven Sorrows, the queen's ladies celebrated Nativity with our guests in the *Grande Salone*, where a lavish tea had been set up. I had invited Theodon, and when he finally arrived, I was proud to present him to the other ladies. "May I present the director of the French Academy, Jean Theodon."

"You hardly look like an artist, dressed in such finery," Mariuccia teased him.

"Speaking so boldly, you hardly seem a queen's lady."

"You are right, sir, I am not well-suited to my role as lady, but my loyalty to the queen compensates for my boldness."

"Then your queen is indeed a great judge of character." He smiled and bowed.

"Indeed, our queen is that." Mariuccia pretended to tell me a secret behind her fan but spoke loud enough for Theodon to hear. "Now I understand, Angelica, why your heart remained fixed on this Frenchman. Even *I*, famed for my fickle heart, should have waited an eternity for this handsome sculptor."

I was struck by his ease with women, and when he had charmed them all with his dazzling smile, I led him into the hallway, where we could be alone, standing at a distance from the guards.

Theodon reached into his pocket and handed me a package wrapped in red velvet. Inside were French lace stockings, virgin white, of the finest silk. I blushed deeply, for it was not the sort of gift a man gave a woman unless they were promised to each other. "*Grazie*, Theodon."

Then, nervously, I reached into my purse and handed Theodon my own gift. I had made him the same as the queen but with a different poem.

> *As the feather needs a wing,*
> *As a song needs an ear,*
> *As the infinite needs time,*
> *This your eyes hold in mine.*

I could see he was pleased by my words. Bowing, he kissed my hand, then raised his glass to me. "To our future."

"Enough of your sweet whispers," Mariuccia called to us from the doorway. "Come and join us. My father is handing out the queen's gifts."

Inside the *Grande Salone*, the Marquis del Monte was taking gifts off a table, presenting them to each of us. Mine was the last, and when I opened it, I was astonished to find a silver brush, mirror, and comb, each engraved with a large *A*, underneath the queen's own initials, *CAM*—Christina Alexandra Maria, the name she chose for her conversion to the Catholic faith. Never had I owned anything so fine, and I thought to run upstairs and thank the queen, but the marquis called for music. "Come, Angelica, play for us. Let us raise our voices for the queen, upstairs."

As I began playing the harpsichord, we all joined in singing the Yuletide songs. Watching Theodon sing and sway among my friends, I caught his eye and smiled. For the first time in many months, I was content. It was not the high emotion I had once imagined love to be, but a simple joy...and I preferred it so. Even with the queen ill and my own family far away, for that brief moment, I was happy and thought myself the luckiest girl in all the world.

❧

We did not celebrate the new year, 1689.

Instead we prayed. Prayed for the queen's health, prayed for peace.

Fear gripped us all, as the pope, learning of the queen's illness, poured his soldiers into the queen's quarter. Outside her windows, we heard the clanging swords, marching boots, and pounding drums.

But the queen was too sick to notice. Even with her eyes open, a dullness clung to her gaze. She suffered a dry cough, shallow and persistent, like a wooden wheel riding stones...*ech*... *ech*...*ech*. Her skin grew sour from her feverish sweat, and she had no strength to bathe. To hide the odors, the sibyl filled Her Majesty's chamber with lavender. For eight weeks I stayed beside

Her Majesty, singing softly the religious songs she requested. *"Amo Cristo…I love Christ, whose bedchamber I shall enter… whose mother is a virgin, whose father knows no woman, whose instruments sing to me with harmonious voices…"*

When I wasn't singing, I stayed by Her Majesty's side, embroidering. Outside, the rain hammered against the windows. When the bells tolled evening vespers and dusk fell, I opened the window a crack and sang a hymn. Theodon listened from the street below. When I had finished, I hurried downstairs and sat with him for a short while in a sitting room on the first floor.

Since I was closed off from everything but the queen's illness, Theodon's visits were my only escape. He told me that rumors were circulating that the queen was dying, probably spread by the pope. "His Holiness readies his army for the moment when the bells toll the queen's death." He took the *Gazzetta* from his satchel and read aloud, *"Perhaps God punishes the queen for welcoming the French ambassador to her palace and disregarding the pope's laws—"*

"Do not read more!"

Hearing my sharp tone, Theodon took my hand. "You must take some fresh air. Perhaps when the rains stop, we might stroll in the garden?"

"I cannot *stroll* while my queen lays dying!" I snapped.

Theodon stared at me coldly, as if I were a stranger.

"Pardon me, Theodon. I am undone by the queen's sad state."

But that was only part of it. I had lived too long with an uncertain future, and now, as Theodon sat beside me, I came close to blurting out, "If the queen dies, what will happen to me? Will you marry me?"

But these days, Theodon's mind was on stone, not marriage. He was so consumed with his new commission, he spoke of nothing else. "Today, the stone arrived, beautiful stone...so white, with smooth edges. It took seven men to load it on wheels and push it inside the workshop..."

I wished to confide my fears, to speak openly about my future...*our* future.

But the queen's ladies often reminded me that *an honorable woman never broaches the topic of marriage, but leaves it to the man to decide.*

Even Mariuccia warned me, "Until he announces his intentions publicly, take nothing for granted."

CHAPTER TWENTY-FOUR

And then, the first week in March, we were made hopeful by signs of the queen's recovery. As the warm winds arrived from the sea, the queen sat up, *commanding,* "I must let the pope know that I am still alive, Angelica. I shall throw a music event to honor the French ambassador, and you will sing."

Overnight Her Majesty's breathing deepened, her cheeks gained color, and her strength arrived with a cheeriness that made us giddy. The next morning, the queen lifted her foot to my lap and handed me a porous stone from the Black Sea. "I understand your Frenchman is most attentive these days? Do tell!"

Head bent, I rubbed the rock against the queen's calloused heel. Owing to the abundance of weight around her middle and her poor circulation, the queen's feet were always cold, and she liked nothing better than to have her ladies groom her feet. The other ladies disdained this chore, but I did not mind as it often turned the queen to speaking on her own past, a topic that never bored me.

"Don't be modest, Angelica. Your Frenchman…how goes it?" The queen wiggled her toes. "Enough of the stone…Would you mind squeezing these old boats, a bit under the arch? Yes, there."

"Theodon is very pleased with his new commission."

"You are modest to a fault, Angelica, and tell me nothing of your feeling for the Frenchman." Her Highness smiled peckishly. "There are many windows in my chamber overlooking the garden, and it gives me great pleasure to see what blooms in spring. I shall expect the director of the French Academy to attend my musical event in the garden. And you must have a new dress for the garden party…I shall send the dressmaker to your sitting room immediately. New dresses for all my ladies."

How quickly the world rights itself, I thought later that day, standing before the dressmaker. As he held his measuring tape, Signor Leopaldi stroked the bridge of my ankle. "Ah, delicate doorknob of flesh…blue shoes, I think." Moving his measuring tape to my hip, he said, "Soft dunes of the coast, a pink sash over a green mantle."

I was taken aback until I saw the other ladies holding their hands to their mouths, smothering giggles. Apparently he was known for taking liberties while he took his measurements. And the ladies, wishing a bit of entertainment, had thought it best not to warn me.

Later, as we sat around the table, Mariuccia stroked a pear. "Ah, your hips, Angelica, are the shape of this ripe pear…your lips a velvet cushion, like moss on this stone."

We all laughed.

"We shouldn't mock him," Portia told us. "He's by far the

finest dressmaker. He knows the latest fashions from France and brings the richest silks from Venice, so that we imitate no one but ourselves."

⌒∞⌒

The day of the queen's party, the garden was in full bloom. It was a beautiful spring evening—dense with cherry blossoms, a full moon rising over the hills, fountains splashing. Tables were set under the trees. Mandarin and pineapple sherbet balls were served in cut-glass bowls; champagne from France, bubbly and cold, was poured freely. The tables were laid with bouquets of lilacs and, around the vases, tiers of cannoli with cream, marzipan flowers, candied fruits, and chocolate truffles.

It was a festive occasion, especially because we were all so happy to see the queen in high spirits. I sang my best and was told afterward, I had surpassed perfection. But that was not what made the evening so special. After our songs had ended and we'd curtsied before the queen, Mariuccia tugged me behind the hedges and pushed me up the hill. "Do not ask why, just follow me."

Mariuccia would not let me catch my breath until we had climbed halfway up the hill, and there, coming around a row of bushes, I came to a halt—hundreds of candles surrounded the queen's banqueting house, now draped with chains of lilac boughs. Theodon stood by a pillar, looking very pleased with himself.

"*Bellissima*...It is so beautiful!" I gasped. "You did this?"

He bowed. "With the queen's permission, of course. I wanted it to be a surprise."

Then, surrounded by his own friends and the queen's ladies, Theodon pulled me to a bench and offered me a glass of champagne. "I have finished my commission," he proclaimed, raising his glass to mine. "Now I toast our future, Angelica...*il nostro futuro*...our future together."

My heart leaped....By speaking in public of our future together, he was indeed declaring his intention to marry me.

"To your future together," the queen's ladies cheered.

I had never before been honored in such a way, and now I was dizzied by all the attention. And made shy by it, too. Theodon had prepared a great feast—we picnicked on roast duck, goose pâté, five kinds of olives, prosciutto, cheeses ripened in French caves, white figs, long thin breads, and fruit tarts. I breathed in the scent of the lilacs, and gazed at the flickering torchlights. My heart brimmed so full, I thought I should burst. There was only one thing missing, and that was Lucia, my closest friend. At such a moment, I wished her to be here, too, celebrating with me.

For the first time ever, the thought of the future did not squeeze my heart. I believed myself safe. Safe from my mother's schemes; safe from a loveless marriage. Most of all I felt safe from a future that might deaden my passion for singing.

All at once, trumpets sounded. Theodon leaped to his feet, pulling me behind him. Seeing the trumpeters positioned on the hill, dressed in the French ambassador's livery, we quickly understood—the French ambassador, Lavardin, had planned his own surprise for the queen. As the trumpets played the most popular song, "Flon, Flon," everyone joined in, dancing and singing.

"Look." Mariuccia pointed and giggled. "Her Majesty sways against Cardinal Azzolino."

"And he sways back, joyous at her recovery."

When the song ended, we quenched our thirst with more wine. Only when darkness fell and a footman came to say the queen had retired did I rise from the table, tearing myself away. "I must hurry. The queen often requires a song to fall asleep."

"I, too, require a song," Theodon whispered.

"Come stand below the queen's window, and I'll gladly sing you to sleep."

"I doubt your song will have that effect on me." Theodon pulled me close one last time before releasing my hand.

❧

The queen was waiting, and when I entered her chamber, she patted the side of her bed. "Come sit beside me and tell me everything. Did your Frenchman proclaim his love?"

I blushed. "He toasted our future."

"Even better." The queen smiled. "A successful evening all around. Ambassador Lavardin was greatly pleased. One must have allies as well as friends, Angelica. Never forget that. Friends guard the heart, but allies protect the future."

"Are they not the same, Your Highness?"

"Oh my dear, never!"

The wine turned me bold. "Is the cardinal your friend?"

"Yes, of course."

"And Ambassador Lavardin?"

"An ally."

"But you threw him a great celebration."

"So the pope would see our alliance." The queen took my hand. "Do you love this Frenchman, my dear?"

My eyes fell. "Yes, I believe so."

"Then make a friend of him, not just a husband. Friends are harder to come by, and in the end, they are far dearer."

✦

It was the sweetest night of my life.

And yet, I am sad to say, a happiness short-lived. The following morning, we were all awakened with news of the Marquis del Monte's death. Mariuccia's wails brought us running to the table. I had never seen her so grieved, and I stayed by her side the whole of the day.

When the sun grew warm, we sat in the garden together. I knew she preferred silence, although every so often, she raised her voice softly. "I know my father had many enemies, but with me, he was always kind." She held out her hand and showed me a ring with a tiny gold flower. "He gave me this when I was twelve...I shall never take it off."

I listened as her grief took different shapes—stories, regrets, silence.

At one point, she choked with sobs. "There is no one else. My mother is gone, and now my father. I am alone."

I hugged her close. "I am your friend, Mariuccia. You are not alone."

But no one suffered so much as the queen, who grieved not only the marquis' death but also her own conduct. She had been summoned to the marquis' side as he lay convulsing, and struck with horror by his foaming mouth, she'd failed to rise above her own confusion and did nothing to help her old friend as he lay dying. Afterward, the queen was so distraught, she took ill again and would see no one except Mariuccia, from whom she begged forgiveness.

That night, after Mariuccia had fallen asleep, I waited in the anteroom off the queen's chamber, hoping I might ease the queen's grief with a song. But when the sibyl came through the door, carrying a tray of herbs and jars, she spoke to me in a solemn voice. "No songs tonight, Angelica. This time, our queen suffers grief *and* illness. I fear the worst."

⟨∞⟩

The queen will not live another Sunday. This rumor found its way across the city to Mother. While I sat in the queen's bedroom singing to ease Her Majesty's pain, Mother saw her last chance fading away. Made desperate by her own greed, she sent a note to Bishop Vanini: *If you still desire the treasure for which you have shown so much admiration, meet me behind the prison walls when the church bells strike evening vespers.*

I had not spoken to her since her last visit. But I knew from Lucia that Mother suffered her life. She wandered about the house, doing her chores, ordering Lucia to tend to the harder tasks, all the time muttering, *How dare my daughter abandon this*

*family. She thinks more of the queen than she does of her own
mother. She places herself above me…uses her title against me…
I've wasted my life on that ungrateful wretch!*

Now Mother's anger found its release. It was a secret meeting on the dirt road behind the palace. From there Mother could
see my room. From there she nodded at my window, pointing
out the place of my ruin. "The queen lays dying," Mother told
the bishop. "Time is running out, and I must guarantee my family's future. I can arrange a meeting in my daughter's chamber
Sunday next when the servants go home to their families. But it
will come at a steep price."

"No chaperones?"

"You and I understand each other." Mother never minced
her words. "But afterward, you must promise secrecy. I do not
want her prospects for marriage ruined. I only wish to guarantee my family's future."

I have no doubt the bishop was stunned by the price she
asked. "Such a sum is extreme."

But Mother held firm and reminded him, "She is the queen's
soprano."

"Well worth the sum," the Bishop agreed. Then, pulling out
his pouch, he paid what he could, promising the rest the following day.

I imagine Mother smiled then, thinking how easily a daughter might be replaced by a house across the river.

CHAPTER TWENTY-FIVE

Twice that day, the queen wept while I sang.

Since the Marquis del Monte's death, the queen cried at the slightest thing, sweet or harsh—a bruised plum, her poodles' sneezes, a dead hummingbird on the windowsill. Always prone to swings of moods, the queen's emotions now revealed themselves to everyone, servant and noble alike.

As I held a kerchief and dabbed at the queen's tears, Pascal knocked and entered, bowing deeply. "Signorina Angelica, your mother waits for you in your chamber. She sends a message that she wishes to discuss your brother's marriage."

My brother's marriage! I was well pleased by these words, thinking at last Lucia would be made happy.

The queen smiled weakly. "Go to her, Angelica."

Sunday nights, when the guards and domestics went home to visit their families, the palace was empty—echoing stairs, cold ceilings, dark corners. The smells of soup and eggs rose from the kitchen, as the queen's ladies prepared a light dinner to serve to the queen. Later, Theodon would come and stand in the garden, listening while I sang the queen to sleep. These days he talked openly of our future, assuring me that as soon as the queen was well and would not suffer my departure, we would be married.

Bracing myself, I hurried up the second flight of stairs, and opening the door, took a deep breath. "Mother?"

She sat at the table, a lovely meal laid out before her.

A footstep came from behind, and I heard a familiar voice. "Your mother has graced us with a great feast!"

Spinning around, I saw Bishop Vanini, smiling.

I turned and faced Mother. "He is banned from this palace...Why do you bring *him* here to my own chamber?" I was so astonished, I didn't realize that two Neapolitans, brothers from the queen's own guards, blocked the door.

"Your queen lays dying." Her voice was hard. "You plan to marry a sculptor who has no money. You give me no choice, Angelica. You have forced me to take matters into my own hands. You must entertain this man for one evening."

"*Entertain?*" I knew full well her meaning.

"I only wish to share an evening in your good company," the bishop assured me. "To hear you sing."

"And I wish you to leave." Then I raised my voice to the guards, "When the queen hears that you've allowed this man into her palace, you'll be gravely punished. Escort him off the premises immediately."

Mother smiled, holding her chin high. "They've been well paid, and they know the queen's days are numbered."

Then she rose and brushed past me toward the door. When I realized she intended to leave me alone with the bishop, I pleaded, "Mother, please...don't leave me!"

But she did not look back. She slipped out the door with the two Neapolitans, before I heard the bolt slide and click, locking me inside with the bishop.

"Signorina Angelica"—the bishop took a step forward—"your mother accepted my payment, giving me certain hopes."

I backed toward the window, hoping I might open it and call for help. "Perhaps we might reach some kind of agreement."

But the bishop quickly reached for my hands, holding them tightly. "You will rebuke me no longer. Sing or cry out as you like...no one will hear you. A gentleman's generosity has its limits. I've paid enough to guarantee your family's future. I've promised secrecy. Your prospects for marriage will not be ruined."

I pulled away and cried out, "Guards!"

"No one will hear you." The bishop chuckled. "Those who stand guard outside your door have already been bribed." Cornering me, he pinned me against the table.

And I, using all my strength to resist, kicked a chair, toppling it. I slid out from under him and, running toward the divan, put it between us, crying out, "Octavia...Mariuccia...Help me!"

Laughing, he grabbed my arm, tore the lace from my sleeve. Yanking me down onto the divan, he pressed me against the pillows. "Do you know what you are worth? Fifteen hundred scudi." Mashing himself against me, he feigned tenderness. "Our secret will remain a secret, but only if you grant me your favors without resistance. Otherwise"—he squeezed my wrists tighter—"I will take you by force and tell the world I've had you."

I tried to roll out from under him, but he made a game of it, twisting my arms behind me, kissing my neck. "Will you shun me after tonight? When I'm the only man who will have you? So proud you are!"

"The queen will have you killed. I am her favored lady."

"So was Giovanniana." And now, with a boisterous laugh, he turned rough, throwing me to the ground, falling on top. There came, by the weight of his body, such a pressure, I could not lift my chest to breathe and felt my heart pounding for air. My pulse weakened, and yet I was conscious enough to feel horror at what was happening. He yanked up my gown and began ripping my underclothes, gripping my legs apart. Grunting, groping, he was more beast than man in his noises.

I knew well enough of a girl's ruin, for my mother had lectured long about it. But until that night, I'd never understood that the heat of a man might cause a girl to turn to stone. I became stonelike then, weakened under his weight. The air was taken from me. And he, being full of words, which I will never repeat, made me feel like an animal carcass being stripped of its meat. He was the sort of man to wish a girl afraid, and to make her so, before he had his way with her. He meant to bring me low, wishing me to beg for my honor, before he took it from me. And so he taunted me, recounting the story of how my own mother had sent him a note and planned my ruin. He licked me, spit on me, sucked on me as if I were nothing but a flask being emptied. There was no rapture to him, but force and power that vented itself on me.

I cried for help, thumping my feet against the floor.

At the noise in our room, the queen complained, and Mariuccia, knowing of my mother's visit, wondered why we would make such a fuss. She grew suspicious, but not wanting to arouse the queen's worry, sent a guard upstairs. When the guard saw the Neapolitans run away and heard the cries inside, he threw open the window and called to the other guards outside, then burst into the room. Seeing Vanini half naked, with me trapped underneath, he drew his sword and pressed it to the bishop's back. "You'll pay for this!"

Theodon had been waiting in the garden and, hearing the yells, had followed the guards up the stairs and into the room. Seeing my dress torn away, my body exposed as I sat trembling on the floor, he didn't flinch but grabbed a blanket, draping it over me. Then he tried to hold me close.

But seeing him, I suffered twice my ruin. I could not bear his touch nor having my shame so exposed. I pushed him away, crying out, "Leave me…Go away…Go!"

"I'll kill you!" Theodon lunged at Vanini and, throwing him to the floor, began choking the bishop. It took four guards to pry Theodon's hands from Vanini's neck, and all the while Theodon cried, "You'll die for this!"

Mariuccia came rushing in, and seeing Vanini's pants around his knees and my disheveled gown, her mouth fell open. "Your mother brought him here?"

Hearing her words, I collapsed. I was told later that Theodon would let no one but himself carry me down the stairs to the ground floor. There he left me in Mariuccia's arms. Revived, I found myself in the queen's washroom, in a tub of hot water. "I cannot dirty the queen's tubs." I tried to raise myself.

"Stop this weeping." Mariuccia spoke gently. "The queen will never know, and you must cleanse yourself at once."

Her voice was firm but her hands were gentle. Mariuccia placed a soft cloth between my legs. "There's no blood. A good sign. You fought hard, and by your own strength, lost nothing to this evil man."

"I have lost everything...my honor." I wept until I could not catch my breath. "I'm disgraced. Better to die, than this." And then I fell to crying harder. "Let me die now...Let me never wake up."

Mariuccia held my wet, naked body. She, too, wept. "This happened by no fault of your own, Angelica. In God's eyes, you're innocent."

She wrapped me in a soft robe, helped me upstairs. Then tucking me between the covers, she crawled in next to me, held me in her arms, humming softly. When I could not stop my shuddering, she went in search of the sibyl, who came at once and gave me something sweet to drink. I remember nothing else.

∞

When I woke the next morning, Mariuccia was sitting beside my bed.

"Where is *he*?"

"Vanini spent the night locked in a basement closet among the rats. Captain Caponi sent for Cardinal Azzolino, but the cardinal was away on business, so his nephew, Signor Pompei, came quickly by horse." Mariuccia took my hand, squeezing. "Signor Pompei wanted the guards to tear Vanini limb to limb and make it look like a street battle. But it was decided they would let him escape and then call Merula, so that the pope would not hear of this scandal."

"He is *free*?" My voice trembled.

"Merula will see to him, Angelica."

"And the queen...Does she know?"

"She suspects nothing. She inquired about the noise and was told the sound came from cats that overturned utensils in the ladies' serving room. We have told her you suffer a sore throat, and that is the reason you have not come to see her today."

Cardinal Azzolino returned that afternoon and met with us, the queen's ladies, in secret. "No one is to know what happened." Glancing at me, Azzolino's face turned red. "My nephew made a grave error, letting the bishop escape. But we will find him, and he shall pay dearly."

I returned to my room, where the sibyl tended me. She rubbed herbs on my bruises and cuts, then made me drink a strong elixir. Almost at once, I fell asleep.

But each time I awakened, memories flashed before my eyes—Bishop Vanini's hands around my throat, his voice rough. *"Do you know what you are worth? Fifteen hundred scudi!"*

Mariuccia stayed by my side. She brought me tea and soup and begged me to eat something so I would regain my strength.

The day after, Theodon came and stood outside my window. Mariuccia gently shook me awake. "Angelica, Theodon is out-side. He sends you this message and waits for an answer. What shall I tell him?"

I sat up, my heart beating wildly. "I won't see him. Tell him to go away."

She handed me a small sketch of my window, the window he stared at now. On the back he had written:

> *Dearest,*
> *I wish to offer you comfort. I can think of nothing but the violence you have suffered. I wish to show you that I am steadfast in my affection and prove to you that my love can help you regain your strength.*
>
> > *Yours forever,*
> > *Theodon*

I handed Mariuccia the sketch and turned over, curling into a small ball under the covers. "Send him away. Tell him not to come back."

"Angelica, it is your grief speaking," Mariuccia whispered. "Please, reconsider—"

"Leave me alone."

For the next five days, Mariuccia gave me notes from Theodon, each one saying the same thing. *Your suffering is my own! I wait to see you...I do not understand your silence. Please, my darling, let me come and see you.* All of them signed the same, *Yours forever, my love. Theodon.*

Mariuccia urged me to see him. "He doesn't leave the place beneath your window but waits outside for a sign from you. All day he stands there waiting. At least go to the window and smile to him, Angelica."

"I can't!" I cried out. "He was there...He saw what happened."

On the seventh day, he sent me a stack of sketches of the

queen's garden—those he had drawn while waiting. At the top was an envelope with a note inside:

> *Dearest Angelica,*
> *I can think of nothing else but you, dearest. I have sought your company each afternoon, but you refuse to see me. Your desire for distance has made me see that I serve only to remind you of your pain. My love for you is so great that I would do nothing to ever hurt you, but I cannot go on this way. If you hold any hope for our future, I must see you. If you do not come, I will leave you alone, as you wish. I wait now, faithfully, in the queen's garden, hoping that you will come to me and let me show you the depth of my love.*
>
> > *Yours forever,*
> > *Theodon*

"He waits in the garden." Mariuccia pleaded for me to see him. "I'll go with you if you'd like. I'll stay beside you. Don't throw his love away, Angelica! Try to remember the good things you once felt."

She didn't understand. Nobody understood.

I wanted to forget everything…everything that came before.

If I remembered Theodon, if I let my heart open up to him, then I'd also have to remember Vanini…the hairy knuckles on Vanini's hand as he gripped my throat; his privates rubbing against my thighs. His jowled face, red and bloated, beading with sweat that dripped upon my own face. His smell, especially that—a sweet perfumed smell, to cover up the rest.

From that day on, I sent back his letters unopened.

I had no appetite. I had no desire to get out of bed. I kept my eyes closed and didn't move.

I made myself small, putting a pillow between myself and the world.

⚭

It was the sibyl who finally confessed to the queen that it was grief, not illness that kept me in my bed. She didn't mean to betray my situation, but the queen had grown impatient for my songs and had asked the sibyl of my condition. The sibyl replied that she had no medicine to cure grief. Furious that the truth had been kept from her, the queen ordered me to come at once to her chamber.

My body had not left the bed for the space between Sundays, and now it took three ladies to help me down the stairs. At the sight of me, the queen's eyes widened. "What has happened to you, my child?"

My eyes had swelled to buttonholes, and my face was still bruised. I stood shivering, despite the heavy robes I wore. I could not raise my eyes to meet the queen's gaze. I believed Her Highness would look at me and know—*soiled, compromised, worthless.* I believed that once she discovered the truth, she would banish me from the palace.

"Tell me what has happened, Angelica," the queen asked gently.

Bursting into tears, I threw myself at the queen's feet. I couldn't raise my gaze, so great was my shame. *Oh please… please don't command me to tell you the truth, for I cannot.*

Mouth open, grief poured wordlessly from my mouth, a dry clicking at the back of my throat.

"Angelica," Her Majesty pleaded, "tell me the reason for your tears."

"Queen Christina," I cried, "my misfortune is already too public."

The queen, glancing at her other ladies, and seeing their eyes averted, addressed Octavia. "I command you to tell me."

Octavia swallowed. "Perhaps Her Highness should direct her question to Cardinal Azzolino."

"Send for him," the queen ordered. "Except for Octavia and Angelica, the rest of you may leave. Your silence makes me think you have betrayed my trust."

Cardinal Azzolino came quickly and, when he heard what had happened, told the queen, "A man, unknown to yourself, entered Angelica's room by way of two Neapolitans in the queen's own service, now escaped, with the man."

"What happened?"

"Nothing grave, Your Highness. But the shock seems to have overwhelmed the girl."

The queen stared at her old friend. "You are protecting me, Cardinal. I know it. I feel it. I am not satisfied with this account. Do not take me for stupid, my friend. I fear you hide the greatest part of the story from me. Send back my ladies."

Solemnly the others returned to the queen's chamber.

Greatly angered, the queen cried out, "I command you to tell me the entire truth…or risk banishment from this palace." Her eyes glanced darkly at each of us. "Do not think my affections so great that I would not turn each of you out my doors, if you lie to my face!"

The cardinal glared at us to hold our tongues.

I was greatly torn, for I had never before held the truth from the queen. Now, in her presence, I could not bear to see her anger grow. I began trembling, and Mariuccia, seeing my condition, stepped forward.

"Your Majesty." She curtsied. "I don't want Angelica to suffer a second time by having to describe what she's already suffered once. It was Bishop Vanini who dishonored Angelica, by way of her own mother's cunning. She arranged the meeting on Sunday evening last, when she knew all the servants would be away. He did all but compromise Angelica, and only God knows the guards saved her from the worst, Your Majesty. She's not to blame but nevertheless suffers greatly."

"Who was in charge that night?" the queen cried out. "Why was I not informed?"

"My husband sent for Cardinal Azzolino as soon as Vanini was discovered. But…but he was away," Octavia stammered.

The queen raised her voice. "If your husband let Vanini escape alive, he is a worthless fool!"

Octavia flushed. "He wished to avoid a scandal for Her Majesty and feared the shock could cause the queen's illness to return."

"I want Merula in my chamber immediately." The queen looked at her ladies. "You may all leave except for Angelica." Then her eyes fell on me. "Vanini will pay for his crime against you…pay with his life."

Merula had already been summoned by Cardinal Azzolino and was quickly led up the back staircase. When he appeared, he bowed before the queen. "At your service, Your Majesty. I've already begun inquiries." He glanced at me, his eyes like stone. "Vanini has already fled Rome, in one of Barberini's coaches. He hides in Subiaco in an abbey."

"I want Vanini's head," she shouted. "I want you to find him, and when you are finished, I want proof of your blow. You will have what men and money you need, Merula. Just make sure this is done...and quickly, before he escapes."

Merula took out his knife and rubbed it against his cheek, drawing blood. Then he nodded. "The queen's wish will be done."

"This man will know no safety," the queen roared. "His head, Merula, whatever the cost!"

Then, as soon as the doors closed behind him, Queen Christina collapsed with a heavy gasp onto her chair. I rushed to her side, and when she did not open her eyes but merely squeezed my hand, I sent the valet for the sibyl. With the help of her guards, she was carried to her bed. There she gripped my hand. "Do not leave, Angelica. I wish you to stay."

As I sat, head bowed, beside her, I heard a sniffling cry, and when I looked up, I saw the queen mopping tears from her own cheeks. "Forgive me, Angelica, it was my duty to protect you." She pulled me close so that she could rest her hand on my hair. "I have failed you as surely as your own mother has betrayed you."

CHAPTER TWENTY-SIX

§ A few days later, Mariuccia came into the ladies' apartment with a grim face.

Octavia put down her sewing. "Is it our queen?"

Shaking her head, Mariuccia fastened her eyes on me. "I fear it shall pain you excessively, Angelica."

"Nothing can be so harmful as what has already happened... Tell me."

She hesitated, unable to speak.

"Say it!"

"Lucien brought a letter and told me its meaning...Theodon has married another woman this very morning." Mariuccia handed me the envelope with the French Academy seal.

Octavia gasped. "It can't be true. He loves you, Angelica. We heard him declare it in public!"

"Tell me who." I gripped Mariuccia's arm. "I want to know!"

"Her name is Rosanna. I am told his wife has neither your talent nor your beauty."

"Nor my reputation!" I cried out.

"He didn't marry her for love, Angelica. Lucien told me—"

"Tell me more, tell me enough so that I might hate him."

Mariuccia spoke softly. "This daughter brought to their marriage a considerable dowry, along with a new position for Theodon. Today, following the wedding, Theodon will be made the director of the Works of Architecture and Painting at the Saint Peter's workshop. He is the first Frenchman to receive such a position. This woman's father, I was told, was greatly influential in the appointment."

Theodon is married.

So deep was my grief, I couldn't cry. Nor could I face the ladies' sad stares. I hurried to my room, where I could be alone. There I lay on my bed, staring at his words:

> *My dearest Angelica,*
> *I did not want our end to come to this. I have not slept these nights, for I do not know how to behave in this matter. Sometimes, when pain is shared, as is ours, Angelica, the absence of feeling is the only relief. Surely what happened to you suffers me as well, for I did nothing to stop this beastly man from inflicting pain on you. I shall never forgive myself. I should have killed Vanini that night. I know there is no way for me to ever look you in the face and make up for my failure. I know that you wish me gone from your life. Though it pains me greatly, I have accepted your decision. Perhaps this news will come as a shock, but I have decided to marry. I do not love Rosanna as I love you, and I have admit-*

ted this truth to her. She is good and decent and leaves me free to do my work. Strange as it may sound, I have found comfort in her friendship. And perhaps that is all I can hope for in your absence. Believe me when I say that you shall always be my inspiration.

Yours in spirit forever,
Jean Theodon

෴

When the queen heard the news, she summoned me.

I sent word that I didn't feel well and preferred to be alone, but Octavia returned and knocked gently. "The queen insists, Angelica."

When I entered the queen's chamber, she took my hand, pulling me next to her. "Endings exist in the world, Angelica, but not in our hearts."

Yes, Your Majesty. Yes, Your Highness. Yes, my queen. That is how I always answered the queen, but not today. Today my heart was not ready to be comforted. Today I could not listen to the queen list all the reasons my life might continue without him. "Please, Your Highness, I must be alone."

She stared at me, her large eyes full of sympathy. Then she nodded.

Alone, in my own bedroom, I wept. Wept for the life that would never be mine. Not mine, the black curls, gleaning sunlight...Not mine, his voice like feathers...*Je t'adore,* Angelica. Not mine, his soft kisses.

Believing my shame greater than his compassion, I had thrown away his love.

Now I wept alone.

᷒᷒᷒᷒

Ten days later, news arrived that two cardinals, close to the pope, had paid Merula to let Vanini escape. So grieved was the queen that she'd not brought justice to the man who had attacked me, she took ill again.

Overnight, the queen's legs swelled double. Her Majesty refused water, refused broth, refused ice. Only after the sibyl gave the queen a heavy brew of valerian tea did Her Majesty fall into a deep sleep. I stayed at her side, singing hymns to bring her comfort, trying to forget my own sorrow.

Outside her room, I asked the sibyl, "What do you say?"

She stared at me with kind eyes. "I believe the end is near."

Still I refused to believe it. That is until I woke at daylight, in a chair near the queen's bed, and heard Cardinal Azzolino whispering, "The pope comes directly, Christina. He will give audience to the queen this morning."

The pope comes here? I was stunned by his words, but even more shocked when I saw the queen nod and smile. Though I stood a few feet away, the cardinal didn't acknowledge my presence. I knew he wished to be alone with her, so I removed the queen's tray to the adjoining room, where I remained, in case the queen should ask for me.

I was still there when the pope arrived with two cardinals

and an escort of guards. The sibyl tiptoed into the room where I sat and, taking the seat beside me, nodded at the pope and the queen. "Standing at death's door makes friends out of even the worst of enemies."

The pope took the queen's hand in his own and greeted Her Majesty, *not* as a former enemy, but as an old friend, smiling. "Do you call me Mignon to my face?"

The queen laughed softly. "That would be most disrespect-ful...especially when His Holiness has come to do the last rites."

*Last rites....*Tears sprang to my eyes. *The queen knows she is dying.*

The pope spoke clearly, as if he wished for others to hear what he'd come to say. "Though our differences be public, Queen Christina, I have always held you in highest esteem, for you did the Catholic Church a great service in your conversion to Catholicism. It pains me to see you so weakened."

The queen responded, "His Holiness suffers as well, which makes his visit all the more compassionate."

After years of harsh words for one another, I thought, *now they speak with such warmth.*

"Something troubles me greatly," the pope said. "It concerns the queen's soprano and a certain bishop. I am told that this in-cident caused your illness to return."

My face burned—*all of Rome knows!*

"So you *do* have spies among my guards." The queen's chortle erupted into coughing. "My fault...I did not keep her safe."

"She will know no safety until she is enclosed in a convent. Perhaps this is God's way of guiding you, Queen Christina. This singer was born with an uncommon talent, an uncommon beauty. Such God-given gifts should be used in the service of the church. Even under the protection of a queen as powerful as yourself, this soprano has suffered great harm. Her honor is tarnished, and her future is at risk. Think what will happen when you are no longer able to offer her refuge—"

The sibyl whispered in my ear, "No one blames you, Angelica...The pope wishes to use you as an example...to help enforce his laws."

The queen cleared her throat. "We should not punish the innocent, but the guilty. Your bishop should be put to death!"

"If he enters the Ecclesiastic States again, and if the facts be proven, he shall be condemned to death." The pope's voice rose. "The church tries to punish such criminals, especially if they wear a priest's robes."

The queen sighed. "Angelica is innocent. Even Your Holiness knows she suffers more misfortune than misconduct."

"Women performing in public will always risk their own ruin," the pope replied. "Such a voice moves men beyond their senses, beyond their judgment. They cannot control themselves. I would gladly protect women born with God's gifts, by nurturing their talents in the safety of walled convents." Again, the pope's voice rose so that all those gathered in the room might hear. "You would do well to save this woman's soul by putting her talent to work for God. You may redeem all wrongs by acting rightly now, Queen Christina. It is never too late to act in God's name. If you truly care for this girl's future, place her in a convent."

"I am not long for this world." The queen turned her head

toward the window, blinking in the orange glare of the midday sun. "Perhaps Angelica must be protected, for her own good."

"Of course she must," the pope agreed. "Saint Agatha's, in the mountains, away from the scandals of the city. The abbess there will teach her the ways of God."

Oh no... I gripped the sibyl's hand. Saint Agatha's, in the mountains, was where the courtesans and whores were sent. *Please, Your Highness, I am not one for the enclosed life...Please, do not make me go there.*

The queen closed her eyes. "Upon my death, Angelica will be placed in a convent, where she shall live the remainder of her life. But I shall tell her myself, so she may know my reasons."

"I will send a coach for her when you are safely in God's embrace, Your Majesty."

"We are not always who we hoped to be, Your Holiness," the queen rasped. "Especially for those we love most."

The pope nodded and straightened himself. "Queen Christina, is there something you wish to say this day before God and His Holy Servants?"

The queen, propping herself up, cleared her throat. "I am deeply sorry for my failures in this life, and I pray you forgive me all our differences, which have not hindered me from fixing myself upon the interests of the Holy See. Though I have not always agreed in words and deeds, I have always held the greatest respect and esteem for His Holiness, Innocent XI."

The pope made the sign of the cross on her forehead, offering his benediction, and the queen took her last communion by his own hand.

I fled the queen's chamber and met Mariuccia on the stairs.

"Is it true?" she asked. "The pope gives the queen last rites?"

As I nodded, my eyes teared. "The queen agreed to put me in a convent."

"No!" Mariuccia's eyes widened. "The queen would never make such a promise."

"Go and hear it for yourself," I said sadly. "The sibyl was there beside me."

I hurried down the stairs and out the door, then hid myself in the garden. I needed time to think, and there was no place better than the center of the maze—a series of hedges that formed a puzzle. That is where I sat, listening to the fountains.

"Angelica!" Mariuccia called out a short time later. "Angelica…I know you're here."

She was the only one who knew the maze well enough to find me. Now she hurried to my side and sat with me on the marble bench. "The sibyl said the only reason the queen agreed to place you in a convent was because her own salvation depended upon it."

I stared at the hills. "No one loves Her Majesty more than I. But I have lost everything—my mother, my future husband, and now the queen. I can't lose the freedom of my song. It's all I have left."

"What will you do?"

I had no answer.

"You must find a way to escape before the pope's guards come for you."

I shook my head. "The queen needs me by her side."

"There is always a way, Angelica."

"Perhaps, but I have not slept in two nights. I am tired. I cannot scheme while the queen lays dying."

"You have no choice." Mariuccia lifted my chin. "You're no longer a child. You must face tne future. You have been in this palace long enough to know how decisions are made, how the future is charted…You need someone with power to help you."

I stared into her eyes.

Mariuccia leaned over and whispered a name in my ear.

I sat back, my eyes wide. "But he's a cardinal. He would never go against the pope."

"Have you learned nothing in this palace?" Mariuccia replied. "This cardinal would never go against the pope in public, but in private is another matter. His passion for your songs is well known. As I remember, there were posters placed on his gate!" She smiled. "I have a good friend among the guards. If you wish, I'll ask him to take me to the cardinal's palace after dark."

I threw my arms around Mariuccia. "Oh, you are a *true* friend. Tell him I wish to leave Rome…see if the cardinal will arrange a way."

That night, I waited…waited until the doorkeeper rang the bell twenty-five times and the crickets had ceased their nightly songs. Finally I heard the faint sound of footsteps and my door opened. Mariuccia tiptoed into my room and sat beside me on the bed. "I told him you wish to leave for another country, beyond the pope's rule, and I asked if he could arrange something."

I took a deep breath. "What did he say?"

"He cautioned secrecy at all cost." She leaned closer. "When the bells toll the queen's death, a coach will come for you at the Ponte Sisto. Disguise yourself well."

CHAPTER TWENTY-SEVEN

"Oh great mystery, oh deepest wounds, oh bitter passion, oh sweetness of Godhead, help me reach eternal happiness... Alleluia."

The next morning, before light, I sang the "Magnum Mysterium," the last song I would ever sing for my queen. With her hair scattered, thin and gray, upon her white pillow, Her Majesty blinked her eyes open and cleared her throat. "I called you here to tell you myself...I have agreed to place you in a convent, Angelica." Her voice lacked air and swam shallow toward me. "I will not be able to give you refuge, protection... Still, I ask your forgiveness. I know the walled life is not of your own choosing."

"Your Majesty." I dried my tears, took her swollen fingers in my own hands. "You have no need for my forgiveness. I have only gratitude for your kindness. You are like a mother to me... Always, forever!"

She stared at me, and I at her. *How close we had become.*

Then, lightly, ever so lightly, she squeezed my hand and pulled me close. "No matter what others decide for you, in the end you must choose for yourself. Never betray your talent, my dear." Such a small pressure, such a brief nod. And yet I knew the meaning of her words.

Then the queen closed her eyes and did not open them again in my presence. So frail. So weak. So much greatness reduced to so much helplessness.

Portia brought the queen a bowl of sherbet—mandarin, Her Majesty's favorite—and after offering her a spoonful, mopped the orange liquid spilling down her chin. "Our queen swallows nothing more." She wept.

The sibyl stood outside the door and told us the queen's pulse was still strong and it would be hours yet.

∞

I didn't sleep that night but lay awake listening.

When the bells tolled six times the following morning, April 19, 1689, the turnstile bell also rang. Tears flowing, the sibyl stood at my door. "Our queen is dead."

I knew I must hurry, before the pope sent his guards to take me, and I shook Mariuccia awake. "Our queen has died."

She embraced me, then handed me her own black cape, the simple one she used to disguise herself when she didn't wish to be seen as a lady, and pushed me through the door. "Go quickly... *buona fortuna*...good luck!"

I hurried down the stairs—*good-bye to frescoed ceilings, silk drapes. Good-bye to roasted chestnuts, champagne, marzipan.*

Good-bye to the bannister curved like a lock of hair. Good-bye to the music room with velvet stools.

Outside, I glanced back once. There, in the window, Anthony and Cleopatra, the queen's beloved poodles, sat in the queen's own room, their mournful eyes staring out, their noses pressed to the glass. *Who will love you so well as our queen,* I wondered.

Then I hurried onto the street. From behind my black veil, the world, in its grief, moved slowly. But I moved fast…then slowed so as not to be noticed. The queen's pages came running through the gate, calling out, "*La nostra regina e morta!*… Queen Christina is dead!"

As news of the queen's death traveled, bells began to toll in every church across the city, ringing a tribute to the queen. I'd never walked alone on a public street. I moved toward the bridge, my heart beating so fast, I could hardly catch my breath.

Bells…more bells, now from the hills, from either side of the river, as if the heavens had opened up. *Oh, Your Highness, I miss you already. Watch over me.*

When I heard horses' hooves galloping down the Lungara, I feared it was the pope's guards come to cart me away. I quickly turned down a narrow alleyway and waited. I could hear the guards shouting as they rode their horses up and down the streets. I knew my only hope was to reach the Ponte Sisto quickly, the bridge where I was supposed to meet the cardinal's coach.

When I peeked around the corner of a building, I could see a black coach coming to a halt on this side of the bridge. Alongside rode guards dressed in Spanish liveries. Taking a deep breath, I picked up my skirts and ran.

But as soon as I darted into the street, I heard the sound of horses' hooves coming fast from behind and felt the pope's soldiers riding at my heels, yelling, "*Ferma!*...Halt!" Fearing they might run me down with their horses, I darted to the side but refused to stop, not until I had reached the coach and was surrounded by the Spanish guards, who numbered at least a dozen.

The head of the pope's soldiers rode up to their captain. "Who goes there inside the coach?"

"The Duke of Medina Celi," the Spanish captain replied, "ambassador of Spain." Then, the Spanish captain took my arm and lifted me into the coach.

"Sir," called the pope's captain, "by what rights do you stop this coach and pick up this woman?"

The Spanish captain mounted his horse. "The Spanish ambassador has sent this coach to pick up the family's *duenna*. She is nurse to his children and returns from visiting her sick mother on this side of the city."

"Let us see her face." The pope's captain rode his horse closer to the coach.

But the Spanish captain blocked his way. "You are outnumbered four to one. Let us go our way, unless you wish to lose a battle."

Perhaps because the bells were ringing the death of the queen, and perhaps because the pope's soldiers did not wish to risk their lives, they let us go. Inside, Cardinal de Cabrera remained hidden behind curtains, his head bent in prayer. When the coach began moving, he looked up and, breathing a great sigh of relief, said a prayer for our safety.

The Spanish ambassador took my gloved hand and bowed

his head. "Allow me to present myself. Duke of Medina Celi, ambassador of Spain to the Holy See. We met once last year." He had a white brow, shiny pink cheeks, and a receding chin—the friendliest of faces. Yes, I remembered him. "In a short time, we shall return to Spain, and if you choose, you may come with us and begin a new life there. Until then, you must remain in hiding."

The cardinal did not speak to me until we had ridden the short distance to the ambassador's palace. Once we were safely inside the Spanish gates, the cardinal took my hands and spoke hurriedly. "I doubt we will see each other again, Angelica. You are safe with the ambassador, and I am pleased to know you will make a new home in the country where I was born."

I gazed at his kind face. "Why have you been so kind to me?"

"Although I am obliged to honor his authority, I do not agree with the strict rules this pope imposes." The cardinal handed me an envelope. "My family is from Madrid. This is a letter of introduction. If you ever need anything, they will help you."

"I shall never forget your kindness." I knelt on the floor of the coach and kissed his ring.

"Nor I, your voice, Angelica." The cardinal gave me his blessing, then stepped down from our coach and into another and was quickly carried away, leaving only a cloud of dust behind.

⁂

The ambassador's wife, Duchess of Medina Celi, came to the top of the stairs and greeted me warmly. "How happy I am to welcome you, Angelica, even on such a sad day. Your grief over the queen must be great. All of Rome is mourning." She took my arm, speaking softly. "I heard you sing at Palazzo Riario for Lord Castlemaine's arrival. What a gift, your voice! When my husband told me that you would take refuge in our palace and might join us on our trip to Spain, I was ever so pleased."

As she opened the door to my new room, I was taken aback—the bed, desk, and chairs were carved from mahogany. Across the floor were rugs from the Far East, an intricate weave of deep blues and reds. *More elegant than the queen's palace!*

She studied my face. "The room does not please you?"

"Oh, it pleases me greatly." I felt tongue-tied, afraid of saying the wrong thing.

"You shall be first lady of honor." The duchess smiled. "If such a position pleases you."

"First lady to yourself, Duchess?" I curtsied low. "I *am* honored."

A beautiful young woman, with wild black curls and dimpled cheeks, the duchess seemed only slightly older than myself. Her curls, held back with a gold ribbon, fell down her back. She carried herself elegantly, yet dressed simply by the standards of palace life, her gown a single color of blue, cut tight and flat across the bust, falling in pleats to the floor.

She sat beside me on the bed. "Cardinal de Cabrera is an old friend of my father's. He's risked his reputation so that you might begin a new life, so for his sake, we must keep your presence here a secret. You must remain secluded until we arrive in Spain. That is, if you choose to come with us."

"When do you expect to leave?"

"We wait for the ship to be readied. Three weeks at most."

*Three weeks…*My heart tightened. Spain was far, far away, and if I left, who could say if I would ever see my family again.

I had not slept for two nights, and now my heart was such a tumble of feelings—grief for the queen, relief at having escaped the pope's guards—that I felt a great fatigue. The duchess saw me hold back a yawn. "No doubt you tended the queen with great loyalty. You must be exhausted. I will leave you to rest. If you need anything, just ring this bell."

I slept the whole of that day and night.

❧

For four days, the queen's body lay embalmed and exposed at Palazzo Riario. On the fifth day, I stood on the balcony, next to the duke, the duchess, and their two children, watching the queen's funeral march. Well-disguised in a black mourning gown, I remained hidden by the thick black veil over my face.

The queen herself had told me she preferred a small, dignified funeral. And yet, her wish had been denied. His Holiness led the procession, joined by all sixty-seven cardinals, and behind followed the members of seventeen ecclesiastical orders. Only Cardinal Azzolino could not make the full journey. He collapsed from grief and had to return in a coach to his palace.

With a heavy heart, I watched the queen's body being carried along the street below, a crown upon her head, scepter in her hand. I couldn't see her face, but I glimpsed her white dress—the same dress she'd displayed on the Eve of Nativity. I had been told by the queen's ladies that Her Majesty would leave a good sum of money to pay a crowd to shed tears at her funeral. True enough, there were many shedding tears, but I didn't believe they'd been paid to mourn.

Watching the procession move toward the river, I remembered the queen's own words. *Every concert…every parade. It is all to a purpose.… That is how the powers in this city make their voices heard.* No doubt this parade was meant to display to the world that, in the end, the queen had bowed her will to the pope's. Through the streets, across the river, they carried the queen's body to Saint Peter's, where Queen Christina was inhumed, an honor done to no other person but cardinals and archbishops.

CHAPTER TWENTY-EIGHT

From that day on, I didn't leave the Spanish ambassador's palace.

My heart felt like a door—half open, half closed. I wore a veil and stared at the world through black lace: dark rooms, dark windows, dark sky. Alone in my room, I lifted the veil from my face. "Ah, to breathe again."

I couldn't be seen. Too dangerous, too risky. Rumors had spread that I'd left the city. Left the pope's land. The *Gazzetta* had printed a story, probably leaked by Cardinal de Cabrera, that I'd fled to France, where women could perform more freely.

Yes, I grew to care for Duchess Francesca. In some ways, she reminded me of myself before I'd taken refuge in the queen's palace. Despite her title as duchess, she was well protected from the world. And yet, she was curious and often asked me questions. "What topics did the ladies in the queen's palace discuss? Did they read books? Did they speak of their husbands?"

"In what way?"

She blushed and leaned close. "Did they say what pleases a husband?"

I laughed out loud. "Only one of the ladies was married, and I don't think she cared much if she pleased her husband."

But as the days passed and our departure grew nearer, my heart grew heavier every time the duchess spoke of our future in Spain. When she saw that my grief did not lift, nor vent itself in words, she tried to pry it from me. "Angelica, what is it?"

I shook my head. "It's my grief for the queen."

In truth, I wasn't sure. Though I mourned the queen, this weight inside was something else...and grew heavier by the day. But the duchess had been so generous and kind, I feared speaking of my sadness. I didn't want to seem ungrateful.

But one morning she arrived in the highest spirits. "In ten days, our ship sails."

At that, I burst into tears.

"Angelica, what is wrong? You must speak frankly...Do you wish to stay here? Surely you realize we are not forcing you to leave—"

"I wish to say good-bye to my family...and yet, I cannot leave the palace."

The duchess clasped my hands. "Of course you must say good-bye. We must invite them here but keep their visit a secret...You must tell me where they live, and I'll send a page." And, then, seeing my face flood with relief, she laughed. "Tell me about them."

"My papa is a glazier," I said proudly. "The best in Rome. And my brothers, Franco and Pietro, work beside him. My sister, Bianca, is pious and has always dreamed of entering a convent. My younger brother, Pietro, was born with a deformed chin, but he has such a kind heart, I hardly notice." Speaking of them brought back all the feelings I'd pushed down deep the past year, all the memories I'd tried to forget. But when I told her about Lucia, tears sprang free. "She is the truest friend I know."

"And your mother?"

I'd imagined the entire city knew of my mother and her scheme to destroy me. I shook my head, but I couldn't bring myself to speak of her.

The duchess sensed my reluctance. "She is alive?"

I nodded. "But she won't be invited to your palace."

Her eyes grew wide. "Will you never see her again?"

I stared at the toes of my shoes.

The duchess spoke from curiosity. She spoke from wishing to know me better. "Have you no feeling toward your own mother?"

"Please, let us leave this subject."

"You must tell me what happened to make you despise her so."

"Duchess"—I was losing my patience—"if you wish to bleed me, then call a doctor and have him slice me open. Otherwise, let me bury this sadness away from my new life."

"But she's your own mother!"

"*My* curse!" My voice rose sharply. "I don't wish to speak of her."

Wishing to coax the truth from me, the duchess took my hand. "I, too, had a mother so strict she allowed me no thoughts of my own. And yet, now that I am far away, I realize she only meant to protect me."

"Then *your* mother deserves your love," I cried out. "Mine does not! Do not speak of what you cannot understand. She meant to destroy my happiness, my future." Tears ran down my cheeks. "It hurts...hurts like a death!"

A guard knocked. "Duchess?"

"Take your leave," she commanded the guard.

Then, grabbing my hands, she begged my forgiveness. I let her hug me and dry my eyes. I let her bring me a bowl of lemon soup. Then I listened as she talked of the future, our future in Spain.

I stared outside the window—two hills, and in between, the setting sun. *She is not my queen,* I thought. *I cannot compare her to my queen. Different ages, different titles, different lives. And yet, how to cross over—to be here.*

There was a knock, then the sound of slippers padding softly. Her son and daughter, Tomaso and Maria, came to give us good-night hugs after their baths. "Good night, Mother... Good night, Zia." Auntie, they called me.

I loved their high squeaky voices and wet eyelashes. I loved the way their hair was slicked back behind their scrubbed ears, as their shiny cheeks pressed to my own. I breathed in their scent—soap and damp skin. The duchess whispered, "Give Zia another kiss."

Feeling their little wrists around my neck, I ached. *Could I really leave my own family behind...could I?*

❦

The duchess sent her most trusted maid, Carlita, to my house. Carlita had strict instructions to give my letter only to

Lucia. The letter requested that Lucia come and visit me, so that I might find out how best to arrange a secret visit with the rest of my family.

Lucia arrived the next morning and threw her arms around me. "Oh, Miss, we heard the rumors you'd fled to France and greatly feared we might never see you again. When I got word you were here and wished to see me, I nearly burst my buttons."

I saw, right away, she was nearly bursting her buttons, anyway. By the curve of her belly, she was with child. Following my eyes, she blushed deeply. "I hope you aren't disappointed in me…We mean to marry soon. Your papa has given us his blessing."

"Oh, Lucia." I embraced her. "I'm happy for you."

Then I told her to sit, and she stared at the room where I spent all my time. "Oh, my, this is grand."

"Nothing pleases me so much as your company. How good it is to see you. Tell me everything, Lucia."

Her smile faded. "We know what happened, Miss. Your papa found the money. Then rumors floated about the bishop." Here her eyes fell, and she shook her head. "And when we heard the Frenchman had married another, we guessed the truth, although your mother wasn't willing to say it until Signor Giorgino forced it from her." Lucia shook her head, not wishing to say more, fearing it would cause me more pain.

"Please, Lucia," I whispered. "I need to hear it."

"Your mother confessed she'd arranged for the bishop to enter your room…claiming she did so for her family. Your papa took the money and gave it to charity. Said he'd not touch a single coin of it, nor would anyone else in the family, for it was

305

earned by the sacrifice of your happiness." Lucia nodded. "Your brothers and Bianca felt the same. As did I, Miss."

"Don't call me Miss, Lucia. I'm soon to be your sister-in-law."

"Don't know as I can stop…Angelica sounds too formal." She laughed and hugged me hard. "After your papa gave the money away, your mother took to wandering the streets, thinking guards are coming for her…She talks to the stray dogs. The neighbors mock her. Only the widow takes pity and invites her inside for tea. At night, Pietro has to go and lead her home."

"Poor Papa," I whispered.

"Don't worry about him. Franco and I will take good care of him." Lucia patted her belly. "And soon he'll be a grandpa."

When the duchess arrived, her eyes grew wide at the sight of Lucia's belly. Even so, I was proud to introduce Lucia as my brother's future wife. "My brother is a lucky man, Duchess."

Blushing, Lucia curtsied, then turned her smile to me. "You'll come to the wedding, won't you?"

I glanced at the duchess, who shook her head and explained to Lucia, "She cannot leave this palace. It's too risky." Then, a smile sprang to her lips. "But I have an idea. Why not have the wedding here? You can marry in our private chapel Sunday next, and then Angelica might attend the wedding." She spoke excitedly. "Afterward we can have a great celebration in the garden. That way, Angelica could see her family before—"

"Lucia?" I interrupted the duchess. "Would a wedding here please you?" I didn't want the duchess to mention my journey to

Spain. Not yet. I didn't want our good-byes to dampen the celebration.

"Our wedding here?" Lucia's eyes rose to the high ceiling, the chandeliers. "That would be grand!"

"Then it's done." The duchess clapped her hands. "I will take care of everything."

CHAPTER TWENTY-NINE

The Sunday before we were set to depart for Naples, where we would board the ship for Spain, Franco and Lucia were married in the small private chapel of the ambassador's palace. Papa, Franco, Lucia, Bianca, and Pietro all came dressed in their finest clothes. I also invited Mariuccia, who announced her engagement to marry Prince Colombiere, my former suitor—the goat. "The prince is old, but he adores me." Mariuccia laughed. "And I quite adore being adored."

Bishop de Sevilla, well-known to the duke, married my brother and Lucia in the chapel. Afterward, we went to the garden, where the duchess had ordered a lovely table prepared—a white tablecloth, silver goblets, vases filled with bouquets of giant peonies, all in shades of red. We feasted on trout, large platters of clams, chickpeas and rice, greens with tiny sweet tomatoes, sculpted pastries filled with cream, and bowls of sweet fruit. It was the happiest of occasions.

After we had eaten, the duke and duchess joined us in the

garden, but their presence stifled Papa and my brothers, who were not used to mixing with nobles. Clinging to silence to avoid mistakes, they kept their eyes lowered.

The duke and duchess immediately understood, and toasting Franco and Lucia with champagne, the duke raised his glass to Papa. "I promise to keep Angelica well-protected, as I would my own wife or daughter, on our journey to Spain."

My family stared at me wide-eyed, confused. But not wishing to offend the duke, they raised their glasses awkwardly, searching my face for an explanation.

Mariuccia broke the silence. "When do you leave, Angelica?"

"Three days' time." I stood up, blinking back tears. "Forgive me. I didn't want to cast a sad mood over this wedding, so I intended to tell you after our celebration. It pains me greatly to leave you all behind. And I wanted to lessen the pain by sharing this news at the last moment. I shall miss you…but the duke and duchess have offered me a position as first lady of honor to the duchess. They have promised to help me start a new life in Spain, with much opportunity to sing."

Papa stared at me, reading my face. And though his smile could not hide his sadness, he raised his glass. "You will always have a place to return to! May God keep you safe and happy!"

Oh, Papa…Thank you! I set down my glass and embraced him, then was engulfed in all their hugs. Touching glasses all around, their voices echoed, "*Al futuro*…to your future, Angelica!"

After the duke and duchess graciously left us, we sat in the sun the whole of the afternoon and into the evening. I didn't want to think of saying good-bye, not yet.

Mariuccia told me all the gossip of the queen's ladies. "Cardinal Azzolino inherited all of the queen's money and belongings, along with her debts. He believed the queen was overly generous in her life and owed us nothing after her death, so her ladies were left penniless." Mariuccia rolled her eyes, then giggled. "Portia plans to marry the dressmaker, Signor Leopaldi. She'll be the best-dressed among us. Octavia and Captain Caponi found positions with a noble family who bought their title… Octavia is forced to do everything but empty the chamber pots, but at least her children have a roof over their heads." Pulling me aside, she said, "Having predicted the pope's death, the sibyl sits in his prison. Her only hope is that her prediction will come true and the pope will die soon." Then, brightening, she said, "Perhaps you should wait, Angelica. The next pope may welcome our songs."

I hugged my friend. "Even with a new pope, my reputation in this city is too well-known. Though it pains me greatly to leave, I cannot stay."

When shade had covered the garden, and the church bells tolled seven times, I pulled Lucia under a tree. "More than anyone, it grieves me to leave you, Lucia."

Her eyes filled with tears, and taking my hands, she touched them to her belly. "If it's a girl, Angelica…and if it's a boy, Angelo."

Then reaching into my pocket, I pulled out a package and opened it. Inside were Theodon's sketches and the queen's brooch. "Get Franco to sell these for you, Lucia. Take half for the family, and with the rest, pay the dowry so Bianca can enter a convent."

"We'll be all right." She pushed the package back into my hands. "You might need them someday."

But I refused to take them back. And as we stood hugging each other one last time, Lucia whispered, "We'll be waiting for you...I mean to have a flock of Angelicas and Angelinos waiting to hear their *zia* sing them to sleep."

∽∾∾

Those last nights before we were set to leave Rome, I couldn't sleep. I tossed and turned, my heart growing heavier each night. I felt as if I were circling a great sadness. There is many a girl ruined, but few, I think, by their own mother's cunning. This, I believe, was my hardest pain, the one that sat inside me like a cliff, as my thoughts and feelings whipped around it like a great wind. A girl can despise her mother, but not without wondering at her own mark, her own worth. My mother had sacrificed me, and though she always claimed to have my own interests at heart, I knew greed when I saw it.

Only when the sun had risen on my last morning in Rome, when time was running out, did I know what I had to do. I leaped from my bed, dressed quickly, then hurried to the chapel, where I found the duchess praying, as she did every morning at sunrise.

"Please don't ask me questions," I whispered. "I must go and tend to something...but I promise I'll return by the time the wagons have been loaded."

She nodded, as if she knew where I was going. "Take four guards with you, and disguise yourself well. Borrow one of Carlita's cloaks."

I did as she asked, then made my way across the river to the Piazza Santa Cecilia. One last time I needed to see my mother. As I wove through the crowded piazza, my eyes found her. Even in the warm sun, she wore a heavy coat. I watched Mother kick the ground until dust rose around her ankles. Watched her smack her lips, as if she were tasting the dust. She kept her eyes lowered, staring at the cobbled stone. Only when I stood a few feet away did she sense my presence. She glanced up and stared in my direction. But if she knew me, she didn't let on.

Around her, the neighbors left a distance. Their eyes said, *Curse you, Caterina. Take your bad luck someplace else.*

Mother stopped in front of the fishmonger.

"What do you want, Signora Voglia?" He showed no smile, no respect.

Mother stared at the dead fish, then turned away, her basket empty, her lips moving. She paced first this way, then the opposite way, around the fountain. Two dogs panted at her heels, and every few feet, she stopped to shoo them away.

My heart tightened, as I stood there, breathing in my old neighborhood. Laundry flapped in the sun, birds cawed, fountains splashed.

Then—I don't know why—I hummed, softly, one of the hymns Mother always favored when I was a child. She looked up, stared at my veiled face, then noticed the guards at my side. She knew. *Yes, she knew.*

Our eyes met, and for a moment I thought she might embrace me. Might say she was sorry. Might even beg my forgiveness.

I wanted to grab her, shake her, make her explain why she'd turned against me. I wanted to ask her why. Was it for the money? Or was it because she couldn't stand to be left behind? But as I stepped forward, wishing to speak, Mother lifted her arm and made a fist, then swung around, shooing flies. I stared as she hurried away from me, her hands jabbed deep in her pockets, her eyes searching the ground.

I stood frozen, wishing I could arrive at the other side of this feeling…this great blanket of sadness on top of my heart. Watching her walk away was not enough. Would never be enough. I needed an ending. And yet, this was *our* good-bye, the only good-bye I would ever share with my mother.

Hearing the bells toll the end of morning mass, I knew the wagons would soon be loaded, and I had to return or risk having the duke and his family leave without me. I hurried across the bridge. I cannot say the burden was lifted.…A mother's love cannot be replaced. And so I had no choice but to be strong, as the queen would have me be, and to live with Mother's mark upon my heart.

When I arrived at the palace, the wagons and coaches were hitched, and the duchess was pacing inside the gate. How grateful I was when she took me in her arms but asked me nothing.

CHAPTER THIRTY

What will I carry with me?

Besides the unsung songs bursting inside me.

One suitcase. Inside that suitcase—Theodon's letters. One mourning gown. Three day frocks. Underclothes. A plum-colored shawl. A hairpin for protection. A silver hairbrush, comb, and mirror.

So little. In the end, leaving is not so hard as staying.

Later that morning, we began the long journey by coach to the customs docks in Naples. It was my first time beyond the gates of Rome, beyond the pope's laws. As the children napped, the duchess and I were like young girls, staring out the coach windows, gawking at the villages and farms we passed. The duke laughed at us, enjoying our delight in the new scenery.

Was I afraid? Just a little.

It took three days to arrive at the bay of Naples. The hills stood behind us, the islands visible in the distance. Never had I imagined such a different world. In Rome the pope welcomed pilgrims from every Christian country, and those who came—on knees, on bared feet, in coaches—worshiped the Holy See.

Here, the ports welcomed ships from many different cultures. My head filled with the scents of other worlds—saffron, turmeric, clove, mint. Each time the wind shifted, the smell of fish carcasses grew strong. A mendicant friar stood nearby, begging for food, his face covered in sores. An old woman sold almond pastries—"*Dolci…*Cakes…a good price!*" Dogs, their noses to the ground, were everywhere, hunting scraps.

Exhausted from the journey overland, I stood waiting to board the ship, surrounded by the duke's guards. The duke and duchess and their children waited inside the coach. I'd been warned the journey would not be easy—rocks, storms, moldy bread, soup that floated slivers of wood, dried meat hard as stone. Before we boarded the ship, I'd wanted to step outside, to breathe the salty wind and see a bit of this new world. As I stared at a huge vessel docked along the great harbor, I saw dark-skinned men, chained on deck. Slaves, I realized. As they unloaded sacks of cocoa beans, they stared at me, the whites of their eyes brighter than the foamy crests of waves.

I couldn't read their faces. Couldn't read their hearts. But I knew…knew what it was *not* to choose for yourself. To have your fate chosen by someone else. I'd always believed that freedom came from rising up in society. But now I understood—there were many kinds of freedom, and the most important for me was the freedom to look inside my own heart and speak the truths I found there.

When it was time and the plank on our smaller ship had

been lowered, the duke and duchess got out of their coach, lifting their children to the ground.

"Come, Angelica! It's time!" The duchess linked her arm through mine.

Quickly we boarded. Quickly the plank was lifted.

The uniformed quartermaster stood above. Around us the coxswain called out orders and the sailors pulled and coiled ropes. The ship's bell tolled. And then, as fishermen rowed their small boats below us, tugging our ship out of the bay, Naples grew small in the distance. All at once, the wind caught the sails, and the ship seemed to fly across the water. The duke and duchess stood on deck, arms around their children.

The duchess waved. "Angelica, come join us!"

But I waved back and made my way beyond the bulkhead, toward the back of the ship. I needed to be alone, to say goodbye in my own way. I felt the wind in my hair, as I stared at the hills growing smaller. I was flying across the water, away from my family, away from everything I knew and loved. How my heart pounded!

I breathed deeply. *It will take time to know myself in a new world.*

But I'd learned that my heart filled more quickly when I didn't try to imagine the future, didn't fill my mind with dreams. I would not hope.

I would trust. *My song. My truth.*

Below, the waves washed away the past. Above, the wind took me toward the future.

I lifted my head and let my voice rise, singing to the salt spray, singing to the crashing waves, singing whatever I wanted to sing.

AUTHOR'S NOTE

Angelica Voglia, sometimes referred to in history books as Angelica Quadretti, really did exist, as did the members of her family, and many of the main characters in this novel. The events described, particularly those dealing with politics and the brutal attack of Angelica by Bishop Vanini, are taken from recorded diaries and biographies of Queen Christina. So, you might ask, what is fact and what is fiction? There are no journals written by Angelica, nor are there any accounts of her life. Indeed, very little was written about girls from the lower middle classes during that time. Angelica's life was pieced together from books written about Queen Christina and her court, as well as from historical texts about baroque music, nunneries, and Roman life during the seventeenth century. I used my own imagination to embellish the story and to develop many of the characters within it. Nevertheless, throughout the writing process, I kept discovering more facts, and I was often surprised to see how closely my imagined story was to the factual history. The most remarkable example of this occurred after I had finished writing my first draft. While doing additional research, I learned that the bas-relief of Queen Christina's tomb in Saint Peter's Basilica was carved by Jean Theodon several years after Angelica had left the city. It seems a fitting ending to this story.